Bloodmist and Bonedust

COSA NOSFERATI BOOK I

K.L. Rasmussen

Crimson Cult Media

WRONG TIME, WRONG PLACE, RIGHT VAMPIRE?

LENORA HOLMWOOD'S BLOOD IS MARKED FOR A HIGH PRICE. ONE THAT VAMPIRE MOB BOSS SERLANOS IS WILLING TO PAY, NO MATTER THE RISK. WITH HER LIFE AT STAKE, LENORA MAKES A RUN FOR IT, ONLY TO FIND HERSELF LOOKING FOR PROTECTION FROM THE ONE PERSON SHE KNOWS SHE SHOULDN'T TRUST, MUCH LESS FALL IN LOVE WITH. WITH NOTHING ELSE TO LOSE AND ENDLESS TIME TO KILL,

VAMPIRE UNDERBOSS LLEWYN HELLSINGER LOOKS FOR A WEAK LINK IN HIS MASTER, SERLANOS, AND HE FINDS IT IN THE FRIGHTENED MORTAL THAT JUST WALKED IN THE MIDDLE OF A HAILSTORM OF BULLETS IN THE CENTER OF A RESTAURANT-LENORA HOLMWOOD.
WILL LENORA ESCAPE OR WILL SHE FIND HERSELF DEEP IN THE VAMPIRE UNDERWORLD HER PARENTS DIED TO PROTECT HER FROM?

This book is for entertainment purposes only.

Printed in Oliver Springs, Tennessee, United States of America

Library of Congress Control Number:

Description: Crimson Cult Media, 2025 | 344 pages printed text. | Series: Cosa Nosferati. | Audience. Adult. | Summary: Vampire Mafia Romance.

Ebook ISBN: 979-8-89467-029-4

Hardcover ISBN: 979-8-89467-031-7

Paperback ISBN: 979-8-89467-030-0

For all those that struggle to believe in the light,
When it's most dark, we carry on.

For my cat, Minerva,
who incessantly pawed at me for pets and cuddles
during the entirety of my writing this.
The only claws and fangs I allow,
as they only mean love
...and give me more treats.

Contents

Content Warning

This is a dark romance that explores many taboo and explicit themes of the genre which generally explores themes of obsession, sexually explicit and dangerous situations. If any of the following themes are triggering, I do not recommend this book for you. Mental health is vital and as the author it is my responsibility to let you know that this book is not for the faint of heart.

Trigger Warnings

Vampires
   Taboo Fetishes (Blood, gore, BDSM)
   Sexual Assault
   Body Dismemberment/Body Gore (chainsaws, beheadings, vampire violence)
   Gruesome Deaths (Mother + Child)
   Forced Marriage
   Human Trafficking
   Organized Crime
   Drug Trafficking
   Alcohol abuse
   Domestic Abuse

Narcissistic abuse

Playlist

Link: SPOTIFY PLAYLIST:

https://open.spotify.com/playlist/4ima7ViWQb8GJco5KV2RfH?si=
xgRY9PlwRLmA6JOEY4FNJw

Kiss the Ring - My Chemical Romance

Vampire Money -My Chemical Romance

This is How I Disappear - My Chemical Romance

The Ghost of You - My Chemical Romance

Boy Division - My Chemical Romance

Blood - My Chemical Romance

Sleep - My Chemical Romance

Breathe - Tommee Profit Ft. Fleurie

The World Is Ugly - My Chemical Romance

Art of Survival - Bishop Briggs

Honey This Mirror Aint' Big Enough for the Two of Us - My Chemical Romance

Bat Country - Avenged Sevenfold

You Know What They Do To Guys Like Us In Prison - My Chemical Romance

Sunlight - Hozier

House of the Wolves - My Chemical Romance

Monster - Mumford & Sons

A Little Piece of Heaven - Avenged Sevenfold

Helena - My Chemical Romance

Blackbird - Beatles

Hungry Heart - Laura O'Connell

I Found - Amber Run

I Never Told You What I Do For A Living - My Chemical Romance

It Will Come Back - Hozier

Lover, Please Stay - Nothing But Thieves

If I Had A Heart - Fever Ray

My Name Is Carnival - Jackson C. Frank

I Will Follow You Into the Dark - Daniela Andrade

Party Poison - My Chemical Romance

Too Sweet - Hozier

Look After You - Aaron Wright

How to Be Human - Amber Run

Man Or Monster - Sam Tinnesz

The Pit - Silversun Pickups

Dark Paradise - Lana Del Rey

Come Follow Me Down - George Taylor

Blood//Water - Grandson

Carousel - Melanie Martinez

Somewhere Only We Know - Lily Allen

Vampires Will Never Hurt You - My Chemical Romance

Emily - My Chemical Romance

Laura - Bat For Lashes

Sing- My Chemical Romance

Secrets & Lies - Ruelle

Soldier - Fleurie & Tommee Profit

Color of Blood - Chelsea Wolfe

Cemetery Drive - My Chemical Romance

Heaven Help Us - My Chemical Romance

Kill All Your Friends - My Chemical Romance

Horizon - Alduous Harding

The Only Hope For You Is Me - My Chemical Romance

The Foundations of Decay - My Chemical Romance

Buried Alive - Avenged Sevenfold

Bulletproof Heart - My Chemical Romance

Castle - Halsey

To The End - My Chemical Romance

Don't Fear the Reaper - The Spiritual Machines

My Melancholy Baby - Ella Fitzgerald

Become the Beast - Karliene

Cubicles – My Chemical Romance

leonidas holmwood

Kiss the Ring - My Chemical Romance 2010

*C*rimson streaks bleed through the sky as sundown creeps over the horizon of Lake Michigan. Rosalynd would be back with the kids at any moment. I promised her they wouldn't be here when she came back. And yet Serlanos nor any of his fiends have shown up for the drop off.

I pace the front terrace and stare at the sky. I try not to show too much concern as the neighbors pass on their evening stroll down Sherman Ave. I wave hello to not arouse suspicion. I always feel like I am being watched these days. I am constantly looking over my shoulder, waiting for one of them to strike from the shadows.

I see my neighbor, Jeff Rodham, our local Ned Flanders of the neighborhood inspecting something in his garden. Always so whimsically cheerful. Sometimes I wonder if it is a mask. For something more sinister. I wonder too if he was waiting for someone to arrive that shouldn't be there. Or is he normal? Maybe he hasn't fallen into Serlanos' trap. Once you prove you're useful to him, he will never let you go.

It's no way to live.

This will be the last time.

I promised Rosalynd it would stop, especially after the last drop exchange. I used to have a bagman but the last one quit after that viper Lycidas nearly ripped his throat out.

I was getting involved with something that was beyond me and my family.

Something inhuman. Something I couldn't protect myself against if I tried.

It's putting my whole career and reputation on the line.

It's the right thing to do. And I'm prepared to do anything if it means keeping my family safe.

I've made preparations.

Yet still I fear they will find us. They found me without very little effort the first time, I do not doubt their ability to track.

It's 6:30— they're thirty minutes late. I was about to drag the cooler back into the house when the roar of the large black escalade came screaming down the street for everyone to hear and pulled in the driveway at full speed only to stop before hitting the garage door.

Lycidas and Norryx, two of Serlanos' most ruthless soldiers, get out of the SUV. Dressed in black custom suits and red ties to give the illusion of professionalism to mask they were bloodsucking fiends.

"You're late— my wife and children will be home any moment. I don't want you here when they arrive. Take it and go. And tell Serlanos that this is the last time," I shove the medical cooler into one of the brutes arms.

They exchanged heated glances and snarls. Lycidas approaches, closing the gap and looming over me.

"Those are some brave words for a mortal," Lycidas jeers, backing me against our freshly painted front door. I shake the trembling fear and regather my confidence that was burrowing deep inside.

"I've got more if he wants to hear. Just because he owns half of the Northside doesn't mean he gets to own me. Now get the fuck off my property," I seeth through my teeth.

The two snarling beasts bared their pointed teeth at me, ready to tear into me but back down. They turn and leave, glaring bullets into me.

I've just made enemies with them. Which was probably a really stupid thing to do but I've had enough.

They've been less than kind over the previous years. Each visit is more daunting and vicious than the last.

The last one was the worst, leaving me pale and shaken after they were done with me.

I learned my lesson about leaving orders unfulfilled. I would have to fill them myself. If I were to refuse, my wife or children would be next. I would let them bleed me to death before I let them harm one of my children.

I watch them pull out of the driveway, their glaring eyes not leaving me as they drive away to go report to their master.

Serlanos, the bloody devil of the Northside. I regret ever being so weak to need his help, but it was an arrangement that made sense at the time. But now I am paying with blood sweat and tears. It's just not worth it.

I found someone, on a darker side of town, who said they could help. Had a cabin that was so off grid, no one could trace us there. New identities. The whole nine yards. Just had to pay fifty-thousand which was just handed to me. Serlanos just paid for our way out of here.

Away from him and his poison that has been haunting my family for decades.

My heart races as I carry the duffle bag into the house and set it on the floor. Pacing the foyer, I run my hands through my hair and jump up and down.

My plan will work.

My family will be safe from these bloodthirsty monsters. And I will do everything in my power to make it up to them for putting them in harm's way.

Sweat drips down my brow as I wait on the bottom stairs for the click of the door handle and for my family to walk in and tell me about their day. Pretend as if nothing is wrong and as if I haven't put all of our lives in mortal danger.

I can't wait to tell Rosalynd that the nightmare is over, almost— I stare at the duffle bag by the door, feeling thankful that my sacrifices were not for naught. I had done my part and my efforts paid off.

But we aren't out of the woods yet. I have to take some precautions. If I don't make it out of here alive, I have to ensure something for my children—someone I can trust.

Dad.

He's always been there. He may be a hard ass but he will understand. At least, I hope.

I dial his number.

"Artemis speaking."

"Dad, it's me. I need to ask you a favor. I can't say much. But whatever happens to me or Rosalynd, please take care of Theo and Lenora."

"Son, what's going on? What have you gotten yourself into?" Dad barks into the phone.

I don't know how to answer that question. How can I tell him that I've brought this curse upon our family.

"Just promise me? Please."

"Son, you're makin' no sense. How about I come over there and we talk it over a cold one, ya hear?"

"Dad. Please, don't let them sink their teeth into them." There's a pause and then he responds.

"Okay, kiddo. I promise."

I hang up, feeling the tears well in my eyes, knowing that may be the last time I talk to him.

It's easier this way.

Say nothing and ghost the world.

But will Rosalynd take to the idea? Will she think me mad for wanting to just disappear off the face of the Earth? Leaving behind family and friends and leaving them confused and wondering what became of us? What drove us away? they will ask. No one will know.

I am sure the kids have some idea something is up.

They've met these brutes before. They're aware of the daunting presence in our lives. When my daughter was three she greeted Serlanos at the door when he arrived unexpectedly for a little chat.

She ran up to him like she would one of her aunts or uncles and hugged his leg.

He picked her up and had her on his hip like she was his little girl.

I wanted to rip him apart for even putting his hands on her.

Then I knew I was in something bad and I let it into my home.

I should have known better.

His teeth shined with desire, I knew he was ready to sink his teeth into her. And that was not about to happen.

Not on my fucking watch.

The front door handle turns and the door flies open to let in the hustle and bustle of my wife and our two children carrying shopping bags filled to the brim of whatever Michigan Avenue had to tempt them with. I've never been so relieved to see them.

I bar them from pushing past me and pull them into a hug.

"Dad, we were only gone for a few hours," Theo wheezed under my arm.

I know, son.

Rosalynd looked me in the eyes and knew that something was wrong but left it alone until we could have a moment of privacy. She didn't want to scare the children, even though she herself was scared. Since she told me she wanted to be done with it, she's been nervous. Setting a boundary has always been difficult. Even with me.

"I just missed you guys. Come on, show me what you got?" I say loosening my grip and blinking my tears away.

The children couldn't know yet.

The kids begged for a movie night after a fashion show of back-to-school clothes and pizza to which I couldn't say no to.

I knew Rosalynd was grateful for family time, but I knew every part of her was wondering what happened when I told Serlanos' fiendish consorts that I was done.

While the kids prepped the fort, Rosalynd pulled me aside in the office and closed the door.

"So? How did it go?" she asked with her arms crossed, her naive hopes that they will take no for an answer bouncing back at me.

"It's not over. Not until we get out of here."

I will be forever haunted by the tearful, terrified look in my wife's eyes as I tell her that we have to leave our home. Our lives. Everything.

I am a coward. In the worst possible way.

I've destroyed the life we worked hard to build. The one we dreamt of. A nice cushy life on the northside of Chicago, like we dreamed about in college. Up in smoke now.

She grabs my hand and pulls me back. I shake back tears, I have to be strong.

The kids are right outside, they will know something is wrong.

"Wherever we go, we'll always be together right?" she asks with tears in her eyes.

"Always and forever, baby."
She trusts me. And yet she shouldn't.

2

lenora holmwood

Vampire Money - My Chemical Romance

*S**even Years Later*

Stabbing red-to-blue lights pierce through the broken shade panel of the boarded-up window followed by the screaming siren waking up half our street on a grimmer part of southside Chicago. Clutching the itchy blankets and holding my chilled breath, I sit up as straight as a bullet. Theo creeps to the window to catch a peek through the jagged cracks of wood.

"It's just the drug den in the apartment building next door - they're getting busted. Go back to sleep, Lenora," Theo said from his spot by the window. He doesn't sleep anymore, he stays up and watches the night go by.

I don't know if I can force myself to go back to sleep again. The wire metal bed frame was at its frailest. I could feel the support bar digging into my shoulder blade.. It was a bit much between that, the screaming sirens out on the street and the sounds of Grandpa shouting and smashing Gram's porcelain to bits against the wall in the room next door.

We stayed quiet, praying his rage wouldn't turn on us. Staying in our small bedroom that we've shared since we came here.

It was our fault. We ruined everything.

8

Grandpa was at the end of his rope. He had to be, that would be the only reason he would've done such a thing. He wouldn't have broken Father's promise if he hadn't completely lost it.

The thud of the battering ram and the crunch of the wooden door echoed in my ear drum as if I had been right against the door. Only a million times I've imagined that sound at the entrance of our condemned apartment building. It will only be a matter of time before they come busting down the boarded-up door, as most clients come to rent a room from Grandpa to nod off in. But I fear that I will never hear that sound.

We don't plan to wait around for it. I know Theo has a plan and a packed rucksack just in case. We are waiting for Grandpa to succumb to the bottle and be knocked out long enough for us to escape unnoticed.

Grandpa must've been desperate. He wouldn't have done this otherwise. He promised our father that he wouldn't ever let us be involved with Serlanos or his crew.

He promised to protect us from these fiends from haunting our doorstep ever again.

Gave him his word. And tonight he went back on it. He went back on a lot of things, like taking care of us and staying sober. I keep trying to tell myself this, it is easier to believe than the horrible truth.

It wasn't always like this.

I remember bouncing on Grandpa's knee as a little girl. Visiting him and Gram in their big house on the upper northside near Hawthorne was a treat. It was surrounded by pines and a large lake that I loved to venture out to to see if there were any ducks to feed. Theo would accompany me when my adventure would take me into the woods and off the beaten path, climbing over wild thickets and bramble. We would return to the back patio with scraped knees and torn clothes giggling.

I'd visit Grandpa in his workshop and he would teach me how to use a drill. After dinner he would submit himself to my playing with his thin white hair. He was always a good sport about playing dress-up with me, tolerating a few barrettes in his paper-thin wisps that were left up there. I sat on his shoulder the day he bought this property. He was so proud of his purchase.

One of many.

"An investment is worth all the while if you treat it well," Dad would say as we drove from the Northside to the South Side of the city. We spent nearly the whole summer there with Dad and Grandpa renovating and preparing the place for tenancy.

Dad and Grandpa argued over paint color while Theo and I chased each other through the various apartments and rooms, jumping out and spooking each other.

Now we don't dare go into the other apartments. Anything could be lurking in the corner.

We stick to our apartment.

Our bedroom, where it's safe.

For now.

Grandpa flew violently at some intruders when he found one of the new tenants ransacking our fridge and taking his beer. We didn't see their faces around here again. Grandpa installed the deadbolt for our safety. That's what he told us when he decided to keep us locked inside.

Theo and I were no longer allowed to roam free in the building, nor could we leave without his permission —one of the many freedoms ripped from us since coming to live with our grandparents.

I wished we had a deadbolt on our bedroom door.

To keep Grandpa out.

To keep the world out.

Here in our bedroom we were safe. So long as Grandpa's drunken rage was focused on the last of Gram's fine porcelain that shattered the floor.

At moments of brevity, Gram stepped in and could diffuse the rampage fueled by failure and bootlegged liquor. Sometimes she would instigate a fight, and antagonize him by reminding him of the failures that brought them into this mess.

It was his fault and she put her blind faith in him. Which only made it worse and then we became the targets.

I don't blame her.

She was just as broken down as we were - if not more. Having endured this brutish man-of-the-house behavior from him since before I was even conceived, I sympathized with her.

She was tied to him. If he goes down - so does she.

Until only hours ago, I didn't think she had any fight left in her at all. Being such a small woman she was easy to dismiss for having a strong voice. But she made herself heard.

How could he? How could Grandpa do this?

There's a lot that Grandpa has done that I don't know if I can forgive him for.

He's not been himself.

Not for the last five years.

Not since the day we lost our parents in the car bomb.

Or that we were forced to move from our grandparent's estate into this rundown apartment building. At least when we lived at our grandparent's home it was a familiar setting. Theo and I had spent weekends there before while Mother and Father went to Paris or some other marvelous adventure he had planned. Father was a romantic like that.

Grandpa blamed us for a lot of things. But he couldn't blame us for what transpired tonight.

Theo stared out the window and watched the madness unfold across the street. A few shadows and hurried footprints sprinted past the boarded-up window and down the alley behind the apartment building.

The perfect getaway.

We say nothing if we want to keep our tongues.

That's the deal.

Until they come knocking for more - like tonight.

"Come in here, *girl*" Grandpa beckoned me into the room earlier this evening. He no longer called me by my name, just 'girl' to remind me that he's forgotten the love he once had for me and Theo. Theo is lucky if he is directly acknowledged without a fist to the face.

Theo followed. He wasn't going to let me be alone with any man if he could help it. His protective brotherly instincts kicked into hyperdrive whenever our grandfather addressed us.

Standing in our dimly yellow-lit living room was a great wall of a man, dressed in a dark fine satin suit, smoking a cigar. His silver hair was slicked back and he wore a hungry smile with dark devouring eyes to match.

I recognized the acrid scent as if from a distant memory - when the men with pale faces and endowed in black suits would knock on the front door and Mother would pull us away while Father would go out to meet with them privately, only to return pale-faced, shaking, and sweating and clutching his neck. One time his nose was bloodied and his eye was black and purple.

Grandpa sat in a chair at the table and gestured for me to join.

I refuse. I don't want to be near anyone on *that* side of the room.

"Lenora, this is Mr. Serlanos Gyanstazi." His eyes shined as his name was spoken, as if it would have summoned him had he not already been in the room. *I knew who he was. How could I not?*

A monster.

A fiend.

A dangerous criminal that will have his will be done at the snap of two fingers and some brute muscle. But this time he came alone. Which seemed odd, as he doesn't seem like someone who would do his dirty work.

That's what his brute force was for. Like Callum or Lycidas or any one of the others that have shown their pale-ugly mugs at our door.

This must be important.

He's been looking at me like a piece of meat to be devoured ever since I've come of a mature age. Like he'd always plan on getting his claws in me. He smiles wildly at me, his teeth white and shiny. I could have sworn I could make out two beastly fangs protruding where normal human canines would be.

I nod at him nervously, acknowledging his daunting presence. He's like a shadow that has followed my brother and me from the day we were born. Always lurking, leaching from our family. Whatever deal that was struck between Serlanos and our father became a string of many that became impossible to sever.

It blew up in our faces one day, taking Mother and Father with it.

Something Grandpa reminds us of constantly in his verbal attacks upon us for why the apartment has failed.

Since our father cannot pay his debt, it's fallen to Grandpa's doorstep. Robbing us blind. Taking everything except our thumbs, even when threatened.

The apartment complex that was once full of tenants has now fallen into condemnation.

Grandpa will only be able to get it out of disrepair with the help of the Gyanstazi now. Selling me to Serlanos was his last hope.

And then Theo nearly ruined it.

"Let me take a look at you. Go on, spin around," Serlanos ordered, approaching me, exhaling musty smoke as he spoke.

Grandpa glowered at me, ordering me to obey the monster before me.

I spun slowly, my knees shaking. I could already feel *his gazes* crawling up my skin and devouring everything there was to be seen. Undressing me with his eyes and violating me with his mind. I avoided eye contact.

Especially with Gram who had been slowly inching herself towards the table.

Where the handgun had sat out for weeks.

Mostly as a scare tactic for us to obey everything Grandpa said. It worked. He was not afraid to use it.

He is the head of the house. What he says, goes.

I wish she would grab it and use it on both of these bastards. Then we would be free. I urge her with every fiber of my being that she just ends it all.

"Yes, she is perfect. Fucking sexy as hell. Beautiful fine pouty lips. Very fine figure. She will do nicely. I'll take her."

Take her?

"Take her? Take her where?!" Theo exploded, launching himself between me and Serlanos.

"To wherever the fuck I want, boy," Serlanos snarled reaching for the briefcase that sat out of view.

He sets it on the table in front of Grandpa and opens it. Loaded with cash. A briefcase of cash.

That's what I was worth to Grandpa.

A fuckton of money and I would belong to anyone for whatever reason.

And I didn't want to know what Serlanos had in mind for me. Something foul and beyond any worst nightmare.

"YOU'RE NOT TAKING HER ANYWHERE." Theo roars, stepping in front of me as a human shield.

Serlanos snickers mockingly. "That's sweet. You're the big brother, right? I bet your Daddy told you to always look after your little sister. It's admirable. Expected. But unfortunately for you, you have no say in the matter. You're a little bitch. Just like your father, and your grandfather here. Did you ask them how we got here?"

"ENOUGH!" Gram shrieks. Everyone looks at her.

Gram shook with a dangerous combination of fear and anger. I could have sworn she nearly reached for the gun that sat on the table. "She is your granddaughter. How could you even consider this?" she shouts at Grandpa, who sits stone-faced in his chair.

"The deal is struck. The girl belongs to me now. And I am not known for backing out on a deal. So, you have your money. I will give you till tomorrow to pack your things and say your goodbyes," Serlanos says, staring me down.

I am speechless. Everything was happening way too fast to even seem real.

Theo doesn't wait for him to take two steps towards the door before lunging at him, wielding a shard of broken glass, which pierces the monstrous man in the forearm. With little effort, Serlanos shoves Theo who crashed into the side table, which crumbles beneath Theos' weight.

"You're either brave or fucking stupid. Neither is going to get you anywhere. I will be back tomorrow, either for the girl or my money. It's your choice. And believe me, you won't like my choice." Serlanos flick the butt of a cigar at Theo who flinches.

Serlanos' phone rings once and he answers. "Serlanos."

He listens for a moment and then hangs up.

"You're in luck. I have a business to attend to. I will be coming back to collect what is *mine* tomorrow evening," he says, enclosing me, lifting my chin with two fingers so my eyes are forced to meet him. He winks at me and then turns away, scowling at Theo who hadn't dared get up as he passes.

Grandpa sits at the table, the angry vein in his head popping out, pulsing to the echo of the tension in the room. No one says a word as we watch Serlanos leave through the front door.

The silence hangs like a dagger waiting to take a plunge, any one of us its target. I could form no words as I was still processing the fact that Grandpa had sold me off to the very monster our father vowed to escape from. The one Grandpa swore to protect us from.

But he was weak. The money was too tempting. I was another mouth to feed. It was only too easy of a choice for his pickled mind.

Tomorrow was just around the corner.

And by then Theo and I will be on a bus away from here. Away from this nightmare.

If Mother and Father had known that this was what would've become of us, would they have made other plans for us?

What feels like only seconds later, I am shaken awake.

"Lenora, it's time."

I shake myself awake, surprised that I'd been able to fall asleep to begin with. I slipped on the only pair of shoes that stood a chance of surviving being on the run - doc martens. I miss the way they used to look with my school uniform - when we went to school. Unfortunately, our attendance has been tenuous because Grandpa didn't want to lose the checks he received from the state for caring for us, yet didn't want to address the administrator's concerns about our deteriorating condition.

Our clothes were tattered and our bodies were nearly emaciated from lack of food. I had gotten by on what my friends had brought me.

It's been almost three years since we left.

Two since the calls from child services came to an end.

I was in the eleventh grade and was going to finish strong - but that didn't matter for Grandpa. It was ripped away from me - the dream and future I was going to make for myself. I don't even remember what that was at this point.

Theo whispers low, "I think he's out cold. Gram gave us the green light about an hour ago - but I wanted to be sure he wasn't faking it. Do you have everything?"

There wasn't much I wanted that was here. This room was a prison and held no sentimental value other than the demons that followed us here. When some of the more fucked up tenants tried renting me, Theo and I hardly left this room.

It became a solace which I have resented. Every good memory of this place has been soiled. Every hope of having a normal life was up in smoke like the crack being smoked in an apartment a couple of doors over.

I nod and quietly follow his lead out the door.

Grandpa's chainsaw-like snore rattled the shattered frames on the walls. I am relieved to know that I would never hear that again, or any other noise that may emulate from him. I hope Theo has stolen enough cash for us to get far enough away that no one would ever dare come looking for us again. But I have a price on my head - and Serlanos will not give up so easily. He's followed us here, what's stopping him from getting what he wants?

Creeping down the hall, Gram waits for us at the very end, glancing back and forth between Grandpa fast asleep in the chair holding his rifle. Gram is holding the pistol that was left on the table. She was no longer shaking. Approaching us before we reach the door she smiles weakly and whispers, "I wish there was more I could have done for you."

She slides a wad of cash into Theo's hand.

"Now go. Get as far away from you as you can. Don't tell anyone who you are, or else there will be trouble wherever you go. Don't come back for me. I am as good as dead."

Without glancing back, we step out into the dark corridor and Gram shuts the door behind us, quietly bolting the lock. An attempt to give us more time.

It feels odd walking these halls once more. It was as if no time had passed at all, yet everything changed at once. The once newly painted colonialized panel walls were now dry rot and peeling. Wasting away from the inside out.

The ornate cast-iron lanterns hung in the hall, casting an eerie yellow glow as if to illuminate the toxicity of this shithole. Bugs fly around piles of old rotten food. Needles and foil are scattered amongst the other debris and beer bottles left behind by the freeloaders. I cling to Theo's side, scared to let go for even a moment that he might disappear into the darkness of one of these apartments. Who knew if anyone was still lurking in some corner?

Most of the usual squatters have fled the scene since the police had raided their supplier a few hours earlier. It would be stupid to be caught around here, which is why we must be careful and fast when leaving.

Leaving through the front entrance was no longer an option. The doors have been sealed shut by whatever Grandpa had available.

How the fuck does Grandpa leave this building to get more beer? Somehow I don't see Grandpa climbing through windows and through holes to get in and out of here. Gram leaves to go peddle so she has to be able to get out.

I start feeling around for a seam or something that would unseal the door. But Grandpa had caulked it well.

What a dick. What kind of an asshole keeps his family prisoner in a biohazardous prison?

Theo looks at me saying to give up. He's right - we have to move fast and give up on lost causes. Find another way.

Stepping over fallen insulation and crumbling ceiling tiles, Theo leads us to the very end of the hall and into an apartment that had a small part of a compromised wall crumbled away enough that we could crawl through. There was just a small bit of foundation that needed to be cut away, quickly and silently.

I could see grass and feel the fresh cool night air, it was just out of arm's reach.

We are so close.

Picking up an abandoned hack saw, Theo begins cutting away, praying that the noise wasn't enough to stir Grandpa from his intoxicated slumber. The walls are paper thin and it is hauntingly quiet. The sawing seesaws loudly in my ears. I close my eyes and wait for Theo to finish.

"Are you ready?"

I suck in a breath and nod nervously, knowing life outside these walls will be very different, and sometimes scary. I felt lucky to have -

A gunshot echoes from the apartment down the hall and then the frantic sounds of the door opening and Grandpa's cruel cursing.

With one teary glance, Theo looks me dead in the eye, hands me the wad of cash Gram had given us, and says "Go. I'll be right behind you."

I want to resist, but if we can escape, I must listen and move quickly.

I shove myself through the hole, scraping my wrists and hands as I pull my way through the opening. Fragments of concrete and other debris are lodged into my hand. I feel the grass beneath me for the first time and immediately want to cry. I move to make room for Theo to crawl through and hold out my hand to take his pack. He pushes it through and then crawls halfway before getting stuck.

"Fuck! My belt loop is caught on a nail or something." Theo pulls violently, panic setting in as we hear Grandpa approach the apartment door.

The roar of a chainsaw growls in the background.

Grandpa has found a toy.

"Nora - Nora, I need you to listen to me," Theo's voice quivers as he speaks, I shake my head - I know what he's about to say and I don't want to fucking hear it. He's coming with me. We are in this together. Just as we have been from the beginning. I've never been without him. Not for a moment it seems.

"Don't. Stop - don't fucking say it," I hiss as I tug more on his arms, desperate to release him.

"Whatever happens - I love you. You gotta keep running. You deserve so much more than what he has to offer," he cries. He's been so strong for so long. For me, I need to be strong for him and pull him through this fucking hole so he stops talking like this.

BANG! We both shudder as the apartment door flies open and the snarl of the electric saw announces what we feared most.

"That fucking stupid bitch helped you - like I thought she would. You thought getting out would be easy. You forgot that you're both mine."

"Over my dead body," Theo smiles through his tears. He shoves me away mouthing 'GO' and I climb to my feet scampering across the lawn, away from Theo. Away from everything.

I freeze as a scream of sheer terror rips through the night muffled by a chainsaw growling and ripping through flesh like a rabid animal.

I sprint in the first direction I see clearly in front of me barely catching the name of the street I was on. The air is dewy and a soft blue glow hangs over the neighborhood.

My heart is pounding in my chest.

He was right behind me. He was right there.

Grandpa got Theo, and he was certainly coming for me.

I choke down my grief. Tears pricked and stung my eyes, blinding me as I ran, disappearing into the night.

3

llewyn hellsinger

This is How I Disappear - My Chemical Romance

It has been a long time since I have felt remorse for killing people. That was trained out of me long before I became the monster that I am today. Serving in the British Army during the first Great War watching your soldiers get blown to bits next to you will desensitize you real quick. It makes returning fire on the fucker that pulled the trigger first feel less controversial.

Trained to kill as a soldier and then a creature of the night, I am now a lethal weapon. Employed and enslaved to the beast that created me. Getting caught wasn't a concern, there was no way that they could trace it back to me. A ghostlike assassin that can absorb the very life essence of someone only just a few feet away leaves very little evidence.

In a sense, I am invincible from life's natural consequences, like remorse and guilt. Trivial emotions of a mortal mind and heart. Something that I've relinquished along with my soul. This mentality works well for a war-seasoned soldier as it does for a personal hitman for a vampire mafia family. It is not my job to feel remorse.

I await my target's arrival at the terminal, leaning against a pillar, pretending to check my phone like everyone else. When really the conversation

I had with the beast that created me is playing like a broken record, a tension in my hollow chest growing more taut as the day comes to an end.

Getting called to headquarters for a private chat was never a good sign.

Especially by Serlanos himself. It usually means you're in the shithouse, and for me he had a private matter for me to handle.

Today it was both.

This was my first job of the night, and my last is my worst.

I am a man of many nightmares, but I must keep that to myself. Not even my wife knows of my true nature, and it's better that way. She doesn't ask questions about where I go or what I do. No one should know what this curse has pushed me to do. I don't think that even mere mortals could compare to the damage I have done to humanity as a whole.

I'm not human, not anymore. I was once a man and now a beast. All thanks to the *man* who did this to me. Sitting across from me to deliver the harsh news is the very man who has me indulged in the art of our blood-thirsty kind: Serlanos Gyanstazi.

A Vampire. A mob boss. And complete asshole.

"Kill them," he orders, releasing the brume of his cigar, filling the private room with a thick musty stench that couldn't tickle the fancy of a primate.

Them as in my family. My human family. The wife and son that I've kept hidden from him in plainsight for the last seven years. He found Emily and Calvin.

How? Who knows. Could've been that he had someone follow me or someone saw me playing-house; mowing the lawn, shoveling the driveway or doing something domestic.

Either way, Serlanos knows and he is pissed.

"But why? What is the point?" I asked, a shocking sense of fury pulsing through my body.

"By Khor's Blood, I don't need to have a point, the point is that I need them gone. Not just me but the entire Blood Syndicate wants them gone," he growled, fangs extending as more smoke plumes out of his sharp nose.

"They are not a threat to you. They don't know anything about us. I've kept it that way," I retort against my better judgement. Talking back to a boss as ruthless as Serlanos is a dumb move. But this is my wife and child. Who are being reduced to nothing collateral damage. I am almost begging.

"But they are. The fact that you don't see that is a problem. I need them gone. You're lucky I am on the board otherwise we wouldn't be having this conversation, Llewyn. Without me, you'd be fucked. "

I couldn't negotiate with that. If I don't comply with his wishes then his efforts to help me would have gone to waste. No more kickbacks from the House of Gyanstazi. Or even worse. The Blood Syndicate will have my head.

"But why can't I just leave them behind, why do they have to die?"

"Because you broke the oath. Not only that but your contract to me. And you got married without my blessing. You are a ghost. An assassin. Emotional ties only result in turmoil. Do not make me regret helping you," he growled.

He's not just talking about now. He's talking about back then. That night in the dark alley where he gave me a choice after throwing a punch at his wingman. To bleed out in the alleyway or to serve him.

He loves holding that over my head. He's the only reason I am still walking this plane. He could have left me to die in that alley way if he so chose. But he decided to make me part of his little blood sucking family.

Seein' that I was a trained soldier proved to be of good use for him.

"Mr.Serlanos, how many times do I have to tell you? No smoking in the Private rooms!" the stern waitress scolded before sashaying away. Serlanos watches closely as she leaves.

I wasn't much of a fan of hers myself, but I hoped that he would listen to her. I could feel the secondhand smoke settling in, not that it would matter anyway.

"Another drink," he barked at her, and she reluctantly marched over to the mini bar and prepared his usual gin and tonic.

I observed her as she murmured under her breath, her brow furrowed and I felt every urge that she withheld to spit into the glass. She slammed the bottle down and threw a plastic cocktail straw into it, marched over, rashly set the drink on the table, and sashayed through the curtain.

"She knows too much," he said, with no feeling of embarrassment in his voice. He enjoyed pushing people's buttons, always had, always will.

"Well maybe you should keep your circle smaller," I snarked.

"Why do you think I have you around?" he laughed, his big belly heaving, which threw him into a fit of coughing.

"Maybe you should quit smoking, I am getting whiplash from the way you cough every time you let out that piggish squeal you call a laugh," I jeered.

"Not in this lifetime."

I couldn't help but laugh at that comment.

That cocktail dress never suited her anyway, I thought, looking down at her uninhabited body. She didn't have the right curves, she was built straight as an arrow, and it seemed that look of disgust wasn't a constant emotion. It was just her face. Her lips which were once a tacky shade of red were now colorless. Her eyes looked more livelier than when she was alive. I sat next to her body and observed the way she just lay there.

She may have been happier if she didn't have to deal with Serlanos. She may have still been alive.

In reality, I feel more so embarrassed for the people who fall for our tactics of manipulation, they really should have known better. She didn't put up much of a fight, I think she had known that this was a long time coming. When I tasted her blood, it seemed in a way that she thanked me, the look in her eyes showed that she wished she had done something different. I had never learned her name, even though she wore a nametag on her dress. I unclipped it and examined it carefully. Brenda. It was such a simple name, for a simple person. Simple, that was a word that was misleading to me.

"It's simple," he told me when describing how he did it.

"I'm not a cold-blooded killer," I said.

"No, not yet. Eventually, your blood will feel no heat nor cold."

When I entered the cabin, Serlanos was pouring his drink.

"I never did like her," he said.

"She wasn't too fond of you either," I said.

"Well, at least she died knowing that the feeling was mutual."

This was life, if that's what you could call it.

The plane landed in Chicago just as the sun was starting to rise. It was about 7 am. I stepped into the busy terminal, my target mark in my peripherals. People pushed past me to get to their gate. I, on the other hand, was in no rush ro get anywhere.

I had time to kill. And so did my target.

I ambled my way down the terminal toward the baggage claim, observing passing businessmen, families with mothers fussing at their small children to catch up with them, fathers scooping them up, and jogging with a small child hanging off their shoulder. Several older gentlemen sat in a waiting area, fast asleep and snoring. My mark has taken a seat with them, hoping to blend in. 'He had to know he couldn't escape the Gyanstazi family. Not when you're of value to them. He can't hide, not even if he tried.

I lurk on the outskirts of the terminal lobby. My distraction is split. I found myself fixated on one particular gentleman who was being doted on by his fussy wife, who kept checking the message board for the terminal train they were waiting by, most likely making sure that they were not getting on the wrong one that will take them to the other side of O'Hare.

I envied what they had. A lifetime of happiness together. Something I doubt I will ever get to experience.

I was amused by the way my target swung from the electrical cord, the way his legs dangled and recoiled from side to side. Luring my mark into the bathroom was no trouble, it seems that when you grow older, your bladder shrinks down to the size of a hamster. I search his gasping and gurgling corpse for his wallet, finding it in his back pocket. His passport was in his briefcase. Both went into my bag and I continued with my trek back home. Job completed.

I followed the small older couple onto the L and sat behind them as they dozed off to eternal sleep.

On the walk home from the station, my mind was rattled with plots to avoid Serlanos' request.

How could I just do away with my wife and child? He was the boss. Head of the Gyanstazi family and spokesperson for the Blood Syndicate. His word was law. Doing his bidding was what I had agreed to when accepting this life. As if I really had a choice in the matter.

I would need a plan. A plan to finally break free from him.

Unfortunately, every thought ended with the small family I had built being destroyed. There was no escaping Serlanos' wrath. If he wants someone dead, he will do it himself. In the most brutal way possible.

I walked the three blocks to where the cement met with the cobblestone and took a detour. I needed more time. I needed to give them more time to live.

I felt the warmth of the air escape into nothing as the sun set over the lake. The metal railing around the dock creaked along with the tide under the platform. I crossed my arms as I leaned against the railing, hanging my head. I may not be able to retain body heat. But when I feel warm against my body for a moment I feel alive again. Real. I want to feel something real.

This spot used to be a place of happy and memorable thoughts, but now I questioned every moment of positive reflection. Here was where I made the decision to ask Emily, a humble bookseller, to marry me. It's where I cried tears of joy when I learned that she was pregnant.

I had once been a human myself.

Life is precious. Fleeting when you're a mortal. It passes by you and before you know it, it's over. Like for that couple I left to their last moments together on the L, hands intertwined as they entered the beyond. It was bittersweet.

A better ending than I could say for my wife and son.

Emily and Calvin were curled together under a heap of blankets on our couch. She had called me earlier saying Cal had the chills and a slight fever. Quietly, I snuck into the linen closet and pulled out our ratchet-looking heating pad.

The cheap baby blue fabric had been shredded by our asshole cat. I always feared that it would one day catch on fire. I returned the heating pad and retrieved our space heater from the basement. Setting it on the side table, I checked the temperature of their feet.

They were like an iceberg, with a magma plume pounding its way through. I turned the space heater on medium and removed my jacket and pants and joined them in this cuddle puddle.

Emily stirred and smiled as I wrapped my arms around her and the small fussy boy.

I lay there, holding them close to me, inhaling their scent with every intent to imprint it in my mind. My body synced with their rhythm of breath, as if I were the last puzzle piece.

The only thing that mattered was this moment.

I ignore the smoke billowing around us and the flames licking up the walls. The walls crash in on us as we enjoy this last moment together as a family.

I wish I could die. But it's impossible. I've tried. Numerous times. Serlanos says it's normal for those like us to test the limits of mortality in the beginning. But I haven't given up.

Each time more gorier than the last. I've walked away unscathed every time, whether by fire or impalement. Nothing works. It fucking pisses me off. I want to die. I regret my moment of mortal weakness. I begged for the life that Serlanos was draining from me in that alleyway in London. He gave me another option and I took it, selling my soul, or what was left of it to him.

I crawl away from the burning house as it starts to crumble from the inside out and dart down an alleyway as the fire brigade weewoos past towards the billowing smoke cloud. Passerby stopped in shock and awe *"How horrible! I hope everyone got out okay"* and some rushed over to see what was happening. I continued towards the lake once I was sure no one had seen me.

A man covered in ash in smoke is bound to draw the wrong amount of attention. I need to rinse off and blend in.

Lay low for a while and bunker down.

I know— it's callous of me. Cold. I say I am not a cold-blooded killer but I just left my wife Emily and son Cal, who was just learning to walk, burn to death in our home. We just paid it off. What a fucking waste. But they were as good as dead. It was a kindness. If I didn't do it— Serlanos was going to. And he likes to play with his food.

Let them know exactly what is happening and how it's going to happen in every gruesome detail. I had some control and let them die of what would appear to be faulty wiring in an electric heating pad. It was a mercy killing.

The least I could do for them.

If they knew what a monster I was, I don't think I could live to eternity. And now the best thing I can do for myself is disappear.

Grabbing a shirt from a bodega while the clerk was distracted by the lights and sirens, I tugged on some new threads, grabbed a cap, and slipped in with the crowd, dissipating like black smoke into the night sky.

4

lenora holmwood

The Ghost of You - My Chemical Romance

High winds blowing in from the lakeshore ruffle my ravenlike hair and I basque in the feeling of fresh air filling my lungs. I soaked in each breath and each step. I embraced the uneven concrete matching my feet. The world is welcoming me back. Six fucking years. No human being is meant to be kept inside that long.

The world feels foreign and surreal as it rushes past me, as it always has been. Life didn't stop just because I wasn't there to witness it. The rail system rattles and clunks high above the surface roads. Shady characters hide in the shadows of the alleys.

People looked different - expressionless. Dead. Like the light behind their eyes has just fizzled out.

The fashions have changed. Some I could recognize, others were new and bizarre. Sometimes I forget how long it's been since I've seen another actual human being. Talked to someone else that wasn't my brother Theo. Or laid eyes on someone that wasn't as revolting as Grandpa, who lost his belief in general hygiene.

Six years is a long time.

I see two men wearing flamingo colored skin suits walking down Broadway and realize I have a lot to learn about today's culture and fashion.

Buildings with large billboards of the latest fashions closed in on me, making me feel outdated and worn out. I felt underdressed.

People are gawking as I pass.

I know I look terrible. My tights and skirt are torn. My jacket is tattered and I haven't had a proper bath or shower in - dare I say. A time capsule of the day I was yanked away from the world and hidden until it was the right time to turn me loose on the world. There's something about the way I look that says that I never thought that day would come.

I don't want to bring too much attention. Word of my escape has surely reached Serlanos.

Grandpa would have rung him first thing. They will be looking for a lost looking woman.

And I am super fucking lost.

I was never too familiar with the southside of Chicago to begin with and everythings changed since Grandpa locked us in for good. Run down businesses were new and thriving establishments. Yoga studios that I'd seen on the Northside had opened up here, along with Starbucks and other bougie bars and shops. The city was cleaning up.

I need to do the same. I am desperate to find a bathroom. And something to eat.

I found a gas station that had a bathroom. I make an attempt to clean up in the grim and yellow stained bathroom, scrubbing my hand and face with the flimsy paper towel and some hand soap. I locked the door so I knew I had total privacy. The clerk had hardly noticed my presence and I highly doubt he's going to come knocking any time soon. I stare into the mirror but I don't recognize the girl in front of me.

My eyes are bloodshot from lack of sleep and crying. I look gaunt and pale from months of being imprisoned in a condemned apartment building. My long dark tousled hair is messy and dry. I pull it back and toss it in a ponytail. Better for travel.

I need to be prepared to brave the streets of Chicago. I turn down one street hoping it would lead somewhere that would give me some sort of idea of how to get elsewhere. But each turn I make I become more disoriented.

I only have so much cash to get me to the next town - I need to conserve until I have a plan.

I need to find my bearings.

I couldn't run anymore. I haven't eaten anything in god knows how long, and my stomach is growling at me for something.

I am running low on energy, I need to find somewhere to rest. somewhere familiar.

Using some of the cash to buy a ticket for the L train back to Northside, I find a seat and kick back and watch the world pass by until I recognize the street names.

Davis Street. I could wait to get back to my neighborhood. Find a place to stay and to have a fucking shower and feel human again.

The shower in Grandpa's apartment worked sporadically, so it wasn't guaranteed we'd get water flowing through the broken pipes. Gram would usually put a bucket out on the back patio to collect fresh rainwater. Looking back now, the way that woman survived living in shambles and squalor was an art. After living in luxury and the limelight of Michigan Avenue, moving to a dilapidated apartment building was the lowest of the low.

My lip trembles with horror and tears start to form knowing what has become of Gram.

There's no way she's alive. We—I heard the gunshot.

She helped us escape. He could never forgive that.

Not with so much money on the line. That was their ticket out of the trenches and she just tore it up in front of him.

The one act of grandmotherly love she could give us.

She had nothing left.

And she gave her last moments alive to me, as did Theo who's now - no, I can't think about it.

He's going to come looking for me. I have to keep moving.

I fell asleep on the train and awoke to some homeless guy jerking off in the seat diagonal from mine, staring at me. Disturbed, I get up and stumble off the train at the next stop.

On the platform, I am lost and look around for anything familiar.

Anywhere that I could go. I find the stairs, but my balance is off. I feel my legs shake with each step down and I hug the railing.

My stomach grows heavy with bile, my body hot and my vision blurs. My eyes roll to the back of my head as I feel my legs give out from exhaustion.

The cold hard pavement feels hard and cold as I collapse there at the bottom of the platform stairs.

Blurred figures start crowding around me. I hear voices of concern but I cannot understand them.

A soothing hand caresses my face as I slip into unconsciousness.

I don't know if I will be okay, I want to disappear.

5

llewyn hellsinger

Boy Division - My Chemical Romance

My phone buzzed sharply in my pocket, startling me as I fell into a disassociating daze at the cafe table I'd been camping at for a few hours. It was either my neighbors calling frantically about my house being on fire. Or it was Serlanos.

Checking the screen, I see it's the latter. I don't answer. The call dies only to start up again.

I still don't answer. I am debating my options here.

I have choices. I could walk away. Start over, leave this life behind, and try to find a quiet place to spend the rest of eternity. Or I could answer my fucking phone and succumb to whatever bullshit Serlanos has in mind for me now.

I pull the phone out and stare at it momentarily before answering. Fuck it.

"Llewyn."

"Where the fuck have you been?! I've been calling you for thirty minutes," Serlanos roars into the speaker, I hold the phone away from my ear. "Get your ass on the streets. The Holmwood girl, she's escaped. I just left that shithole her grandpa owns. Put a bullet in the old man's head. Said he'd shot his wife and the grandson for letting her get away. I told him that he missed one."

Damn, that's cold. What is it about this girl— Lenora Holmwood. Sounds like some uptight Northside girl. Which that's exactly what she is. Her family lived on the nicer side of Evanston on Sheridan Avenue. Not far from where the remnants of my double life lay smoldering in ash.

Serlanos has been terrorizing the Holmwoods for as long as I can remember.

It was only a matter of time before Serlanos was to take one as his bride.

This family fucked with the wrong vampire.

"What does she look like? Send me a picture."

"Already on your phone. I will be waiting by the phone for updates. Bring her to me alive. Her blood and flesh are mine."

The line falls dead. His word is law.

How the fuck am I going to find this girl?

She's a ghost in the wind. If she could escape that hell hole her grandfather owned then certainly she would be smart enough to lay low. She wouldn't be stupid enough to go back to her home, there's nothing left of it thanks to Serlanos and his men. They burn it to the ground after the assassination.

I scroll to my messages and open up a stream of texts.

Photos that Serlanos has collected over the years of stalking the poor girl up until her grandfather locked her up.

Lenora Holmwood, now of age, is hot as fuck— but you could see that she was going to be a drop-dead knockout from her school photos.

I feel a little less like a century-old pervert.

Where would she go?

She literally has nowhere to go. Everyone she's ever known is dead or has abandoned her. She's probably lost somewhere on the southside, which is not somewhere you want to get lost. Especially nowadays.

Crime - thanks to us- has been booming and Chicago PD can't keep up. Nor can our enemies. Serlanos has been dominating the region's blood banks and hospitals. Ordelia and Talon are pulling all of their resources together to bargain with Serlanos, something no one ever wants to have to do. Serlanos is under the illusion that he is a fair vampire to do business with. Tensions are high with the Blood War on the rise. We can only keep our enemies at bay for so long. Ordelia has been dominating the trafficking racket, cutting off their tribes for fresh and willing vassals.

For now.

Rumor is Cynfael is making his move soon. He's just opened a new club he's been begging me to check out.

I pay for my coffee - the girl at the counter winks at me and leaves her number on my cup sleeve.

She looks like my wife.

The one I just left in a burning house with our son.

The wailing of the sirens still echo in the background as I exit the coffee house, sipping my overpriced cup of coffee.

I've had to kill off my family before— it's not new. I've started over numerous times, hoping that time would be different and Serlanos would never find out.

But he always did.

Every time.

Ten wives I've disposed of in numerous ways. All at his demand.

He always found me despite my numerous hideouts around town. I'm convinced he's either having me followed or there's some power he has that he's kept hidden from me. To my enemies, I am quick and agile and three steps ahead at all times. I am there before they even walk in the room. But with Serlanos, it's like he knows my every move. He lives freely in my head and I can't shake him. I cannot block him out. He's like cancer, his malignant influence spreading like disease.

I would have never done these things if it weren't for him.

My life would have been completely different if I hadn't given into a moment of weakness and gone home to my mother. It could have been normal, I would have died when I should have instead of watching life as I know it crumble before my eyes and transform into what is known now.

If I am going to shake Serlanos and I am going to have to get further from Chicago to do that.

And maybe that's exactly what Ms.Holmwood had planned.

Stepping out onto the street from the coffee shop, I notice a large commotion of panic just down the street on Davis outside the L Station staircase. Blaring police and emergency lights flashed from around the corner as the paramedics worked and the police controlled the crowd. "Back it up—give us some room."

I can't resist the urge to find out what was happening.

Blending in with the crowd, I camp out behind two chattering hens that couldn't help but gossip and cluck on.

"She was found unconscious in the street. Some thought she was dead but when we found a registered nurse, we were able to find a pulse and get the paramedics here. Police say that Ms. Holmwood has been missing for several years and that she was lucky someone found her."

"Did she say about where she's been all this time?"

"No. She hadn't said anything. Rumors are that she went to live with her grandparents. From there, no one has heard anything until now."

"What about the boy?"

"The what?"

"The Holmwoods had a son, Theodore - I think was his name."

"Time will tell. I am sure there will be a full investigation into this."

Well, looks like Ms. Holmwood is going to be a bit harder to get to than I thought. I watch as they wheel the poor girl on the stretcher. Despite how terrible she looked, she was beautiful. Her skin pale like frost and her hair dark as night with hints of amber like embers of a coal burning out. She was pale and thin and unconscious. An oxygen mask has been placed over her plump rosebud lips.

I want to bite those lips. Taste her.

Her neck was exposed and there was a clear path through the crowd.

The frenzy burned inside me.

But I can't risk it. Not when I have a crowd of witnesses.

Calm down, I tell myself.

I know where they're taking her— Ingalls Memorial. I will just have to get there and improvise.

I turn to leave the scene but am met with a cloth bag and am tossed into the back of a limo that speeds away before anyone could say a word.

6

llewyn hellsinger

Blood - My Chemical Romance

"You're an idiot for showing your face around here, Llew," a snide voice sneers at me as the cloth blind is pulled off and I am offered a goblet of garnet red blood.

"As are you, you're on our turf. Serlanos will certainly hear about this. Especially when the Holmwood girl is his mark," I retort before taking a sip. The moment the blood touches my lips I am frenzied with a ferocious thirst and guzzle it down. Riskel, Cynfael's big silent brute sits next to me, eyeing me suspiciously. He never enjoyed these little entourages between me and Cynfael. He still doesn't trust me. I ignore his judgment. I can't ignore fresh blood when it is offered to me. Not in the middle of a drought. The revenant soldiers are chomping at the bit and enforcing Serlanos' mandatory fasting order. Since Chief Warren has been cracking down on organized crime, keeping our organization in his focus, Serlanos has been mandating strict rules for us to not attract attention.

"Easy, easy boy. There's plenty more where that comes from," Cynfael chuckles as he takes my goblet before I drop it and opens up a wound like a wine bottle cork on the unconscious woman that lay across the back bench of the limousine.

I nearly tear it out of his hands when he fills it to the brim. Beads of crimson poured over his hand and I was half tempted to lick it off. Since our supply has run dry— things have gotten a bit desperate.

"You better hold up your end of the deal or so help me God, Cyn, I'll drive a stake through that smug face of yours," I sneer wiping my face with a kerchief.

"Everything will go just as planned, Llew. Don't worry, I have no plans of stirring the pot so long as Callum doesn't."

"I cannot make any promises for that crazy fucker."

And Cyn is counting on that. He wants to have a reason to hold power over Callum's head. The fact that Callum is desperate for blood, yet victims are harder to come by for him.

It comes down to Serlanos who has lost a main blood supply. Serlanos lost a lot when he ordered the death of the Holmwoods. A decision made in a moment of rage and malice. Mr. Holmwood was our main supplier. But what could he want with his daughter - other than to cast further insult on his grave. It was bad enough the brutal way he had murdered them. Drained them of their blood right there in the theater, leaving the employees to find them there - empty of all life.

"The Holmwood girl is not going to solve his problems— he's focused on the wrong things right now. He's thinking emotionally and that's dangerous. You know it won't be long until you'll come crawling over to us, Llew," Cynfael teases.

He's right— I don't know what Serlanos thinks that girl has that's going to solve anything. Declaring her blood as his property in front of the whole syndicate makes her off-limits to other members and makes her a delicious target.

She's a mortal. Just a mortal. And we aren't in the practice of taking on mortal brides.

So I thought.

With the exception of Serlanos' succubus that he had turned and sold off to Ordelia, Serlanos preferred to be untethered. Believes that emotional attachment as a hindrance. And as his personal hitman, I need to be disposable. A ghost.

Usually he paid no attention to women with the exception of satisfying his sadistic needs. It was never just one woman either. I've never seen him target one mortal like he has with Lenora Holmwood.

"How close to war are we?"

"Very, my friend. Just make sure you're on the right side when shit goes down.

7

lenora holmwood

Sleep - My Chemical Romance

Stirred awake by a cacophony of beeps and rasps it takes me only seconds to realize that I am indeed in a hospital. Laid up in a bed that's attached to a series of machines beeping. Which is a good sign. Means I am relatively alive. The room around me spinned and my vision was blurred. But I could sense someone else was in here.

I could feel another presence in my room - I could have sworn to have seen a shadow outline of a man with long dark hair looming in the corner, watching me closely like a wolf stares down its prey.

It must be a trick of the light. The night guard was still on duty outside my door. He hasn't noticed that I was conscious.

I had nothing to worry about. For now, it seemed.

I pass out, half believing it's Theo watching over me. Stroking my face like the angel that's watched over me since this nightmare began in childhood. Always there's been a presence, looming over. No matter how bad it got, that phantom feeling of a hand caressing my cheek was there in nights of terrible nightmares.

I want to believe it was all just a terrible nightmare and the police came and rescued us too when busting the drug den next door.

Maybe when I wake up again, I will be greeted with open arms and Theo's wide goofy grin - everything fades to black.

"Theo."

"What's that, sweetheart," a foreign voice replies.

"Theo," my throat is dry and my eyes are weighed shut.

"I am right here, honey. You're in the hospital. I am Nurse Kylee. Can you tell me your name?" Nurse Kylee asks calmly, taking my hand in hers.

"Le-Lenora Holmwood," I rasp, blinking my eyes aggressively. Everything starts to come into view. Nurse Kylee is young and petite with a bandana and dark long hair falling underneath it.

"Good. Good job. Can you tell me your birthday, Lenora?"

"October 24th." Why aren't you answering my question, Nurse Kylee?

Nurse Kylee radios for the doctor to come at once while she stands by my side and takes notes as I struggle to keep awake.

Whatever they got me on is kicking my ass. But perhaps it's necessary.

The doctor rushes in and Nurse Kylee takes him aside and whispers to him before he attends to me. He repeats the same questions as he pokes and prods at me. I wanted to smack the shit out of him when he peeled my eyes open and shined a flashlight in them.

"Nurse Kylee, get her in for an MRI. I am concerned about there being retinal damage when she took the fall. Might be linked to a concussion. Forward me the results and I will come back after lunch.

"Where's Theo?!" I say again loudly, catching them off guard.

The nurse gives a sympathetic smile. " Come on sweetheart, let's get you in for the MRI."

Where the fuck is my brother? Is he in the next room?

My body wants to go in every direction as I lie dead still in the MRI machine. I need to know why my brother isn't here. Why is he not by my side?

What could be keeping him from me? We've not been apart. Never.

Back in my private room, the nurse has me set up with a tv remote and a tv tray of soft foods. Due to my malnourishment, they're concerned I might reject solid foods, unsure of the last time I actually ate. The doctor informed me that I was severely underweight and was suffering from a vitamin d deficiency.

Which is all important news - however, he's been avoiding the number one question: where the fuck is Theo?

I shovel the food around on my tray. Impatient. Antsy. I don't want the food, even though I know my stomach is physically screaming at me to eat something. But I need to know that Theo was found and is okay before I take one bite.

I lay in my hospital bed, and watched the tv, my mind spiraling. Has anyone made any efforts to find my brother? Surely since my escape someone would have thought to go look for him?

My spiraling thoughts are once again interrupted.

The doctor walks in with Nurse Kylee.

"Hi Lenora, I am Dr. Biederman. How are you feeling today?"

I am already sick and tired of asking that question.

"I'll be better when I know where my brother is."

"Yes, Nurse Kylee mentioned you were asking for him as you woke up. The authorities -"

The nurse knocks on the door before entering and two men in suits follow behind. "Pardon the interruption, doctor. The detectives are here and would like a word in private with Ms. Holmwood."

My body tenses up.

Everything I've been dreading comes to the surface as they approach cautiously - my heart is pounding in my ears so loud I barely heard their names.

"Ms. Holmwood, I am Chief Deputy Warren of the Chicago P.D Organized Crime Unit and my partner Sergeant Peterson. I am sorry to intrude at a time like this but it is of great importance. We would like to speak about the events that occurred at the residence of Artemis Holmwood two nights ago. We've recovered three bodies that we believe may have been victims of fowl play. We have some photos we'd like you to take a look at - I do warn you they are graphic."

"It's okay to say no," the other detective adds.

No, I need to see this.

The detectives set the crime scene photos on the table in front of me - each of them gorier than the last. Gram's eyes are still open, yet she looked unsurprised. She knew what she'd done and accepted her fate.

Grandpa got less than he deserved. I stare at the man that was supposed to be my grandfather and feel nothing at the sight of his brains splattered against the wall. I wish I had been there. He broke his promise to Dad. I don't think there's a worse sin than that.

The last photo.

I can't.

The nurse hurries the detectives out of the room as my cries and screams of grief carry through the corridor.

8

lenora holmwood

Breathe - Tommee Profit Ft Fleurie

I don't recall when I fell asleep, but it was restless. Each time I closed my eyes I was back in that small dank dilapidated room with the peeling wallpaper and frightening lights flashing on the walls, creating silhouettes of monsters so frightening that I would hide under the covers. Theo would always remind me they weren't real. " It's just a trick of our minds to find the worst in the darkness."

Sometimes he would use the light to his advantage and make shadow puppets with his hands and tell stories to pass the time.

Each time I woke up I had to reprocess reality again.

Theo is gone. Ripped to pieces. By our own grandfather. I can still hear the whirring of the chainsaw.

I'll never see Theo's goofy grin again. Feel the comfort that I wasn't alone in this world.

When we lost our parents, we at least had each other. Now I have nothing. No one except strangers that claim to be my friend. It's like waking up into a nightmare that never ends.

Moments from my rescue come back jumbled. Sometimes in moments of clarity, others in my unconscious. Sometimes all at once, or spaced out.

Sometimes it's as if it's happening in real time— the red and blue lights and the commotion and whispers from passersby and emergency services all come flooding back.

The poor woman who had found me just at the bottom of the stairs to the subway station shook me awake as best she could but I was fading in and out of consciousness. I heard the panic in her voice as she dialed 9-1-1 and calmly explained to them that she had found me at the bottom of the L station on Davis Street.

'I think it's the Holmwood girl that went missing a few years back,' her voice shook with uncertainty.

I always forget that Theo and I were kept hidden away for so long, imprisoned in our grandfather's hotel hell— nothing seems real.

I count my blessings that she found me and not someone else.

If Serlanos or one of his serpents had found me, who knows if I'd be alive to see the light of day again, which now broke through the window illuminating the high rise in the distance.

I felt as if I had barely slept.

The morning nurse comes in and checks my vitals and asks if I want any breakfast. I nod, feeling the grumble in my stomach grow louder. She nods and leaves to retrieve a tray from the cart that was brought to the Trauma unit.

The tray had a sad helping of wet eggs and fruit that had been cut into bite size pieces. I got a choice of a milk carton or orange juice. I went for orange juice.

As I dig in, I hear a knock at the door. A man with kind eyes and rimmed glasses dressed in a sweater vest enters softly and takes a seat in a chair by my hospital bed.

"Lenora, I am Dr. Fanguido, a licensed trauma therapist. I've been referred to you by the hospital. During these sessions I don't want you to think of me as a doctor but rather just an open ear to listen. No judgment. You've a lot to process and I am here to listen and give you coping strategies. How does that sound?"

I nod but continue to stare out the window, disassociating. I wanted to be anywhere but here right now. Facing reality sounded like anything but calming.

I haven't seen a shrink since my parents died. The school insisted as did some of our extended family. Gram sourced one for us. I think Theo and I went at least twice before we stopped going altogether. We knew the threat wasn't over.

No amount of talking was going to fix that whoever killed our parents was going to come after us too.

The shrink and I sat there in silence. I couldn't even look him in the eye. Sure, his eyes were kind. But how did I know that he wasn't going to just sell this information to any reporter. I cannot trust anyone. Especially when my name continues to be the headline news, people reporting on my discovery and rescue. The nurse who found me has had her fifteen minutes of fame. I see a card resting among the other bouquets and gifts that I can only assume is from her. It seemed personal.

I may reach out. I may not.

I really don't want to talk to anyone.

I miss being in hiding.

A few hours later I have yet another visitor. A tall man in a suit with dark hair and glasses begs for entry and I nod to my stern security guard to allow him in.

"Ms. Holmwood, I am Roderick Remus. I managed your father's estate. I am so, so sorry for your loss and what you've endured. You have mine and my office's full support through your recovery."

"Thanks, I guess." I don't really know what to say anymore when people say that. Like it's not their fault? I think.

"I know things may seem overwhelming right now, but I was hoping you'd be open to discuss the matter of your estate. Since you are of age, you are the sole inheritor of the Holmwood fortune."

I gesture for him to take a seat in the chair by the window.

He pulls it closer and sets his briefcase on his lap and begins rifling through it.

" Given that it's a large sum of money, I do advise that you consult someone who knows what they're doing. Invest. Or I could even make a note of guardianship and you will be given an allowance to cover living expenses until you get on your feet."

This guy gets right to it. I look him over, wondering if I can trust this man that just walked in claiming to know so much about me and my family's money. I don't know what Dad set aside for us. Dad had so many secrets.

I know I am skeptical, maybe for the right reasons, but something else is not right with this guy.

As he speaks, my mind jumps to the wildest conclusions. I try to shake them from my head. I am just being paranoid. But then my eyes land on something that confirms this paranoia. A ring on his right finger, with the same garnet bat emblem that was embossed on the ring that Serlanos wore. The one on the pendant bullet that hung around my neck. The last gift from my father.

He's one of them.

"Do you have plans for when you leave the hospital?"

I shake my head no.

"I know it's so soon, but think about it and get back to me. We can set up a financial plan. You won't have to lift a finger."

I stare at him. I have no words. What do I say or do here? Here's a man I am supposed to trust after all that I've been through, and yet I can't.

For the same reason that I can't trust anyone that crosses my path now.

I have to leave— but I am not going to tell him, or anyone.

9

llewyn hellsinger

The World is Ugly - My Chemical Romance

The city lights blare in through the window casting a halo-like glow around her soft slumber. I sit in the corner, watching over her. Praying she doesn't wake and starts screaming. Which she would have every reason to - I mean, I admit I am being creepy right now. Dark brooding vampire in the corner just drooling over a beautiful unconscious girl, what a pop culture cliche. But I can't help it.

She's perfect.

Pale skin. Soft red lips. Dark cascading hair that frames her neckline perfectly.

I've never wanted anything so bad.

This is why Serlanos had me on this job. To torture me. With flesh and blood he knows that I can never have. Declaring her as his in front of the Blood Syndicate made her off limits, blood and flesh.

I am destined to be alone because he wishes for it.

Just as he has fated her to be enslaved to him. He ripped everything she had away with the snap of his fingers. Leaving her the only choice he's given her, to be his.

I killed my whole family to save them from a fate worse than what awaited them in the afterlife.

Two people— alone because of one monster.

What a bastard.

No one knows I've made this visit when she arrived in the hospital.

Serlanos would have my head on a silver platter stuffed with garlic if he knew I had been this close to her and taken no action to bring her to him.

But I can't.

How can I hand her over to the man who would drain her of her life essence before he ever thought about showing a drop of mercy?

I can't do that.

Not to her. She's lost so much already.

She deserves a fighting chance— so I am going to give it to her.

I will come up with some excuse for Serlanos, convince him that it's not the right time. Too many people have eyes on her and it would bring unwanted attention from the mortals. We cannot have that - we are in the middle of a war.

A war worth more than blood.

My phone buzzes in my pocket and I know that it is time to leave, but not without one more look. I set the rose I stole from the bodega on the street on the night table beside her.

Run while you can, girl.

Roderick didn't give me anything more than what was due when I stopped by to pick up this week's payment. When I asked about his visit to the hospital, Roderick was less than forthcoming.

"She didn't say anything of significance. And as her attorney, I cannot divulge anything pertaining to her estate. If you have questions about your own personal matters, I'd be happy to discuss those."

The smug bastard Roderick sits back in his chair. His pale lips spread thin across his face.

I just want to punch him. He wouldn't help me even if he could. He'd do anything to spite Serlanos, after what he did to him. Brought Roderick back from near death just to serve him. He would've been happier dead, as he so reminds me.

Trust me, me too, asshole.

"Haha, very funny. Still keeping up with the charade of being a lawyer."

"Just because I am one of you now doesn't mean I've lost my integrity as a lawyer." As if he really had any to begin with. Roderick Remus has been ripping off most of the northside, bleeding their estates and trusts long before he was turned.

"No but it does solidify your identity as a blood sucking leech."

"Haha - fuck you, Llewyn. You won't be laughing at Callum's wedding." The words that passed through his spite laced lips had me choking on dead air.

"The fuck are you talking about?"

Roderick doesn't say anything, just smiles to himself, feeling proud of himself for making it into Serlanos' inner circle. Close enough to know information before I do. Serlanos' personal hitman and adoptive son.

Callum isn't the type to take brides. He just fucks the ones Serlanos has made blood bonds with a few of Ordelia's succubi, allowing Callum to do whatever he wants to them. He's a sadistic fuck.

He fucks mortal women and drains them for all their worth.

If he gets his hands on Lenora, she's dead.

My phone buzzes in my pocket.

Speaking of the devil, it's Callum.

"Get your ass back to the hospital. We're bringing her in tonight. Serlanos isn't going to wait on this any longer."

He hangs up before Llewyn could reply.

Duty fucking calls.

"Good luck," Roderick laughs maniacally from his chair, kicking his feet up.

lenora holmwood

Art of Survival - Bishop Briggs

I can't sleep anymore. I've slept all day waiting for three am to roll around. Three days in bed has done me no favors. I am a sitting duck. I lay in bed pretending to sleep and wait for the night nurse to leave for her third smoko break for the evening. The first hour of her shift she took a break and left the nurses station about every fifteen minutes so I knew that it was only a matter of time that the urge struck again. She would return smelling of freshly sprayed cotton candy perfume and chewing mint gum.

I smelled it on her the last time she checked in on me. I've barely bothered her for anything. I didn't want to bring attention to myself. I wanted them to forget I was even there, just enough to slip into the cracks and disappear. I had my drawstring bag under the covers at the foot of my bed. The last bit of everything we -I owned. Which wasn't much. Some old clothes that Theo had and a photo frame of our parents, and a notebook I'd caught Theo reading at night.

Dad's last gift hung around my neck. The silver bullet pendant. I find myself playing with it when I am nervous or focused.

I slip into the sweats and jacket Theo had packed and throw my hair up into a bun. I was unrecognizable. I could blend in with a crowd and slip through unnoticed. At least for a little while. A security guard makes his rounds every half hour so as to make sure paparazzi don't sneak up here to get a shot for the tabloids.

Scoping the floor to the right and left before leaving the ward, I get a lay of the land. I can't risk getting caught. By a nurse, night guard or one of those brutes Serlanos has circling outside. I'd recognize them in a heartbeat.

Dark and brooding. Otherworldly.

I dart through the first set of swinging doors. I hold my breath as I move quickly down the corridor towards the elevators, praying a security guard doesn't come round the corner or that I get stuck at a dead end.

Or worse.

And worse just stepped off the elevator. Callum, one of Serlanos' brutes that has paid our apartment a visit or two. He nearly broke two of Theo's thumbs for speaking to him. I hated him and his very essence.

Tall, blond and brooding he steps into the lobby of the Psyche unit, and looks around. I am trapped in the corridor opposite, with nowhere to run but towards him.

Fuck.

I should have known it would be so long before Serlanos sent someone for me.

To claim what he's deluded to be rightfully his.

I am no fucking prize to be won.

I push through the emergency stairwell door to my left and fly down the stairs.

II

callum gyanstazi

Honey this Mirror Ain't Big Enough for the Two of Us - My Chemical Romance

"How is it that two of my best trackers are being outrun by a human? Are you not vampires? Stalkers of the night? Bring her to me or there will be hell to pay."

Serlanos' disappointment echoed through the empty art gallery as he paced before us like a disappointed father.

"If it weren't for Llew being so soft with humans, we'd have her by now," I grit through my teeth. I am tired of whatever humane part of Llewyn that still lives inside him getting in the way.

Llewyn stands phlegmatic as Serlanos continues to tear into us. As if nothing matters to him anymore. Not the oath that we made. It's like he feels no shame anymore for abandoning his duties.

And that needs to change. We used to be a team. Brothers, and now it's like I don't know him these days.

And tomorrow we have important business to take care of.

A one day truce to make the exchange with Cynfaels horde of shit-heads that defected with him.

58

The roman white showroom echoes with Serlanos' criticisms for the late night art enthusiasts to hear and cower away from. Behind him the father and daughter of the American Gothic look upon us, as if they too disapproved of our failures.

How is Llewyn so unbothered, unphased. He just takes this lashing as if it's nothing. As if Serlanos isn't already punishing us for what happened at the blood bank. And tomorrow we have the exchange with Cynfael and his men at the diner. How is that going to go? When Cynfael has stolen half of our revenants. Finding willing converts for Serlanos has been no problem, but pureblood vampires that were still willing to do his bidding were hard to find. But now with the bid on the Holmwood girl, many have taken interest.

He's been making promises left and right from what I've heard from Lycidas and Norryx.

"You cannot blame this on Llewyn completely. You were there at the hospital too! And somehow she slipped past both of you!"

But it's true. Llewyn dropped the ball. And still he says nothing, he takes no responsibility for his negligence.

What was he doing instead of watching her?

I got off that elevator and found Llewyn in the empty hospital ward. The girl's bed is empty. He supposedly had been watching her around the clock. How did she get past our great assassin? He is supposed to be the ghost, unseen and unavoidable? Is he losing his touch? Has he gone soft since he torched his human wife?

I wait for him to say something, anything. I can tell he senses my impatience, like a small child waiting for the older sibling to cough up the truth. I am not going down for his fuck up. All he had to do was bring the girl to the loading dock at the shift change and we would make away with her without anyone noticing. But somehow he missed her slipping down the stairs and out the emergency exit.

"It won't happen again, sir," Llewyn finally responds.

"It better fucking not! I expect results. And tomorrow at the diner there better not be any fuck ups there. We can't afford anymore attention from the public. Chief Warren is breathing down my neck right now as this blood war has gotten out of control. I told him it was out of my hands," Serlanos continued to yell, spit flying out, his fangs beginning to protrude as his fury released.

The blood war. We've hit the largest shortage in a millenia. It all went downhill once Leonidas Holmwood was murdered. It's what's keeping us all at bay. Only feeding when Serlanos is fed. Serlanos was just as hungry. We were all hungry. Clans across town were struggling. Bodies were found left and right. Covered up in the news as a drug epidemic. But those close to the case knew it was much more horrific than that. Chief Deputy Warren of the Organized Crimes Department has been fighting us every step of the way. Trying to find one reason to break his deal with Serlanos and call in the special forces that knew how to deal with 'leechbags' like us. Vampire hunters.

A few school children found a body that had been turned inside out and planted among the hedges in Lincoln Park. Chief Warren is still paying the family to keep that out of the news and many years of therapy.

"Now get out of my sight and find that girl before someone else does. Bring her back to me alive and unbitten. I need her blood unsoiled."

Llewyn doesn't need to be asked twice before he strides out of the exhibit room leaving Serlanos and I alone in the gallery.

"You know that lately my trust in our dear Llewyn has been waning. Ever since finding out about that sham of a family he kept secret and several moments where he's just fallen down on the job, I worry about him. Keep an eye out for him. Watch him closely. If he so much as makes puppy eyes at a mortal I want to know. ”

"I can do that. And what about the girl? Do you think he can rise up to the task?"

"I will give him the smallest benefit of the doubt, however, if you succeed before he does I can guarantee you first rytes in the blood bonding ceremony."

Serlanos told me in private that once the girl is here, and he's drunk from her, she's mine.

And I have something planned for her. Those sweet voluptuous red lips would look perfect wrapped around my cock right before I drain her until she begs for more. I am not usually this ruthless, but for her I will make an exception.

llewyn hellsinger

Bat Country - Avenged Sevenfold

I know he's behind me. Following me on Serlanos' orders for sure. I am on the hook. I've let Serlanos down again. But not as much as Callum has. He dropped the ball when we raided that blood bank to make this exchange happen. Had it not been for his fuck up, we wouldn't be in as much trouble. But Callum is a hotheaded bastard and the thrill of a blood bath gets the best of him.

Since losing the blood bank in town to another sect of vampires, we've had to make other arrangements. Leonidas Holmwood was our key to holding down the blood banks and hospitals we did have in our control, but Serlanos wanted more and the spread was too thin. Leaving too much room for the enemy to swoop in.

Our blood supply has been bone dry and Callum was fiending fiercely that night. It'd been weeks since we'd been paid, despite the promises for a blood drop at our shadowy doorstep. Yet nothing came.

Drooling at the bit as he slowly loaded the bags of emergency blood into the duffle bag, dying for just one drop. He hesitates as each bag falls into the duffle to never be seen again.

"Later," I urged him to work swiftly. I knew what he was thinking, like I wasn't guilty of sucking down one of these bad boys like a capri sun as I passed a stray cart of blood samples in the hospitals.

I saw the shine of feral starvation crawl across his dark eyes as they glowered over the bags of blood. What came next was nothing short of a rampage of a starved vampire.

Blood is everywhere. Dripping from the walls of the chilled storage room beads of ruby and crimson from the back splash of Callum's carnage. Bags ripped open and devoured in seconds. My throat clenched as the blood poured and trickled down his throat. Dry with hunger. I struggled to restrain myself but temptation took over. All I see is red. And then I am a bloody mess having devoured several packages of blood in seconds.

"I knew you couldn't resist. You're no different than me, Llew. Why can't you accept that?" Callum antagonizes from his blood puddle on the ground. Drunk on blood.

I guess I still have a drop of humanity left in me.

I turn left down a side alley and disappear darting down around sharp corners, knowing he was hot on my trail. This felt like the old days, when we first arrived in the city and prowled at night to get a feel for the territory. Jumping from building to building puts most parkour artists to shame.

I jump a fire escape and climb to the top, and listen for the rattle to follow me from below.

"You took long enough," I taunt as he reaches the top, nearly breathless.

"I admit, Llewyn. You're in better shape than I am."

"What? Are you getting old or something?"

We both laugh. But it dies quickly, unable to ignore the dead body in the room.

"Where are you running off to? Your new boss Cynfael?" I could hear the hurt in his voice. Callum never liked Cynfael. He took more of a shine to me than him. And views him as the enemy, the sense of having stolen his brother from him. Callum's always been possessive of me.

He was there to help me through the trials of vampirism taking over my body. Wiping my face as my mind slipped over into oblivion and then crawlings its way back through hell. He helped me feed for the first time, teaching me how to find an easy target and how to strike. And in turn I taught him. My experience in the military wasn't for nothing. I had been trained to kill long before I had become a vampire and there were strategies that were applicable in any situation.

"Actually, no. I was running off the pressure of carrying the weight of the blood exchange we have tomorrow. Are you and the boys ready?" I retorted, trying to hide my irritation but failed.

"Ready? We have been preparing for this for months."

Have they now? What would they be preparing for? All we do is meet up in a public restaurant to exchange the blood and the money and part ways. No fangs bared and growling.

"No fucking shady business. We promised peace for a day."

"This is stupid. Why are we giving them blood in the middle of a drought?"

"Because paying our dues keeps the peace between the sects."

"We barely have enough for us."

"I know."

We remain silent for a while. "You don't honestly think you've done all the work here? Serlanos personally asked me to pick up the slack on bringing in the Holmwood girl because you haven't yet.

"Which you've also failed to do. Not that easy is it?"

"Fuck off. Be ready for tomorrow. I have a feeling Cynfael is up to something. You can't trust him."

"Really? Because some would say you'd be the one to start shit. I've been enjoying the enemies-to-lovers story unfolding between you two."

"Fuck off, Llew. And don't be late. We meet at 4:30am on the dot."

Cynfael takes the roof stairs, with hopes of finding easy prey to satisfy his thirst. Despite the no-feeding order, Callum always managed to bend the rules somehow. He's my favorite. Serlanos' first. How are we to enforce the no-feed order on the underlings if he's out there ripping through the streets of Chicago?

I don't doubt that he will try to get a head start on bringing in the Holmwood girl. Searching hotels or anywhere someone would lay low. But I don't suggest that. The girl needs a break. She's been on the run all of her life.

Give her one night's rest. A head start. The one that I didn't take when I had the chance.

I let my thoughts carry me away with the hopes I get so lost I can't find my way back to this lonely immortal life.

13

lenora holmwood

You Know What They Do to Guys Like Us In Prison - My Chemical Romance

I wake in the hotel room feeling more rested than ever. The mattress envelops me in a feeling of comfort I haven't felt since living at home with my parents. I almost didn't want to leave but knew I had to get hustling to the bus station.

It felt like the first day of my new life, knowing I was walking out of here and leaving it all behind me. The clock read 3:30 and luckily I was only a block away from the station. Maybe I can find breakfast along the way. Something quick and easy.

It takes me only mere seconds to be ready and out the door.

The front desk receptionist was barely awake when I checked out. I wasn't even sure if they knew that they were awake when processing the payment. Their eyes were dead and empty like they were lost in another world far from here.

It's still dark outside. The air is crisp as it blows in from the lakefront, carrying the chill that settled over the frozen surface to wash over the city. I shiver and force my hands deep into the pockets of the hoodie that was way too big for me. But it smelled of Theo. It was like he was with me. The reality of him being gone is still not real to me.

I will grieve properly when I am safe.

Far away from here like he had planned for us.

The train is delayed in Indiana. I have an hour to kill and my stomach is grumbling. I think I passed a Pepperpod diner just a block over. I bought my train ticket and began to backtrack. I avoid reading the familiar signs of each of the shops my family and I used to frequent. It will only make it harder to stay.

Remembering the last day with Mom is hard. She'd taken us out shopping for school, buying everything we set our eyes on. Which was unusual for her because she likes to add up everything to the penny as we push the cart, making sure we don't go over our budget.

Did she know then that she was going to die? Was she trying to make up for missing the rest of our -my life knowing that it would be stolen away just the next day?

Just the thought of it makes me almost not want breakfast. But I push forward, I should really eat something even being out in the open is not safe. Maybe I can grab it to go and hide at the station until the train comes.

Sitting in a diner eating a four course breakfast is not wise for me. Not when half of Chicago is looking for me.

News of my leaving the hospital had to have gotten out now. The news of my discovery broke out like wildfire, which was overwhelming. It's like you don't realize what hell you've lived through until you see it through the eyes of others. It doesn't necessarily make it better either.

Grandpa had kept us in originally to protect us. He said this every time we begged to go out for just a bit of sunlight. But Grandma was convinced that the media circus would swarm, he didn't want us talking to the press about our parents death. There was still an ongoing investigation.

"You don't need that in your lives."

That's where the manipulation began. Feigned protection.

The neon diner lights glowed against the settling morning dew and cast an exterrestrial light that projected onto the surrounding buildings. I felt relieved, knowing I could find a moment to sit down, process and plan. My stomach gurgles, excited to have a decent meal that wasn't brought to me on a tray or scraps of the previous day's meal. Thoughts of chocolate chip pancakes and crispy bacon lured me in.

The sound of the bell startles me as I open the door and step in from the bitter cold. My cheeks burn red hot as I approach the vacant hostess stand. The air in the room was still and tense. I notice that no one is around.

Except the bodies of unsuspecting diners that lay bleeding out on the tile floor, bent around tables and chairs like ragdolls. What the fuck happened here?

Shouts from the back kitchen startle me.

Sharp pings of bullets rattle through the air and the kitchen door is barreled down as a slim shadowy figure is thrown through it with supernatural force. Pieces of wood fly everywhere.

I freeze in place as he quickly recovers, brushing off his black dress coat with a high collar. Sculpted from marble like a roman statue, his face is next to perfection. Long sharp features and dark eyes cloaked by a long mess of wild ebony hair. He turns and we lock eyes with each other. His dark eyes shine and sink into mine with a veracity that I've never felt from anyone. Time around us seems to slow - despite a hail of gunfire plowing through the diner, riddling the booths with bullets. In seconds, the tall handsome figure was beside me, with one arm around me like a shield and pulled me out of range to take cover behind a toppled table.

"Stay low and close to me," he whispers, his breath felt chilled to the bone against my face. I listened to him - unsure of what exactly I'd walked into. It went from breakfast to crime scene real quick.

He moved fast and low as we crept towards the back hallway past the kitchen doors towards the emergency exit at the far end of the narrow hallway. I had hardly noticed he'd taken my hand and was leading me away like an enthusiastic child with a new balloon.

Behind us, the bell chimes abruptly followed by shattering glass and a storm of Chicago PD floods the diner, throwing flash bombs and shouting "GET DOWN" just as we break through the EXIT door and flee down the back alley.

A shiny black town car waits in idle for us.

There was no time to question whether or not to get in - I just do it when he opens the passenger door for me.

Mindlessly.

The handsome stranger takes the driver's seat that sat close to mine and peels out of the alley like a madman on the run. Holding onto the 'oh shit' handle, I take a deep intake of my situation : I'm fucked.

The Nosferati ring on his finger shines bright against the morning sun bleeding into the windshield.

"You're lucky it was me that got to you first. Any one of those other bloodsucker's would've turned you over to Serlanos for the price he's put on your blood this morning."

Was it really a good thing that this handsome stranger scooped me up and got me out of a room that had been ripped apart by these supernatural beings of chaos?

Blood drips from the man's mouth as he speeds down the alleyway, taking sharp, precise turns. I crash hard into the side door, my arm is numb from the impact. I can feel a bruise forming already.

"Buckle up my dear. I'd hate for your beautiful face to be ruined by a windshield."

I grab the buckle but struggle to pull the strap out as the vehicle darts around another sharp corner before bleeding out into the main road - but then he takes it and buckles me in with ease. One handed. He leans in close and lingers, looking deep into my fearful eyes.

"You should have gotten out of here when you had the chance," he says in a low voice.

"I bought a bus ticket - I was almost-" I trail off. Why am I explaining this to him? Whoever this is? I don't even know his fucking name. And here I am in a fucking car with him driving to who knows where?

"Doesn't matter now. You're too important to them. You'd never make it out of the town limits on your own - you're with me now."

I walked out of a nightmare and straight back into pure chaos.

Only to find myself at the mercy of a man that is covered in blood.

14

llewyn hellsinger

Sunlight - Hozier

*S*he *walked into the fucking diner.* She had to walk right into the diner where everything went to hell because of Callum's fragile fucking ego. Cynfael kept his end of the deal, the cash was there in exchange for the blood. But that didn't mean he was going to keep his mouth shut. Callum couldn't take the taunting.

His blood thirst was too fucking high to keep his cool. Asking him to even shake hands to be civil was asking too much of him right now.

Norryx and Lycidas circled in the back ready to pounce again. They tore through the restaurant like a cat tearing through fine drapes. Scraps of flesh and bone scattered the floor amidst the eggs and bacon. The fry cooks lay bleeding out by the sizzling frier.

Cynfael dips down and wipes some blood off of the cook's face and licks it off his finger.

"Mmm. A little too greasy. Ah, it's really a shame that you have to wait for your boss to give you the okay to mate, or even feed. He's busy chasing down this silly mortal for you to feed on while I am enjoying what walks in my club door. Think about it, Callum. You're a fucking puppet on a string. The lot of you are." He winks at me, I know he can't help it. And he wasn't lying.

But Callum is dumb and loyal, like your best golden retriever. He would've made a better werewolf, in my opinion. But they're more selective than we are. They're survival doesn't depend on reaping the life force from humans. More so depends on hiding from humans. Those fragile fucks are more afraid of something that wants nothing to do with them, while they would gladly invite one my kind in for dinner and a glass of wine.

Only to become the dinner chased by the wine.

Callum's cold veins turned frigid with rigid rage. I could feel it radiating off of him.

Guns and drawn and pointed.

"Come on, guys. We promised. One day. Tomorrow, we can kill each other all we want," I remind them, my hand on my gun but one foot towards the door.

"Fuck that shit. You think I am going to let him -"

"Callum, he's fucking with you. You're giving him exactly what he-"

I didn't get to finish before Callum opened fire and Cynfael and his men returned tenfold.

I can't say I didn't try. But I also did say I wasn't going to back Callum up if he started shit with Cynfael. Cynfael is only telling the truth. I've known about it for a long time. Serlanos' old ways of the original mob outfits are dying. His fucked up views of loyalty and sacrifice for the good of the family.

He's out here chasing the daughter of an old blood bank connection that he murdered in cold blood. What is it about her -

Speaking of her. She just fucking walked in. In the middle of this shit. Stray bullets had riddled the small diner. Bodies ripped apart by silver and gunpowder. Laid to rest in the remnants of maple syrup and bacon. Collateral damage.

I don't feel sorry for leaving. Not one bit as I sit here and drive this small scared, beyond beautiful creature back to where no one will find us. A penthouse that I've arranged to bunker down in when shit hits the fan. A simple luxury that one can afford with connections like mine. It would be a shame to live as long as I have and to not have resources. But maybe that's the pretentiousness of immortality speaking.

I have no plans to hand her over to Serlanos. She's already lost everything at his behest.

I cannot watch it go on any longer.

We drive in hollow silence. She can barely look at me without turning beet red.

"I'm Llewyn, by the way."

"Lenora."

"I know."

She sits on the far edge of her seat as I pull into the below ground parking garage and follow it up to the private sector parking for the penthouse. I pulled into the designated spot and had her door opened before she could even unbuckle her belt.

"Oh. Thank you," she whispers as I offer a hand to help her out. Her tiny hand shakes as she takes mine, making me feel like a giant. She looks up at me with curiosity as we touch, I grab the bag from the back of the car and I start walking us towards the glass elevators.

"We have our private elevator, password protected. Each resident makes their own number and provides one for guests. There are no guests of mine. Only residents."

No one knows I own this place. I made sure of that. I purchased it under another name. One that hasn't been associated with me in a long time. One that not even Serlanos knows that I've used in past jobs.

We all have our secrets. This was mine.

My peace.

Wrapping her arms around herself, she timidly follows me into the glass elevator. Standing close to the wall. Frightened. I didn't blame her. Here she was alone with a vampire that could've very easily handed her over to the very man who has destroyed every life he's come across like a plague. She didn't know where I was taking her. How does she truly know she is safe with me? For all she knows, he could be waiting at the top of the elevator

I will have to show her that her safety is my top priority.

She's not my prisoner. If anything this is to be a refuge. Her plan failed. That is if she had a plan or was just running in the wind.

I am giving her a chance to recoup and regroup.

But what if I don't want her to leave? Tough shit, I remind myself. She's not a kitten to keep, I remind myself.

Besides, she deserves to be free.

She stares out of the glass elevator window, looking out over the city below her as it becomes smaller and smaller.

I can feel her recoil as I look upon her, so I avert my eyes. She's probably tired of people gawking at her already. At the hospital they picked and prodded at her. Psychiatrists questioned her perception and everything around her. Onlookers at the scene of her collapse took unprecedented photos of the unconscious girl on the ground. The media circus has been flashing her face on the screen as much as they can. I would be surprised if she wanted anything but my devout attention.

She knows I am anything but human - or so I hope. She does know right? I mean she recognizes the bat shaped emblem on my ring. It matches the one on the necklace she wears. It's wrapped around a silver bullet pendant and set with garnet diamonds.

Ironic. I could never wear that. Literally.

So why is our emblem on something we could never wear?

She catches me staring again and shudders. I avert my eyes and clear my throat to break the hostile tension.

"No one else has been here but me. You're safe here. No one else has the code."

She nods to show she's listening. I don't know if that bit of information made it better or worse.

The elevator door opened into the grand foyer that bleeds out into the luxurious living and dining spaces.

Her heart skipped a beat before the gasp that followed when she caught sight of the view of the Chicago Skyline from the large window that wraps around the entirety of the room. An overcast of blue clouds have swept in from over the lake only to be broken up by the early rays of sunlight.

I let her explore a bit, watching her curiosity flourish like a cat. Her fingers tracing the surface of the organ in the corner, the black and gold painted dining table. She marvels at the collection of musical instruments that I've hung on the walls or perched on a display stand.

She circled the kitchen island. She pressed against the black marbelized counter top that I would love to bend her over and fuck her brains out on.

I'm getting ahead of myself.

She has to invite me first.

"You can stay here. For as long as you like. And if you wish to leave, I can arrange for a safe pathway out. You just have to trust me," I tell her.

Her eyes wide with disbelief. She really was lucky that it was me that picked her up. I can see her realizing that now as her eyes sparkle with unvocalized gratitude.

"Let me show you to your room."

I led her down the hall. Her room is the first door on the right. Mine just to the left across the hall.

She deserves her privacy but I am nearby if she needs anything.

"I am right across the hall. Don't hesitate to knock on my door if you need anything. I don't sleep much." I hope she gets that joke later, this is too much to process to start the jokes now. I am not even sure she is aware yet that I am what I am.

The bedroom isn't that impressive.

Cool and modernized painted walls and matching privacy curtains. Satin black bedding with blood red trim on a king size bed. A large window overlooked the south end of the building. I should let her redecorate. When was the last time she got to choose something for herself?

She needs more clothes. The clothes she has on hang on her like she dressed from a lost and found bin.

She looks around carefully, taking the room in.

Opening each of the drawers and touching the surfaces as if she's checking to make sure this is all real.

I can only imagine her disbelief. Everything happened so quickly. She went from on the run from a horde of bloodcrazed morons to bunkering down in a penthouse with me. One of those bloodcrazed morons.

"If you need anything, do not hesitate to ask. I can have it sent here. I will let you settle in."

I go to close the door behind me, but then I hear her soft angelic voice utter the first sentence.

"You're different from the others. You were there in my hospital room, weren't you? You had every chance then to turn me in and now. Why?"

Her large innocent eyes pour into mine. I cannot lie to her, they command the truth, and that's what she deserves.

"Because, my dear, I cannot fathom the idea of anyone else sinking their fangs into that divine ass before me, Nor will I let anyone take away your free will to choose to do so. And if you were to choose, I want it to be me. If not, you should be free."

Chivalry is undead.

callum gyanstazi

House of the Wolves - My Chemical Romance

The fucker bailed on me again. Right when Cynfael unleashed the complete asshole that he is. Serlanos wouldn't fail me. He never has. But Llewyn walked out.

The holding cell was cold and dark. I lay there sticking my nose up at the stench of the human horde of police that hauled me, Lycidas and Norryx out of the diner, throwing us in the back of the police cruisers like wild rabid animals being carried away by animal control. Cynfael was able to escape in time before the media and paramedics addressed the massacre left inside. The walls dripped with blood of the diners that were victims of a gang of uncontrollable bloodthirsty vampires. Norryx nor Lycidas had fed and being around that many humans in one room waiting for Cynfael to show up was too much to bear.

Cynfael was late.

I lay on the bench seething. Llewyn ditched us. He should be here in the shit with us. Serlanos is going to have a field day when he finds all five of us here in the custody of mortals. The media is going to riot over the deaths of those in the diner. Llewyn was just as much a part of this as us. And where the fuck is he? Who knows.

How will this be explained to the public? Only so much of Serlanos' money can explain away vicious crimes carried out by the hands of vampires.

We fucked up. Hard.

The clang of the gate opening broke my spiraling thoughts.

"You lucky assholes are free." The officer looks exhausted and horrified. He's seen what we've done. And in his futile mind he believes we should be locked in a cage, like the animals that we are. As if we can be contained. It's hard to catch smoke.

Serlanos waits in the center of the bullpen of the police station. A frown is carved into his face as he glares silver bullets into all three of us. But he does not speak, he just starts walking towards the exit and we follow, like guilty pups with their tails between their legs.

Once in the limousine waiting for us out front, Serlanos begins to rip in

"What happened there with Cynfael? There were supposed to be no casualties. You are making a spectacle of us. I only have so much cash to bail your ass out of mortal prison."

Serlanos lays into us the second we are in the back of the limousine and he's poured himself a glass of blood and lit himself a cigar.

"That's because you're spending it on finding that Holmwood girl."

"Silence - you damn well that is your future I am investing in. And if you don't cool your chops you're going to find yourself alone forever, Callum," he spits a mouthful of blood in my direction, it hits me in the face.

Serlanos bailed my ass out so many times before this. Once as I'd been thrown over the hood of the police cruiser, brazen with new shiny cufflinks. Serlanos worked his magic and got them to let me off with a warning, while Cynfael is carted off in the back of a cop car shouting obscenities at the officers who were happy to ignore him.

This was nothing new to him.

"Where's Llewyn?" Serlanos inquires, setting his stogie into the ashtray attachment. It was piled high. .

"Who the fuck knows. He bailed. I didn't even see him leave.," Lycidas pipes up, taking the focus of Serlanos' wrath away from me.

Sharing the blame, like a true brother.

"Hmm."

"Hmm? That's all you have to say? It'd better have been fucking important! If the mortal swines hadn't shown, Cynfael would have siphoned off my head."

"And all of this began unprovoked - I have a hard time believing that considering your history with Cynfael, Callum. I don't need your drama spoiling any further exchanges with the southside. We count on this on-going arrangement to keep the peace."

"What do we get in return?"

"Time,"Serlanos answered.

Time means nothing to a vampire. His answer is invaluable to me. I don't wait for the limo to stop. I open the door right then.

"Sir - please do not open the door when-" the driver shouts out at me through the window as I light a cigarette and stalk away.

I needed answers.

I need more. Of everything and anything.

But first, I need to feed.

Serlanos has been stingy on the payouts on the recent blood bank rob-beries so I've had to ration what I have in stock at my crib. But that's for emergencies.

I want something fresh.

I met her in a hole-in-the wall bar on the South Side. Outside our sect's turf. I relished it. Taking a woman that Cynfael could never have and leaving her for dead. Her lips tasted of red wine, but her blood was even sweeter. The burning frenzy in my head relinquished as I drained her as I held her in the bathroom stall. Leaving her there to be found by the bar keep, only wanting more.

Nothing satisfies my thirst anymore.

Will anything suffice?

lenora holmwood

Monster - Mumford & Sons

The last thing he said to me before leaving me replays in my head. *If anyone were to sink their fangs into that divine ass of yours, I want it to be me.*

His hauntingly dark eyes and perfect cupid's bow lips are all I can see when I close my eyes. His seductive drawling voice sings to me at night like a lullaby.

He's not human. That's quite obvious at this point.

He's too perfect to be human. He's sculpted like a god, and moves so precisely. Like everything he does comes with such grace and poise that no human possesses.

At least not from what I've seen from other humans. We are too gangly and fragile. Easily broken.

Personally, I am anything but graceful. I trip on air or fall where I am standing.

I can't believe my luck though when I fell into his arms at the diner.

Here I am in this plush penthouse. Hidden from the world once more. Only this time, I've never felt more free.

Llewyn has been very gracious to me. He's given me space to just be. Exist without question. I couldn't be more grateful for that. For the first time in what seemed like eternity, I had my own room. and bathroom. With an enormous bed and breathtaking view of the city skyline. I find it hard to believe that I was trying to leave this behind hours ago.

I don't remember falling asleep. I lay down on the bed and that was the last thing I remember. Feeling the coolness of the sheets and the mattress support and meet my body. The weight of exhaustion taking over.

It was the rustle of a brown take-out bag and the weight of someone sitting on the end of my bed that stirred me awake.

"Any Chicagoan knows that the trip to Chinatown is worth the effort. But this came from Koi. It's a favorite of mine. Best chicken fried rice in town."

He's in my room.

I freeze in bed, my eyes still closed.

Nora?" No one else but my father has called me that. Everyone insisted on Lenora because of how pretty it sounded. Which I get. But I also loved 'Nora'.

My eyes fluttered open but my vision was blurred. My body felt heavy and tired. Sitting up was a struggle but I feel a hand behind me for support. The touch of his skin sends a shock through my body. His very presence was intoxicating.

"Come on, sit up. You should eat something. You need to regain your strength."

He was right and this chicken fried rice smelled pretty fucking good. Handing me the styrofoam box I tear into it like a rabid beast.

"I went to the store and picked up some clothes for you. I hope they're the right size. If not, let me know and I can exchange them."

He went shopping for me. Where did this man come from?

Llewyn pulls a large shopping bag from nowhere and pulls out the contents and sets it before me. This man understands more about me than I can comprehend right now. A few cute skirts that reminded me of what I used to wear back in school. Some nice blouses. And a few pairs of leggings and sweaters.

I was dying to get into the sweater and leggings. The weather outside called for it. A few cozy items fell out of the bag like underwear and fuzzy slippers.

"Why are you doing this for me?"

"Because we all need to feel human from time to time," he responds, his languid voice drawing me in with every word he spoke. Every moment with him felt more intimate than the last.

"Do you not feel human?" I ask, afraid of what the answer might be.

"I've not been human for nearly 100 years."

I nearly dropped my eggroll. How do I even respond to that? I'm sorry? No, that can't be right.

"Oh."

"I'm a vampire. We're all vampires."

"Oh."

"Did you not know?"

"I feel like that would be rude to presume."

I did not expect the belly laugh that came out of the handsome creature beside me. The belly laugh turned into a tea kettle wheeze that I could barely understand the next part.

"You thought it would be rude to presume I wasn't human? That is too sweet," he wipes away tears.

"Well yeah, I mean to be fair most humans can be monsters without supernatural powers."

"True," he said, the laughter dying down.

"I'm sorry, that was rude. I shouldn't have said 'monster'. Fuck, I don't know what I'm say-"

"It's okay. I've heard worse," he stops me before I continue to embarrass myself.

"But you're not - I mean you had the opportunity to, but you didn't. And you haven't."

"And I won't. Not unless you ask," he says in a low sultry voice, leaning in so close. My heart pumps rapidly. His lips just inches away from mine, his dark eyes not breaking their hold. I nearly jump out of my skin as his chilled hand caresses my face.

He runs his thumb over my lip, wiping the bright orange sweet-n-sour sauce and licks it off himself. Without saying another word, he gets up and leaves the room, closing the door behind him.

Um, okay sir, that is really unfair.

A foreign feeling stirs inside of me. Something I thought was locked away.

I had boyfriends in high school. But that feels like ages ago.

When Theo and I moved in with Grandma and Gram, Grandpa was strict about dating, or really having anyone outside the family over. I barely recovered from the embarrassment of Grandpa chasing Daniel Richardson down the street with a shotgun for walking me home. Daniel had his arm around me, pulling me in close to keep me warm from the icy Chicago wind biting through our skin.

Grandpa had been watching from the window and opened the door before Daniel could even think about trying to kiss me, again.

And soon, we were locked in from the outside world for good.

I was sixteen when we became prisoners in Grandpa's house of horrors. It's been six years since I've been in the same room with a male that wasn't family.

Let alone one that was a complete tease.

The feeling of his thumb on my lip lingered like a phantom kiss. Every thought haunted by the idea of what his lips would feel like against mine.

I try to shake this feeling and eat. But I am too distracted. My hunger is replaced by a flutter and nausea.

It's like a grand reawakening. A second puberty.

I set aside my chicken lo mein and hop in the shower. I need to cool down and gather myself.

Try to wash away the thoughts of letting this drop dead creature ravish every part of my body. The waterfall shower fills with steam as I turn the dial to scalding hot. Hotter than Satan's left butt cheek.

I feel a strong sense of comfort. But a deeper desire for touch.

From Llewyn.

That's what it is. The want. Each time I meet his eyes it's like something primal takes over and it makes me fear every part of me that wants him. That's what scares me the most: how much I want him. And how much I shouldn't.

Dad wouldn't approve. But isn't that what makes it more exciting? Heck that's probably why I even bothered making out with half the guys I met up with behind the music store after practice.

It was forbidden. Edgy.

Every part of my life was under the microscope up until now. I had the freedom to choose, yet I still fear to do so.

The water does nothing but entice phantom feelings of him pressing up against my body. I lose myself to thoughts of him pressing me up against the cold tile walls and putting his perfect mouth and strong hands everywhere. Making me his. Sinking those pearly white fangs into my neck. My hand wanders as the fantasy presses further.

Even knowing what I know now - I am not deterred. I am enchanted.

And I've known him for seventy-two hours.

What the fuck, Nora?

Cleaned and pampered with luxury styling gels and lotions, I pull on a comfort outfit of leggings and a pull over hoodie paired with some fuzzy socks and tiptoe out into the hall. The pearlescent vaulted hall echoed each shuffle of my slipper, I could hardly sneak up on anyone in here.

Llewyn is in the kitchen unloading a myriad of groceries that he had delivered, every cabinet door is opened and slowly filling with dry goods.

"It's crazy how food shopping has changed over the decades. Humans have way more available to them now than they ever did. What a time to be alive, or not in my case."

I giggle. "Was that a vampire joke?"

"My sense of humor never died, Nora. If anything it's what's kept me going this long. Aside from the immortality thing and blood."

"Damn. You're on a roll here, sir."

"Like the wheels of a gurney, but don't worry, I'll see myself out now," he smiles to himself as he folds up the paper bags and tucks them into the pantry. He's so pleased with himself. It's honestly cute how much he cracks himself up.

"A vampire that cares about the environment, interesting." I pretend to take notes on an invisible notepad.

"Hey, if I am to walk this planet for all of eternity, I am going to take care of it. You humans can start taking notes," he retorts, wagging his finger on me.

"I'll spread the good word. Is there any coffee?"

"Even better. A smart keurig. K-cups are in the top cabinet."

I let out a small squeal of excitement and skipped over to the counter and opened the cabinet door, feeling the weight of his eyes on me.

He got every flavor. Even the seasonal flavors. My mouth hangs open in basic-bitch-awe.

"Yeah that's right. I did good." He stands behind me smiling smugly. He's so proud of himself. As he should be.

"How do you know so much about mortal-female interests?"

"I had a wife last week."

I blink absentmindedly. I don't know how to acknowledge that with a proper response.

"I'm sorry for your loss," I say feeling rehearsed.

I remember hearing it for a month after my parents were murdered. It felt ingenuine or the wrong thing to say at a time like that. Eventually it didn't make sense anymore. Just like their death. Or it straight up infuriated Theo. After hearing it enough times he would excuse himself from the room to go blow off steam.

I understood his feelings. I took the brunt of it for his sake. Giving the weak smile back in the funeral line as the attendees gave their condolences. Like the funeral goers could even fathom the living nightmare we were all in. Serlanos and his men didn't hesitate to show their faces. Outside the cemetery gates they waited, and then later that night after the funeral they paid very little respect on our doorstep, reminding Grandpa he was to be showing payment by the end of the week.

I remember catching a glimpse of him glowering at the funeral party through the trees from the streets. Coveting me from then, making his plans then to take control of everything the Holmwoods had.

"Don't be. It was my fault for thinking that I could keep up the charade of a double life with Serlanos hot on my tail," he says matter of fact.

Serlanos destroys everything that he comes in contact with, spreading like a plague darker than that imaginable by mankind. He is a family-killer. What is his deal? First mine, and now Llewyn's. I can understand the sadness reflected in his eyes now. They've witnessed so much pain and lost. The ghosts that he carries with him reflect back into the world, through him they can witness the world one last time.

"Did Serlanos kill them?" I ask.

"No, I did. At Serlanos' orders. If I didn't, he would've. If he did it, it would've been worse. As a punishment for me, not so much. I saved them from hell."

Oh fuck. I felt my eyes bulge out of my head as I processed this.

"I know. That's a lot to take in."

"No kidding. Fuck."

Llewyn continues to unpack the groceries and goes to open the fridge to reveal bags and bags of blood. Each of them labeled different types and dates harvested. Some were stacked in the drawers and others lined up in order of type in the shelves in the door of the fridge.

I've never seen anything like it. "I can move them if blood bothers you. I have a mini-fridge."

I looked at the bags closely. It felt strange to hold such a vitality in my hands. It's strange to think Llewyn and I both need it to survive - but in different ways.

"Are some blood types better than others for vampires?"

"Yes. O-Negative is the best. It's also the rarest. Which is why we purge blood banks."

"You rob blood banks?"

"Yes. And sometimes sell what we rob to other clans. Serlanos likes to dabble in darker markets. Always searching for something that will make him stronger."

"I thought vampires were immortal?"

"They are. But we aren't indestructible. Lemme put the groceries away and I'll be happy to answer any and all questions. Better yet, I've not given you the grande tour - I have a place that can answer your questions."

"You have a library hidden somewhere in this maze in the sky?"

"Indeed, my dear, I do."

I see him smile to himself as my jaw drops. He continues to put away the groceries as my brain breaks.

How in the world am I to process all of this at once? A vampire mobster rescued me in a hail of gunfire in the middle of a restaurant and swept me off my feet to his fancy penthouse on Michigan Avenue and has a library.

Okay. I think I got it. I will address the other trauma later. First the library.

I think I did die and go to heaven.

Llewyn led me down the long vaulted hallway towards the double wide oak doors at the very end. He stops and looks at me as I am teeming with excitement, as if to tease me like a dog and his bones. "Inside you will find peace and harmony wrapped into one, my dear."

I expect nothing less, good sir.

He pulls open the doors to reveal his fortress of books. My jaw dropped at the magnificence of the library; high vaulted ceilings, black oak trimmings and hanging black tapestries and the faint hint of bergamot and sandalwood encapsulating me in dark academia heaven. Shelves crawling to the ceiling and spanning from wall to wall leaving a break in the center for an ornate electric fireplace and two large leather arm chairs and side table.

I am lost for words. I know how Belle from the Beauty and the Beast feels now. It was my favorite Disney movie growing up. I appreciated her because she would have cared less about being a princess or winning the guy. She had a strong head on her shoulders and didn't fall for the biggest hunk in town. I hate even being called princess. I just want the library.

"Will it do?"

I don't answer. I don't think I can. I lose my mind as I run my finger tips down the first shelf, looking at each spine carefully. History, art, politics, science and more from all around the world. From floor to ceiling each shelf is filled. It would take me more than a lifetime to get through this. Never have I ever wanted immortality than I do at this moment.

It's foolish and reckless thinking.

But I mean it.

The idea of Llewyn taking my blood in his sensual lips was too tantalizing to cast away. God I hope he doesn't hear these thoughts. Vampires can read thoughts right? Or control minds? I'm not sure which.

I will have to ask.

He said he will answer any and all questions I may have about vampirism. My time has come.

All those years of hiding up in my room with the horror stories that I could sneak past my father who was quick to ban anything that remotely reminded him of vampires.

I was fascinated by them, to his dismay.

"Aren't there better things to occupy your mind with?" Dad would tease me as I would pick up another vampire book from the library, hidden in the stack of other parental approved titles.

"Are you saying that Dracula by Brom Stoker is not worthy of being studied? Was it not worth the nominations and criticisms it has received for decades. Gosh Dad, I thought you cared about my education."

The argument usually ended there. Dad knew not to fight me in my books. I understand his reasoning now. He was trying to create an illusion of a safe family. One that wasn't being terrorized by a fanged mobster. And here I am. His daughter is obsessed with vampires. The one thing he swore to protect us from.

"Come sit with me," he takes my hand and leads me to the chair before I faint from excitement. His hand is cold but so soft.

He takes the seat next to me and lets me take a moment to take all of this in.

"Take your time. It's a lot to take in."

"It's beautiful." I find myself still unable to grasp how many books were on each shelf. I try to count each one but lose track.

"I've spent two lifetimes putting it together. When Serlanos brought us here, I began to visit bookstores on our travels. Picking up what I could along the way. It's accumulated to this. Some titles I've had to hunt for. Stolen even. When we became more settled here in Chicago I was able to start putting this together."

"When did you come over here?"

"Shortly after the end of World War II. We scrammed when they started hunting down some of the Third Reich's alliances. Apparently some of Serlanos' connections were Nazis. He was afraid that would come back to bite us."

I resist the urge to laugh at the irony in his statement there, but sometimes I think he does this on purpose based on his comedy performance in the kitchen. He has a way with words, which shows how much he reads. Such control in his languid irresistible low voice. I could listen to him speak all day.

"Did Serlanos turn you or -"

"Yes. And no, I didn't want to be turned. He found me drinking in a bar just after I returned to London from the first World War. I had just found out that the woman I was to marry had married someone else while I was away. So I went to drown in my sorrows and wait for shellshock to hit."

"And Serlanos was at the bar?"

"And Callum. I started a fight I couldn't finish and they dragged me out into the alley way and nearly ripped me apart before they saw I was a soldier."

Callum, the monster. The one that came after me at the hospital. He was the worst of them all in my opinion.

"Those bastards," I let my intrusive thought slip. Llewyn smiled at that.

"I'll let them know you said so."

"I will be happy if I never have to see them again. Especially Callum."

"He'd be happy to know that considering you're to be betrothed to him."

My mouth drops. "I'm what? You've got to be fucking joking?"

"I wish I was, love. I spoke to that family attorney of yours. The deal has already been written up."

"And no one thought to consider my feelings in this?"

"I'm afraid not."

"Any chance you may break into that attorney's office and tear that up?"

"I can't say that it hasn't crossed my mind."

We both stare at each other for a moment before bursting into a fit of laughter. It felt nice to laugh with someone who got it. The absurdity of it all. How am I supposed to comprehend any of this? It's all far from normal.

"So there's more of you. Other than you, Serlanos and Callum?"

"Oh yes. Many more of us. Too many in fact. Chicago cannot feed all of us. At least not at once"

"And you have your own government?"

"More like an organization. A system of bloodlines. Families."

"So you are like the mafia?"

"Who do you think took over when the old outfits piffled out. The current gangsters work for us now, they just don't realize it. With vampires it's easier to keep us altogether. We all have one thing in common and without each other, we won't get it. With every vampire born, there is a cost."

"So where do I fit into all this? I guess that's where I am lost," I say, wishing that any small bit of that made any sense.

"You and I both. Vampires aren't known for being monogamous. An eternity of various partners makes it all seem meaningless, especially when it comes to mortals. Which is why I don't understand why Callum of all people was chosen to be your betrothed. Serlanos was the one that put the bloodmark on you, I thought he of all people would be the one to -"

"To what?"

"It's an ancient legend. To wed a mortal and turn her to gain everlasting life. To increase the bloodline strength by the pure unity between a vampire and a mortal. Something in the bond between the two makes them an unstoppable force. Serlanos declared your blood as his to the Blood Syndicate, making you off limits to any other vampire that might cross your path."

"So he's basing all of this on legend? Which legend?" I ask.

But Llewyn doesn't respond. Telling me that I will have to find out for myself, like he did.

And I'm going to find out what that is. Llewyn has hundreds upon hundreds of books in this room, and one of them is bound to have the answer.

"So you have magical powers? Right? Like there's no way in hell that you would have been able to have gotten us out of that diner without being caught," I sit on the edge of my seat, having felt that I've only cracked the skull of this mind fuck of a situation.

"I prefer to call them abilities. Every vampire is different. Some don't show any true powers until after some time or never at all. Just leeches of the earth. Others are reborn naturally with many abilities. It depends on the bloodline that turned that vampire."

"Do you burn in the sun?"

"More like show my true form in the direct light."

"What is that?"

"You don't want to see."

"But I do."

Looking deep into my eyes, he sighed and then rose from his chair and walked to the large curtained window and stood far to the side of the window as he pulled open letting the morning sun burst through the library.

Dropping the pull rope, Llewyn hesitates before stepping into the bright rays of morning light. His porcelain skin decays before my eyes, drying up like one's skin would after being in water too long. His eyes sunken in and glowed red. His fangs extended and shined menacingly.

I withhold my gasp. He did warn me, however I wasn't nearly as frightened as I was enticed by him.

He closes the curtain and his appearance returns back to perfection, the skin mending before my eyes like some wicked spell. I was bewitched by his very being. The more he revealed to me the more questions that I have. But he's baring so much to me, with hopes that I don't run screaming from him. I cannot take that for granted.

I stand and approach him. He stops in his tracks and his chest tightens as I draw close. Just as mine does when he is near. I raise my small hand to his pale face and feel the coldness of his cheek.

"Just a handsome vampire," I say with a smile, feeling his fear relieve and escape from his body as he finds comfort in my touch and presses my hand to his face with his hand. He closes his eyes and exhales, releasing everything he's been holding back for a moment. Sharing this tender moment.

He's shared a lot with me already and it's barely been two days. How long has it been since he's bared his soul to anyone? I don't get the impression that he does a lot of opening up to Callum. Least of all Serlanos.

He finds comfort in me in the same way I find comfort in him. Perhaps this could work out.

Perhaps I am not wrong to believe that in just a mere two days two beings can fall in love.

17

lenora holmwood

A Little Piece of Heaven -Avenged Sevenfold

Grandpa hasn't been in the apartment all day. No one knows when he left he was gone before any of us were up. We woke to a dead heater and an empty refrigerator. Maybe that's what stirred him out of bed, but it was doubtful. Rent was due and we had two tenants staying next door that Gram has been working up the courage to collect on the rent. Grandpa normally handles it, as some of the tenants are not the nicest individuals. But Grandpa hasn't been home all day. Our stomachs growl and our breath is bitten with frost. Theo has wrapped me and Gram in all of the blankets on the couch that he could find.

"We have to eat something soon. It's been three days since," Theo begs Gram. Gram, empty-eyed and panic stricken musters up what courage Grandpa hasn't beaten out of her and goes to the front door that Grandpa had forbade us to leave through. She disappears into the dark, dilapidated hallway. Theo and I sit on the edge of our seats, listening closely. This was a bad idea. We should wait for Grandpa to return.

Every part of me cursed Grandpa for abandoning us for the bottle again when we needed him to take control. What happened to the powerful patri-arch of the family. The one that brought down the ironfist that molded my father. To never back down. It was the Holmwood motto, he would say. But he's given up. Everything taken from him. His northside manor, his fortune, and his pride. Serlanos didn't miss a moment to destroy us further. Mom and Dad were barely in the ground when Serlanos paid a visit explaining the terms of his 'protection.' Grandpa didn't take his threats seriously.

'I will not be intimidated in my own home on the day of my son's funeral by some creepshow-Capone wanna-be," Grandpa roared as he slammed the door after Serlanos left, leaving his demands for cash or to relinquish rights to our father's estate. Grandpa turned him away. That was a mistake.

One Grandpa learned to regret as we soon were tossed onto the street, leaving only the failing apartment building Grandpa invested in for shelter. Here we were given another chance to crawl out of the pit and prove our loyalty to Serlanos, who promised in turn to take care of us if we did right by him. Grandpa is running out of collateral to keep him at bay. The rent sitting next door in the hands of unsavory characters is our last hope.

There's a small thud and raised voices followed by the sound of someone running for their life. Gram darts back into the apartment and pulls the door closed but her pursuers are too quick. Kicking the door down, two large brutish grifters crawl into the apartment like sewer vermin venturing out for garbage. Reeking of gas fumes and a few months of body odor, they close in on us. Brandishing knives they either found or made themselves as no sensible person would give them one.

"Get the fuck out of our house now!" Theo roars, stepping up to the plate. He's the only man here. It's his job to protect us. The two men laugh as Theo's voice cracks as he yells at them.

"Ottis, you take the grandma and boy into the family room and make sure they don't make a peep. I'm about to teach this slut who daddy is," the bigger of the two says, his dark and malevolent eyes locked in on me. My body freezes as he grabs me hard by the arm and drags me to the kitchen and throws me to

the floor like a broken ragdoll. Theo and Gram scream in desperate protest. "Touch her and I will fucking kill you!" Theo spits at Ottis who elbows him in the nose, knocking him down into the couch. I could hear the crack of his nose breaking from the kitchen. Gram doesn't move an inch nor say a word.

"I got it covered Brodus. Go on, do her. She's much cleaner than the last one," Otis says, licking his lips at me, all ready for his turn next. Great serial rapists. Grandpa let serial rapists move in next door. It was the only apartment that had working plumbing other than our own. The best that he had to offer.

Brodus climbs on top of me as I hear Gram and Theo scream from the living room where Ottis held them at knife point. Grimey, meaty hands grope me everywhere. I scream at the top of my lungs anything to get someone's attention from the outside to save us from this nightmare, but shoves a towel in my mouth and pins my hands above my head. The tile beneath me is frigid as a grave in winter. Here will lie what's left of my dignity if this grotesque beast has his way with me. Theo manages to slip past Ottis, distracted by Gram's hysterical cries and Brodus' demands to 'Shut the bitch up!' and jumps on Brodus' dirty back as he forces his knee between my legs. Theo gets Brodus in a chokehold but isn't nearly strong enough to subdue him. Otis pulls Theo off, "Sorry about that. Grandma won't shut the fuck up."

"And neither do you. I hear enough of your voice as it is. I don't need to hear it when I am with a slut." Brodus turns to me and leans in close, "Since your old man didn't pay the heating, the least you could do is keep me warm tonight." His rancid breath pouring over me as he forces a kiss on my neck. He's going to rape me. Right here in front of my family. On our kitchen floor. Before he could unzip his stiff pants, the doorway is haunted by the shadow of our grandfather, who's armed with a raised shotgun he keeps by the door. His fierce stare rips through Brodus and Otis, who charges at Grandpa with his knife raised in the air screaming - Grandpa fires two shots, splattering

his brains across the wall and family portraits that adorned the peeling wall. Brodus wasn't as stupid as his counterpart, but that didn't save him from the point blank shot to the head, spraying me and the kitchen floor with brain matter, blood mist and skull fragments. Brodus slumps to the floor beside me with a dead thump. Silence resonates through the apartment. No one moves. The fog from the blast of the shotgun settles in the air. Grandpa puts down the rifle and goes to the dial phone and starts ringing in numbers. The police hopefully? Maybe they will see how bad things have gotten. Grandpa and Gram can be unburdened by us and can have a chance at a life. Gram searches the pockets of the dead fucks as Grandpa dials the one person he knows that can make this disappear overnight.

"Serlanos, it's me, Artemis Holmwood. Something's happened. I need your help."

Asking Serlanos for a favor always comes at a price. And this is a big favor. Making two bodies disappear was something I was certain these men in custom tailored black suits in our apartment were used to by now. Each of them wore evidence of their glory and riches. Members of high society, like we were once.

Serlanos oversaw the cleanup. It didn't take him too long to arrive with a team. Two of his men were dressed in hazmat suits and collected the bodily fluids scattered across the home. Grandpa offers him a drink of whiskey and sits in the armchair as Theo, Gram and I sit frigidly on the sofa, dried blood on our faces and clothes, still in shock. Serlanos isn't watching his men. No - his eyes have been captivated on me since he walked in the door. The cold stare was familiar, the same he gave as the cold-iron gates closed as he left us on the street with the few belongings we have left. Sending the message that this is what happens when you cross him. And yes he can do anything to you.

"Do you not take care of your family, Artemis? How long are you going to let your grandchildren suffer in squalor for your failures? Their father didn't

fall far from the tree, did he? No spine to hold him tall. Men in society have the biggest job of all. Making decisions for the greater good. You're just not up for it, are you?"

Grandpa doesn't respond. He just sips his whiskey in cold-silence. Letting Serlanos admonish him in his own home while making eyes with me. Claiming me. I could take better care of you, they said. And the scary part is, he was probably right. He's done a number on my family, showing how strong he was and could take out anyone that stands in the way of what he wants.

Serlanos reaches into his pocket and pulls out a stack of cash and hands it to Grandpa. "Take care of your family, Artemis. They are all you have. Family is everything and yours is diminishing rather quickly. Which is a shame as your granddaughter is a delicious beauty. She must be protected from scoundrels like these," he gestures to the body bags being carted out by two men. Grandpa's lip curls with shame and anger when Serlanos offers the money, expecting Grandpa to take it. But he refuses his hand. Serlanos shoves the money into Grandpa's shirt pocket, nods to Gram and winks at me before leaving our home. One of them had been kind enough to swap the door that had been torn off its hinges.

All Gram had found in the pockets of our attackers was charred tinfoil and a mangled spoon. Nothing to show for the nightmare we endured.

llewyn hellsinger

Helena - My Chemical Romance

She has nightmares. Almost every night since she arrived. It's been five days and each night has been more intense than the last. I can't make out her screams or what she is saying to ask questions. And she doesn't acknowledge that she even has nightmares.

Not even when I have been there when she wakes sobbing and screaming, drenched in sweat and terror. I would urge her to talk about it more but I can't say I am perfect about opening up. And she has some horrors in her past that I feel she's not entirely ready to face. Like the death of her brother, who had clearly been her best friend for the past six years.

Her only ally and protector. Gone.

I can't even come close to replacing him but the best I can do is assure her that she is safe here with me. And if that means being there when she's reliving something I can't wake her from, then so be it. I don't sleep. Not since my forced sabbatical in the tombs of the Headquarters. A place you don't want to be. Ten years in a coffin was punishment enough. I don't do well with enclosed dark places, surprisingly enough. Hence the large penthouse with wide open spaces. No clutter.

Everything in its place from the ornate candelabras to the trash can placement.

I received permission to live off headquarters property with the agreement that it would not hinder my ability to perform and stay true to the code that keeps us safe. No making a spectacle of oneself that will lead to exposure of our existence and follow no feed orders. Snitches here get rewarded by underbosses. Conformity is important, hence why it was mandatory for newborns and close family members to stay at headquarters.

With what I do, I need my space to decompress. Feed the illusion that I am just some normal person. An eligible bachelor living the high life of the windy city. Callum, Lycidas and Norryx do better at the headquarters. I do not. It feels too much like a frat house. And with my time served in the tombs, Serlanos felt that he could trust me to live on my own in the city. He had Callum and Norryx to wrangle the newborns when they were frenzied.

I was lucky I was permitted to live on my own based on this recent infraction. Which still was being resolved. My phone has been ringing nonstop. Our neighbors called on the hour every hour to see if I would answer.

I was certain that they had their theories about me, none of them got super close. They knew me through Emily as she was the one that attended the block parties and the fundraiser bake sales.

I had hoped that they would assume I too perished in the fire.

Roderick ascertained the estate of my mortal life as Emily's husband. The other day he called to discuss funeral arrangements and if Emily and I had our plans written out.

"Did Emily want to be cremated?" Roderick asked over the phone.

I hoped he felt my death stare through the receiver.

"Sorry, too soon?" Roderick asks, the smile in his voice evident.

I resent the Gyanstazi family for turning him, we should have left him to die. Like he asked.

"A bit, considering the house was just recently hosed down. Emily would've wanted a closed casket. Same for me. Make sure a casket and death certificate are issued for me. I can't have anyone wanting to go look for me."

"Already taken care of at Cynfael's expense. He said "consider it a good will gesture.""

How does Cynfael always find a way to intervene in my business? Being the strong arm of the coroner's office and the death industry, Cynfael would've been the one to have the medical examiner blindly sign off on the evidence that was said to be my remains. He didn't need to pay for it either. It's not like I am concerned about money. However, a charge to an account of a person who is supposed to be dead would look suspicious. I am to lay low for a bit, which works well for welcoming my guests.

The funeral was planned and according to Roderick, Emily's parents want more answers as to what happened, even though it was explained to them by the fire marshal himself after giving his official report. Which included the fabricated evidence Cynfael had planted to resolve any doubt about my death.

"Your father in law sounded like a charmer," Roderick says when he calls with the funeral plans.

"You should have spent the holidays with him. He was a real joy then."

"I take it he did not approve of the marriage then?"

"What father-in-law completely likes his son-in-law?"

"Fair. We're all bastards, every single one of us. My father-in-law still hasn't forgiven me for just existing."

"I haven't either."

"I am starting to understand your father-in-law a bit more. Just do yourself a favor, don't be an asshole and don't go to that funeral." The click of the receiver bites in my ears.

I am not that much of an asshole, not unless it's called for, and when it came to Roderick, I couldn't hold back. I don't have time to pretend to like someone I honestly detest.

Him being a vampire now only made me resent my kind even more.

I went to the graveside service, I had to.

My wife and son are dead and now being put to rest. They deserve the respect from me. I didn't join the other mourners, I am supposed to be dead. If I turned up alive, Emily's father would have my head.

Parked in my SUV just across the street I could see through the wrought iron gates and surrounding bramble to the funeral party for the graveside service. I followed them here from Holy Name Cathedral where my wife was a devout Catholic, much like her parents.

My cold skin prickles with shame as I stand on the outskirts of the hallowed ground watching them bury my wife Emily and my son Calvin, or what remained of them. Cynfael made all of the arrangements, taking each criticism my father-in-law had to give.

I was not bothered a bit when the passenger door opened and Cynfael hopped in the front seat.

"I knew you couldn't resist not coming."

"Roderick said don't. I heard 'go'."

"Like always. You're very stubborn, you know that right?"

"Absolutely," I say, wiping away a sudden tear.

Cynfael pauses before speaking again.

"I'm sorry, man. I really am. But it may be for the best. You know? What would've happened if she had found out? I know you thought you covered your bases but maybe, just maybe she would've blown the whistle on you. All of us. And your son -"

"I know. But do not bring up my son. He deserved a chance at least." My shame corrodes what organ I have left inside of me, eating away. Knowing all of this is my fault.

"Just like everyone, but not everyone gets one."

"It just hurts worse because I did it."

"You did what you had to. If it wasn't you, it'd be someone else. And you did it in the most painless way you knew how to."

My vision blurred as grief strikes and the funeral proceeds in the background. I see the funeral goers toss their roses on the coffins as they are lowered into the ground.

Cynfael always knew how to help me keep my head on straight even when my emotions were driving every action.

"Come on, let's get you out of here before someone sees you," Cynfael says, turning the car on for me. But I fear that I've been spotted. From the top of the hill away from the rest of the dispersing crowd stands Emily's father, Chuck. It was as if he knew I was in this SUV. Even with the black out windows, he knows. A father always does and he has someone to blame for this. Me.

Confirming what he always believed about me, a typical wiseguy. He warned Emily against men like me, having lived the days when Capone ruled the streets of Chicago.

But she loved me. And I loved her.

She wasn't the love of my life, but she deserved that respect. She was simple and didn't expect me to change for her. She didn't want to know if I was up to knowing good, just if it was time to run for the hills.

And I never told her when, because I was naive to think it would never come. I was stupid. Costing me my wife and my son all because of the say so of those who have all the time in the world.

lenora holmwood

Blackbird - The Beatles

During the day, the penthouse is quiet. I stick to the few rooms I know as I fear I wouldn't find my way back without the help of a search party. As far as I know, Llewyn could have a portal to another universe just behind one of these many doors, which must remain locked. Made me only more wondrous of horrors he has locked away. I feel that I've only scratched the surface of questions that I have for him. And locked doors can only mean more secrets.

More questions that seek answers.

At times I feel like a ghost, haunting the empty halls waiting for life to return and haunt me in return. I sip my morning cup of coffee and check in with the news to see if Serlanos has surfaced to the public eye, making a criminal spectacle of himself once more. He was good at crawling in and out of the darkness like a cockroach, infesting the lives of others. Since the diner incident, police activity down below on the street has been more active. People want justice for those that were murdered.

"Sources say that the Chicago Crime Commissioner is cracking down on the violence that is running rampant. Bodies have been turning up all over the city, many of them homeless. Many have gone missing and the numbers are rising. Many of the locals suspect that whoever is killing these unfortunate souls is behind the massacre at the Pepperpod diner last Monday morning...."

I doubt Serlanos nor his men will face the consequences of that massacre.

It will be swept under the rug like everything else they've done.

Being immortal with unlimited financial resources has its perks. Free from the burden of guilt and responsibility to mankind. Political campaigns and poll reports follow so I turn off the television. I wasn't going to learn anything new. Serlanos released what he wanted. He controlled the media. The police. Everything. The only person I knew for sure that would never side with Serlanos completely is Chief Warren. And that's by Llewyn's account of the Blood Syndicate's relationship with the Chicago Crime Commission. Chief Warren has made it his mission to expose them - he's under an oath to never reveal their true nature outright.

"He's just hoping we fuck up somewhere," Llewyn had said. "And we have. The diner incident should have been it. Explaining away a massacre that is public is too much, even for the best conspiracy theorist out there."

I eventually find myself in the library tucked under a blanket and folded into one of the arm chairs I coveted at first sight with a book on ancient lore of vampires, making a list of questions to go over with Llewyn for when he returns. Waiting for him can be agonizing as it's never at the same time when he comes through that door. I wonder what he does while he's gone. He doesn't share much about himself aside from answering my questions about vampirism.

Sometimes I feel we do a lot of talking about me. He loves hearing my mundane childhood stories and will ask very specific questions in explicit detail, almost as if he were there himself watching on the sidelines.

I think back to when I first arrived here and he said, "Sometimes we just need to feel human again."I wonder how often he wishes to be human again. He's not bragged about his sanguine conquests nor does he incite mortal fear in me. He doesn't revel in his nature, unless when forced to do so in a matter of life and death. It wasn't by choice by the way he speaks of the others of his kind. Like referring to the vampires at the diner as 'bloodsuckers' sounded a bit derogatory.

But I too am still learning. I don't know if I could offend him if I tried. I accidentally called him a monster to his face when he first told me of his condition and he laughed instead of ripping my throat out. If it weren't for the fridge of blood and plasma and for him telling me outright, I wouldn't have guessed. He seems more human to me than most.

Llewyn's path of self-discovery is shelved among the many books and records of vampires across history he has neatly organized in a dark corner of the impressive library. His collection was magnificent. Every time I enter through the double doors I am in just as much awe of it as I was the first time Llewyn welcomed me in. There's nothing more romantic than showing a bookworm your personal library. The tense feelings of attraction only heightened as Llewyn and I spent our evenings together in the arm chairs with a lit fire in front of us.

I would catch his eye over the top of my book before he quickly averted his gaze. Pretending as if he weren't distracted with me sitting next to him.

I bite my lip and refocus my wandering thoughts to my book on Eastern European vampirism I was struggling through. I reread the same line over and over. I can feel his dark eyes on me, only making me feel slightly self conscious.

What is he thinking? Is he waiting for me to have questions for him? I have plenty of those. But right now less than pure thoughts were brewing. I had to banish them away and break the tension.

I reach over for a piece of cheese from the charcuterie platter that was delivered with today's groceries. A tall glass of wine sits next to it. Llewyn poured a bag of blood into a glass and wrote NOT WINE with a dry erase marker.

"I appreciate the labeling. I worried I'd get the two mixed up."

"You'd be in for a terrible surprise then."

"Blood doesn't taste that bad."

"You've not drunk it by the glass. It's different, "he says, his mouth red from his last sip.

"Okay when you say it like that, 'I don't finish that sentence.

I withhold a giggle because he reminds me of a small boy with the remnants of a red popsicle on his face.

"What? Do I have something on my face?" He asks, noticing my stifled giggles.

"Just a bit," I say, mirroring on my face in a circular motion with my finger.

He pulls a kerchief from his breast pocket and dabs the blood away from his lips: "How embarrassing."

"By the time I finish this bottle, my mouth will be just as purple as yours."

"Pssssh. You're going to finish the whole bottle?'

"Were you going to chase the blood with a Cabernet?

"I might."

"I doubt that would mix well. Flavor wise."

"You don't want to know."

"So do you eat food on top of drinking blood? Do you choose to eat or do you need blood on top of normal food?"

"I choose to eat 'regular' food. It is not necessary. I can go months with any other sort of meal as long as I have a steady blood supply."

"Can vampires still-you know... experience bowel movements?"

"Yes, we still piss and defecate."

"I'm sorry, it was rude of me to ask that. I'm just trying to wrap my head around this whole vampire thing."

"I know. It's amusing to me. I didn't tell my wife so I never really got to have conversations like this."

"How did you manage? I mean you carried on a double life. One minute you're a bloodthirsty mobster and then the next you're a family man back from a business trip?"

"It wasn't easy. And you're right. I think that's why I am so attracted to you. I don't have to hide who I am."

I blush, using my book to hide my redness rising to the surface.

"You can hide your embarrassment all you want. It only makes you more attractive, Nora."

I am not used to his direct declarations of his interest in me. It commands my arousal, my curiosity. But I wasn't sure how fast I wanted to go. Or even how to respond when he says things like this, I haven't been flirted with in six years.

Grandpa chased the boys away, claiming he was keeping me pure. A few years too late. The boys I had flirted with didn't speak as eloquently as Llewyn. The art of romance in language was a nuance to them. Llewyn's English accent was a bonus. Had I been his prey on some dark street or a forbidden alleyway I would have fallen for his trap. I imagine women swoon when he walks down Michigan Avenue, he looks the part of a model that would steal the spotlights on billboards.

"You know I lose all concept of the English language when you say things like that. I'm not used to it."

"That's because you've never been around a gentleman who knows how to romance a woman like a queen."

He draws his lips to my hand and impresses a sensual kiss before releasing my hand and then leaves the room with the empty wine glass in hand.

He is to me what blood is to him. He loves leaving me wanting more.

20

llewyn hellsinger

Hungry Heart - Lauren O'Connell

It's been hard to keep up appearances for blood runs and drop offs since my new house guest arrived. I admit, it was easier in the suburbs to hide a human away. But my previous wife Emily was able to leave and take care of the house stuff while I was 'at work' and earning a living. No one knew of her existence and she was self-sufficient. Caring for our home and son Calvin was a full-time job but she wanted to do it.

It was what her mother, and grandmother did. She was traditional.

Living in the city with a human-in-hiding from the very person I work for is tedious and dangerous. I couldn't be caught shopping for groceries when of course vampires have not much need for food the way humans do.

I know my absence has been noticed by Callum and Lycidas who have their own opinions about what I do when I'm away but whatever rumors they've conjured have been explained away with lies that I was still tracking 'Ms.Holmwood' down. Lies that could neither be proven nor disproven.

Serlanos knows I have my ways of doing things - but I wasn't so sure that he trusts me right now.

Since Callum followed me just before the diner incident, I had a feeling my every move was being watched. When I was 'back in town', Serlanos seemed to have some dirty work saved for me.

I know I am still being punished. I don't suck up to him like Callum and the others. I have no reason to except for the sake of my own survival.

Had it not been for my skills as a trained soldier, Serlanos wouldn't have kept me alive. As he so likes to remind me every time we meet to ensure my shriveling loyalty to him.

When I am out tracking down a bounty on the lamb or driving blood deliveries to different clans as payment, I wonder what Nora does while I am gone all day. I've taught her how to use the smart TV and there are *plenty* of books but I picture her sitting at the window, tapping at the glass at the city she's just barely rejoined, trapped like a raven in a cage, bursting to take flight at last. Her freedom is the treasure that she seeks.

Driving down Michigan Avenue, I check my rearview mirror every chance I get making sure I'm not being followed back to the penthouse. I hold my chilled breath until I enter the parking garage and am secured in my spot - waiting a few moments anticipating an ambush. At any moment it could come from either side. My allies or my enemies. The Volcolacs are on the move and reaping havoc on the upper north side and leaving prostitutes bleeding out in motel rooms. Serlanos has sent some of our revenant soldiers to his brothels to prevent further attacks on his products. Brothels were the one way we could bring in fresh blood for ourselves without making a spectacle of ourselves. As long as we kept our vassals happy and paid, they would do anything that we wanted. But our desires are dwindling.

The Volcolacs, shape shifting lawless beasts on the fringe of town, are determined to exterminate use from the city since the uprising of our kind in the Chicago Underworld. Surpassing the accomplishments of Capone himself in a short time, Serlanos has made a spectacle with his presence alone for everyone.

Every paranoid thought was left at the door when I entered the penthouse. The moment I see Lenora dancing in the kitchen in nothing but a shirt and sleep shorts as pasta boils on the stove, the thoughts of the poor mortal I bludgeoned to death earlier escapes my mind.

Not even the red tomato sauce she pours daintily on my plate with a warm smile could bring back the sickening squelch of blood spurting through the gouge I left from tearing his throat out with my fangs. Don't feel too sorry for him, he had it coming.

He was hurting one of the girls that worked at one of many clubs owned by Serlanos. That doesn't fly. Part of our duty in gangland is to offer protection to those on the payroll. We can't let mere mortals think Serlanos is a pushover.

I've taken a bit of a soft spot for women in trouble lately. So I had no trouble seeing the fucker into the next life.

Not only that but he'd been holding out on Serlanos for too long.

Time to pay up.

I devoured her food only to lean back and basque in how normal this felt. Like things did when Emily was around. But better. I mean no disrespect to my late wife's memory, nor my son's. But there was something about Nora that was different.

I didn't expect to feel this happy just to have her around. She made life feel normal again. I feel alive in a way that I never did with Emily. Emily was more about companionship and fulfilling the dream of having a family that Serlanos had robbed me of so many times before.

It was the first time I had borne a child that had stayed alive. The first time I felt I had completed something.

Now I take happiness as it comes fleetingly. That's what Lenora brings. Even as an immortal, it's important to enjoy those rare moments of happiness. It takes the mundanity out of living forever.

An escape from my daily life where there were very little responsibilities. I was surprised to see how self-reliant she was. I've been wearing a smile more often than not lately.

She smiles, pleased like a small housewife, waiting for my praise. It's nice to see her smiling too, for once. The curve of her perfect rosebud lips. Her bright green eyes light up when she looks at me.

"That was delicious. Where did you learn to cook?" I ask as I take my clean plate to the dishwasher.

"My parents taught us. Each week we were expected to prepare a meal. I missed it. Considering the last six years was literally survival mode. I am getting back into the swing of things starting with the more simple dishes."

She sits at the table and sips the last bit of wine before pouring another glass. I knew she was itching to head to the library. It seems to be a ritual of hers.

When I look at her, I see such beauty and strength. Even though she has seen such horrible things at the hands of her grandfather and her family ripped away from her, she doesn't let it darken her outlook in the world. I still see hope. You wouldn't have known by looking at her that her last six years were spent in captivity. Dependent on someone who was supposed to care for her but gave her less than nothing. Scraps. Abuse. The scars are still just teeming at the surface.

She doesn't discuss them outloud. Not yet. But her night terrors tell me everything I need to know about what that fucker did to her and her brother. I don't bring up Theo. I know better just from feeling the weight of her nightmares when waking her from them. She clutches me for dear life. Serlanos did one decent thing by taking that piece of shit grandfather out.

Blood sometimes really means nothing.

She has given no indication of wanting to leave. I don't blame her for not wanting to. This place is a complete 180 from where she was. A full cabinet and smart fridge of food. Lounging, entertainment. Quiet.

Nor do I ask her if she wants to.

I don't want to make her think I don't want her here with me. Because I do. I want nothing more than her to stay here forever, with me. But she has a choice. She's always had a choice. She just needs a chance to live and be free. And I am giving her one.

To live freely.

I can hear her crying at night. Sometimes I wake her from a screaming night terror. She's grieving. Everything has caught up to her. The loss, the fear. The reality that she's shacked up with a vampire whom she's trusting with every fiber not to bite her nor turn her over to the one person who would reduce her to beyond nothing.

And that was the last thing I would ever think of doing.

Destroying such a small creature that was so beautiful, pure and innocent.

Fuck, she was worried about offending me. Refusing to call me a monster.

When that's exactly what I am.

llewyn hellsinger

I Found - Amber Run

Lenora is in the far corner of the library, browsing my collection of eastern European vampire lore once again. I know what she's doing. She's looking for answers. The same ones I scoured those pages for, trying to understand where I fit into this whole mess. The question of 'why me'? It was the same question I asked myself so many times. Why me? Why did I go into that bar - I should've just gone home to my mother, who was already forlorning my return?

I didn't see her again. I couldn't.

It was better off leaving it that I had died.

That didn't stop her and my father from searching, while I watched them from afar.

I see those same desperate eyes on my mother as I do in Lenora.

I remember the way Lenora's eyes lit up when I first brought her into my library. The pure awe and admiration. Her big blue eyes nearly bulged out of her head, and tears of bountiful appreciation began to form. Walls upon walls of books shelved on black oak soaring up to the vaulted ceilings. Two large black leather arm chairs placed in front of the fireplace.

"This is where I like to spend a lot of my time. I spent years cultivating this library. I would visit bookstores during my travels in the army and always find something worth taking with me and that habit stuck with me," I told her.

"It's not a bad habit. It's better than collecting a bunch of touristy shirts," she approves as her small hands caress my collected leather bound treasures.

When I'm not home, I imagine Lenora spends her time either sleeping in the armchair by the fire or exploring the maze of a penthouse, weaving in and out of the empty rooms looking for something to spark her curiosity.

The life of a house cat.

I feel bad though. It's almost as if I have trapped her again in some way. I know I am only trying to help her and she hasn't fought me at all on the matter.

I just want to offer her more.

She doesn't have much, nor does she even ask. Even though I know I've told her a million times over in the last few days that if there was anything she needed or wanted to just ask.

I'm in no way short in cash.

I should bring her more entertainment. Maybe an e-reader or something. But I feel hesitant about her leaving any kind of digital footprint. It could lead Serlanos or one of his more tech savvy associates right here.

Thanks to modern technology, grocery delivery has made it easy for her to retrieve items that she may need throughout the day.

Occasionally she will use it for delivery from the Chinese restaurant I ordered from the first night she was here and conscious.

She tried sushi the other day, but sadly the fish didn't keep in transit and she paid for it later.

I stood outside the bathroom in case she needed any emotional support as she emptied out her bowels.

I felt slightly bad since it was my idea for her to try it.

Standing at the doorway, I watch as she stands before the book case, skimming the summary of the book in her delicate little hands. The way her eyes smile as she finds that hint of magic is just too precious. I see the book that she's holding. My first edition of Bram Stoker's Dracula. Of course she picks up Dracula.

"That's all fiction you know?" I tease her from afar. She jumps in my presence, her large beautiful eyes widen and then soften. Sometimes I forget how quiet I am.

"So you say? Vampires are supposed to be fiction, yet here one stands before my very eyes," she says playfully. I love the way her lips purse seductively and her eyes shine as she looks at me. All of this flirting has been building.

"Vampires are real. But I think Bram Stoker was a bit theatrical in his representation of a true vampire."

"Oh? Enlighten me then?" She is standing so close that I can hear the blood pumping in her veins. Is it attraction or fear? It's hard to tell. For some women, it's one and the same. Scared and horny.

"For one, the hairy hands, come on. And I don't crawl up buildings or turn into a bat."

"You don't plan to terrorize me in my dreams or possess me?"

"Not currently," I tease. But I do watch her sleep. Her night terrors are bad. Yet she never acknowledges them.

I can't protect her from her mind, but I can be there when she wakes up.

"So you're telling me that you don't turn into a bat and fly away?"

"No, I don't turn into a bat." I know she's messing with me.

"That's a shame."

"Why?"

"You'd be a cute bat."

She giggles as she hugs the book to her chest, pushing her perfect breasts up - I need to stop staring.

"Don't tell me you're really going to read that?"

"I already have. But it's time for a reread. I have to compare notes with Mr. Stoker," she teases as I lunge for the book, pressing her against the bookcase.

Her poised red lips provoked me to regale them with my own. My desire to feel her soul against what's left of mine haunts me. A slow death-march drum roll builds between us as nothing was spoken yet everything was said. Her soulful eyes look up into mine, her eyelashes fluttering with her hastening heartbeat as I feel the pull.

The tension is taut. Her breathing staggered as I leaned in only centimeters from her plush lips, feeding on her fear mixed with desire - but stopped in my tracks by the incessant ringing coming from my phone.

The screen glows with Serlanos' demand to be answered.

His name is scrawled in big letters across the screen.

Breaking up this moment of tenuous perfection.Threatening our safe haven.

Her eyes widened with real fear when she glanced at the screen.

I must protect her at all costs.

lenora holmwood

I Never Told You What I Do For A Living - My Chemical Romance

It struck me like lightning. Serlanos is just a call away for Llewyn. Seeing the name displayed on the phone screen had me frozen in place. Llewyn's thumb quivers over the answer button. I always knew he worked for Serlanos and was gone most days doing unspeakable things in his service.

But seeing it on the phone screen made it too real.

It was easier to pretend that Llewyn was just leaving for a normal day job and not out on the prowl for victims or shakedowns of innocent business owners for the very man who wants to do god-knows-what to me.

"I'm sorry I have to take this," he says and walks out of the library and closes the door behind him.

Quietly, I follow.

I wanted to know, once and for all - can I trust Llewyn?

When I enter the dimly lit hall, I can hear he's in the kitchen negotiating.

I keep quiet as I hide around the corner listening.

"Yes, yes I know it's important that you find her. I will meet you there to give a full report."

What does he know? Why is he going to meet him? Is this a ruse? Is he going to finally turn me over? Was this all just a clever ruse - to romance me and hand me over once the bid was at its highest?

As soon as he hangs up the phone I step away from my hiding spot and he sees me, a startled expression scrawled on his face.

"I'm sorry, Lenora. I -"

"Leave. Now." The words were out of my mouth before I could stop them.

They weren't my words. Fear was speaking.

He doesn't question it. He leaves the penthouse, securing the door behind him. The click of the latch hung in my ears long after he had left.

I fall to the floor sobbing, realizing I sent the one person I depend on out of his own penthouse.

But the fear that festers inside me is all consuming.

How do I know that one day Serlanos won't be on the other side of that door, ready to tear me away from this safe haven in the sky and marry me off to one of his beasts? How do I know anything except from what Llewyn tells me or I learn from watching the useless news reports.

Am I really all that safe here? I never considered leaving once I got here. I didn't get that far in my plan. But how long will Llewyn be able to hide me away from the world? I got too comfortable here and I've nearly lost track of how long that's been since I arrived. My time in the hospital was disorienting and this place is a bubble in the sky. Llewyn and I have shared this space and it's been completely blissful, until now.

I blew that up.

I ruined everything. And now I feel cornered. I could run but that would be a big mistake. Being out on the street only makes me more vulnerable as I do not know who is with Serlanos and who isn't. And by this time he most likely has everyone in his pocket. But - how do I know Llewyn isn't going to arrange for Serlanos to come get me?

Just throwing him out of the apartment would be enough to say 'fuck this bitch' and turn me over. I am just another human to Llewyn that he felt the need to be responsible for. Not too long ago he had a wife and child and he killed them on his say so? Despite his rebellion, Serlanos still has Llewyn on a string.

How long might Llewyn's rebellion go on? I might've just pushed away the one person that I shouldn't have. Broken his trust and ruined whatever has been brewing between us. That moment in the library - it was the closest we've been. He was going to kiss me. Those perfect cupid's bow lips were about to claim mine when Serlanos called. I don't expect it to progress further than that.

This is too new. Too fragile. And I shattered it into pieces on the floor. A mirror that Llewyn can no longer see himself in. To see a reflection of a future together with me, it was a fantasy I've built up in my head. A place to go when the night terrors get too bad. Llewyn takes me away to a place of bliss that only exists in some alternate universe that is too far out of reach for me. I am limited. A mortal and completely wrong for him. It didn't work out with him and his previous wife. How am I any different?

I don't see a way back from this. I know too much and he will have to kill me or send me away. I wouldn't blame him if he did. I should have thought this through before I let my fear and emotions take over and thrown out the one person that isn't against me in this world.

I pound my head. The fears replay in my head. It was hard to separate his voice from my own at times. I wondered if I would ever separate the two before too many men occupied my thoughts - leaving no room for a voice of my own.

I don't dare to open the door to see if he's waiting. All I can do is assume he will be back at some point.

I feel my chest heave with uncontrollable sobs, my heart pounding loudly. *I fucked up.*

The wait for him to come back is already tortuous. It may have only been minutes since the door shut behind him, the click of the bolt echoes in my ears. Anticipation threads through my veins.

Please come back, please come back.

Silence moves in. Like it has hung in the air waiting to make its move into the empty space to remind me that I am on my own.

llewyn hellsinger

It Will Come Back - Hozier

"Any leads on the Holmwood girl?" Serlanos asks, sipping his whiskey casually, pretending as if he isn't fiending to get his claws in her. He has Norryx and Lycidas searching the Canadian border, and Damascus traveling south to chase one of my false leads.

He finally caught up with me. Sending for me to meet him at the Davis Street Fish Market in Evanston.

"Where've you been?" Serlanos asks, pulling a fresh cigar from his pocket and removes the wrappings.

"I've been taking care of a few things. I don't know if you heard but my wife and son died recently."

"Tragic. By accident of course?"

"Of course," I say. There are people watching around. I have to be careful about what I say in case someone recognizes me. Fortunately I am not in the the newspapers

There's no smoking in here. But the owner doesn't argue with Serlanos as he cuts the tip of a stogie and torches the end. He never has. He knows what we are. He pays the toll for protection from us. We give him business. He's in no position to turn that down.

"I have sources on the south end that say she was seen at a bus stop in Calexico. Headed south.

"And are your sources reliable? I cannot afford to lose her again, Llew." He blows the smoke in my face and gives a sneering smile. He loves to antagonize me when he can. He loves pulling the strings on his favorite puppet.

"Absolutely. I received security footage from a reliable resource of the girl purchasing a ticket the morning of the diner incident."

Chief Warren was kind enough to pass the information to me and to me only.

It feels strange referring to Nora as 'the girl'. *She's my girl.* And *my girl* is somewhat peeved with me right now. I gotta make it up to her somehow. Reassure that the devil in front of me isn't going to get his claws in her.

"And how do you know they didn't turn around and sell that information to someone else."

"Because I trust them."

I am playing a dangerous game mentioning trust - as I doubt Serlanos has much of that these days. Especially concerning myself and Callum. The Gyanstazi family is disappointed.

"I guess that would explain your sudden absence at the diner when Cynfael opened fire on Callum and the entire company."

"Yes."

"Very well. I expect results, Llewyn. I don't want to see your face until you're delivering the girl to me. I trust you, for now. This is your last chance to prove you're worthy of the Gyanstazi name."

Maybe I'm not.

A week ago, I murdered my secret family for this man - and now, I am lying to his face about hiding the very mortal he's hunting for in a secret penthouse. Loyalty is not my strong suit. I don't blame Serlanos for not trusting me.

Our values diverged the minute I took Lenora under my protection.

I trust myself.

And I'm going to get us both out of here.

How am I going to explain this to her? I had to leave to go meet Serlanos but she is surely shaken. And probably has lost trust in me. I didn't tell her what I did for a living just for the same reasons I never told Emily. For protection. Lenora didn't need to know how closely I worked with Serlanos because soon I am hoping to be rid of him for the both of us.

But how?

Serlanos is watching all major transportation. The airports. Roadblocks. There's even an unspoken BOLO and a Missing Persons report out for this girl. Her face is everywhere I go, reminding me of the trouble I possibly put us both in. It would've been easier to have gone the day we escaped the diner rather than put on appearances but I wasn't thinking that far ahead. I wasn't thinking at all.

I just saw her in the diner and acted as one would in a hail of gunfire and an innocent walks in.

Too many innocents had died that day and I couldn't bear another one. Not when we were supposed to leave the diner without bloodshed from either side. And the mortals paid the price for our debauchery.

I stopped at a newsstand with flowers and paid the big man with a cigar and barking dogs twenty bucks for a bouquet of red roses. As he divided out my change, the front page of the Chicago Tribune stares back at me, Lenora's stunning features on the front page.

24

lenora holmwood

Lover, Please Stay - Nothing But Thieves

The new door had industrial-strength locks - locked from the inside and out. Grandpa had the only key. Only he could leave. We were his prisoners under the guise of safety. Completely dependent on him. And he is consistently letting us down. Punishment for making him look like a fool in front of Serlanos. Someone he vowed to never let himself be intimidated by in his own home.

But Serlanos owns him now, just like he owns all of us. The cold gaze of his eyes claims ownership of whatever makes them dilate with greed and malice. The same one when his eyes meet mine. The same ferocious eyes that haunt me in my nightmares every night saying 'You will be mine'. He already owns my family. And all that we have. What more could he want?

Grandad left again. No food, only bottles of liquor from last night's bender. He called us ungrateful when the partially eaten cheeseburger he found in the garbage on his walk home wasn't enough to feed all of us.

"You're the only one with a key. Either let us out so we can go get some or go get us food!" Theo roars at him. "Serlanos gave you all of that cash to take care of your family and you're still here pissing it away. Your granddaughter

130

almost got raped and we are starving and you don't give a single shit. You just want control."

Theo has had enough and he was right. We all watched Serlanos stuff bills into his pocket as Grandpa was too proud to accept the loan himself. It was already spent.

On the door locks. On the liquor fueling his rage and need for control. Being the only one with access to the world, Grandpa is obsessed with controlling the public's opinion of the Holmwood name. The bitter memory of the iron gates, baring the Holmwood family crest, closing on him as Serlanos sneers at him through the gate bars replays in Grandpa's head over and over. I imagine when he leaves the apartment he takes the L-line up to Hawthorn Woods to stand outside of his former home, seething in liquor-laced lament. Only to let it fester on the train ride back to the south side leaving him to take it out on us when he walks in the door.

Sick of his self-pity and neglect from the previous chaos, Gram has found some courage to provide for us. The first challenge would be getting out of the apartment which has become a fortress, starting with our front door.

Grandpa always locks us in when he leaves and when he comes home, storing the skeleton key in his breast pocket along with his dwindling pride. Making the mission seem impossible, without the help of alcohol. Gram was ready to play the long game of waiting out the liquor and rage to reduce him to a whiskey-induced coma in his chair, allowing us to lift the keys and slip out to get food for us all.

Gram insisted it was her that went. She didn't want us to be punished for just trying to survive.

However, I longed to go with her. To leave this horrible building we can barely call home. To feel and breathe fresh air. To see somewhere or someone else.

Just enough to know the world still exists outside these putrid, dilapidated walls. But beggars can't be choosers. I'd just be grateful to have a hot meal.

Grandpa started snoring around 12:23 am. He didn't have much to yell about, he just drank away whatever was grinding his gears today. Gram waits another twenty minutes before lifting the keys from his pocket.

She stands over him, pretending to kiss him on the forehead as her other hand slips into the shirt pocket and slips the keys and remaining cash into her pocket.

She silently tiptoes over to the front door and begins turning each lock. Theo and I watch Grandpa intensely, waiting for him to move or stir awake at the sound of each lock turning.

Gram releases her breath as the door is unlocked and she slowly opens it, praying for the slight squeak in the hinge to remain silent.

Gram looks back at us, seeing our hopeful faces and she motions for us to follow her.

She knows how much we've yearned to go outside, just as much as she has.

Snow falls on the dimly lit street of the southside neighborhood our building is crammed on. Tucked between townhomes and surrounded by dark alleyways haunted by shadowy figures. The streets don't sleep. Phantoms dart down the railroad tracks, escaping the chase of Chicago Police. Police Commissioner Chief Warner's fight against organized crime grows more rampant as Serlanos' influence spreads across the city. Polluting the pockets and warping the minds of government officials, politicians, and anyone else with the smallest bit of power. Commanding the city to his every whim.

We keep to the lit side of the road. Cars roar past us with thumping music and loud engines. Gram walked tense - her body frigid with uncertainty. She was out of her element here on the south side. As we all were. The urban life was very different from what we were used to on the north side of Chicago. Hawthorn Woods, a development of lavish estate homes, sat near a lake and golf course. Most of the owners of these large homes came from old money, like Grandpa who inherited the Holmwood Manor at his father's death. Passed on to the eldest son of seven.

Gram came from a similar background, and she and Grandpa found common interest in going to the Chicago Symphony and other lavish exploits the city offers. Gram needed someone who could provide for her lifestyle. And Grandpa was happy to spend every penny on her.

Dad had a rich upbringing and he wore it proudly. Which only made it so shocking that he would be involved with someone like Serlanos, who took everything and everyone in his path for granted. Dad was a giver. He was a philanthropist. He started his practice to benefit those researching cures for infectious diseases and help scientists develop new ways of extracting DNA. He wanted to make a difference in the world. Serlanos is the antithesis of that.

Seeing Gram in casual clothes was unusual for me and Theo. She loved to make a spectacle of herself, turning heads at her age in the latest in Chicago Fashion. But now, I was sure she wished to be anywhere but on the streets of Chicago in the middle of the night looking for food.

There's an Arby's a few blocks down from where I remember turning and crossing under the L when we first arrived. Gram shivered the whole way but didn't let the cold keep her maternal instincts from kicking in. I know what she's thinking.

Will we have enough pocket change from what Grandpa had in his pocket to get something for all of us?

My stomach lurches with need as the aromas from the restaurant tickle my nose as we approach the front door. Inside, warmth stings my face. Gram stands off to the side to count the wadded bills. I see a smile spread on her face as she whispers her counts.

She turns to us and says, "Fifty dollars. We have fifty dollars here."

The tension releases from her chest as she approaches the counter to order for us while Theo and I find a table by the window and watch the snowfall. With the window reinforcements Grandpa added for security, we couldn't see much from the small bedroom window Theo and I shared.

I tore into my curly fries as soon as Gram reached the table with the tray of food. Together we sat in silence, devouring our food and watching the snow build outside.

For a moment, we felt like a normal family again, like when Gram used to bring us along on one of her shopping sprees on Michigan Avenue.

Time with Gram used to be an hour of frivolity. Where we weren't being terrorized.

Where we were like everyone else.

Is he ever coming back? There's a hollow pit in my stomach. His absence is noticed and it's like he took every part of me with him as he walked out the door. He didn't even look mad when I told him to leave.

He didn't look sad. Expressionless.

He is so hard to read at times. Those dark eyes convey so much yet so little all at once. There's a shine of danger to them that hypnotized me each time they met mine.

I craved his presence. And sending him away now nearly broke me.

God it feels like eternity until he returns.

If he ever does.

I lay on the couch after finishing some breathing exercises to calm my nerves. Those meetings with the hospital trauma therapist actually kind of helped.

Counting to ten inhales. Hold. Exhale. Repeat.

He is coming back.

I have to take my mind off what he's doing and focus on me. Self care is important, especially in the middle of a nervous-emotional breakdown.

I shower, but nearly fall from shaking so that didn't last long.

I wrap myself as a burrito in the extra large towel and toss myself onto the bed, hoping that the compression will calm me down.

But I feel too restless, confined and start to panic and thrash my way out of the cocoon.

I try to read but my mind keeps trailing back to him and sitting still is next to impossible.

Where did he go? What is he doing? Every question repeats in my head on a loop.

How stupid could I be? Here he is trying to protect and hide me, while on the other hand he's lying to Serlanos. The one person that craves my blood more than any beast in the city. Everyone is looking for me. I know that much. And how much someone would pay for my blood is probably in the hundred thousands. I know Llewyn won't tell me. He wouldn't want to worry me with such demeaning information.

Time stands still.

I have to do something otherwise I will go mad waiting for him.

Once again I find myself in the kitchen.

Seeing the full cupboards again seemed odd considering the fridge full of blood bags. He doesn't normally eat. He chooses to. It makes him feel human. Food does nothing for him. It's blood that satisfies him. How often does he have to -? I don't know if I want to know the answer to that question.

Nothing sounds good as I rummage through the refrigerator. There was plenty to choose from but I was looking for comfort food. Something sweet.

Chocolate. I found chocolate in the pantry. Double fudge chocolate brownie mix.

I spread out the ingredients and mixing bowl on the center island and begin with pouring in the brownie mix. The dark fudge powder is strong and suddenly I'm back in the kitchen with Mom baking a hundred kinds of cookies for no reason at all except we could.

I break open the first of three eggs and watch the yolk *plop* into the bowl. Mom used to make the plop sound with her mouth each time she broke a yolk into the bowl. The absence of it was deafening. And I wasn't nearly as good as she was.

On the second egg, I hit the edge of the mixing bowl too hard causing it to tip over - drenching my leggings with bright yellow stickiness. The brownie mix was salvageable. The eggs however - *I yolked myself.*

I peel off my embarrassment and toss it into the fancy washing machine that beeps at me as I activate it, leaving me in nothing but the oversized t-shirt and panties. I shiver and scurry over to the oven and start the preheat hoping it will heat up this chilled tomb. I wonder if he would notice if I turned on the heat. Or is he like most males where it has to be kept to the specific degree? The thermostat is sacred. Dad forbade us, even Mom, from touching the thermostat.

I asked Mom if she was okay with that. She said they came to an agreement years ago and it's in the prenup.

"So is the direction the toilet paper roll must face," Dad interjected without looking up from his paper, smiling to himself like he's proud.

I miss them.

I start again with the eggs and find myself cradling the bowl as I stir the brownie mix, standing closer to the over as it glows to life. I pour the brownie mix into the pan and lose myself in watching the waterfall of chocolate fill the pan, using the spatula to spread it out like Mom showed me. I feel the primal urge to just eat the brownie mix raw, but I wanted to have something to wait for for twenty minutes. Hoping he would be home by the time they are fin-

The door flies open and once again I am taken aback by Llewyn's drop-dead-good looks as he enters walking towards me with ferocity. Every time I see him feels just as startling as the first time. It's like his presence shakes my whole existence, my heart flutters uncontrollably when his eyes fall upon mine. I don't think he ever needed the supernatural charm that comes from being a vampire. He had that already.

He's carrying his jacket over his shoulder and drapes it over the couch, his crimson dress shirt is ruffled and his black neck tie pulled loose. His long dark hair hangs loose and messy, framing his strong jaw long. He barely gives me time before he closes the space between us, pulling me into his embrace. I felt the tears welling up. The guilt poured in after. I pull away and look up at him with tearful eyes,"I am so sorry. I should have never screamed at you like that. I realize that you're putting yourself at a great risk to protect me. I-"

He grabs my chin between his strong fingers and tilts my chin up so I am once again spell bound by his intense hypnotic gaze. His tempestuous lips hovering just above mine, taunting me. I am devoid of all self control around him.

"You of all people do not have to explain yourself to me - nor do you owe me anything, my dear."

"But I-"

He leans in for the kill and his soft lips capture mine, and I let him devour everything I had.

Soft, poised and insistent, he consumes my lips. The bow of his lip fit perfectly to mine like a shard of glass being set into place in a stained glass window pane.

Shivers of ecstasy coarse through my veins as our lips meet, his tongue ensnaring me with a macabre dance of passion.

I fell in love with him, slowly yet all at once. Like a leaf breaking from its stem, twirling and fluttering to the ground.

Enveloping me in his loving embrace, he breaks the spell and whispers, "But I must ask - do you make a habit of baking in your panties? Because if so, you're going to be screaming for more pleasurable reasons."

"No, but I might start just to find out," I say catching my breath, my mind struggling to wrap itself around what is happening right now. The words that are spilling from my mouth. Something else has possessed me. Desire.

My chest rising rapidly, barely keeping up with the speed of my heart.

The tension between us is taut and is speaking more for us than we need. Something deep inside of me has been awakened and refuses to be tamed.

I wanted more with Llewyn.

Had it been anyone besides Llewyn, I would've been embarrassed to be caught in my underwear - but not around him. The instant comfortability. It's unnatural.

Or possibly supernatural, considering the handsome vampire specimen I'm entangled with.

I wanted him to see me.

After being hidden for so long, it felt nice to be seen. And not as a scared little girl but as a woman. A woman that wants to get her brain fucked out onto the floor by a vampire.

"Just say the words, my dear, and I'll have my way with you right here," his languid voice corrupts me as he leaves a trail of kisses down my neck and to my collarbone. My eyes roll to the back of my head and I clutch on to him as I feel my body go limp with euphoria.

The words leave my lips, breathlessly.

"Please."

With one swift move, Llewyn pins my arms behind me and bends me over the edge of the counter. A growl of satisfaction emanates from him. He had full control, and he liked it.

And so did I.

Leaning over me, I feel his chilled breath in my ear. "Are you sure?" He's at my center with two fingers, well aware that my black lace panties were beyond compromised, soaking with desire.

"Yes," the words escaped me before I could catch them.

"That's my good girl."

He rips my panties off in one fluid motion like they were made of tissue paper, I let out a gasp as the silk fabric pulls tightly and then falls away from my skin. He chuckles at my surprise as he unbuckles himself, I hear the jingle of his belt as he unleashes himself. I can feel my heart beat thump against the cold countertop with breathless anticipation.

I melt as he teases me with two fingers, weak to his touch at an instant. He carefully loops his black leather studded belt around my wrists and pulls tightly. "Stay still," he commands.

Llewyn circles the island, like a starved wolf closing in on his prey and unbuttons his shirt revealing his pale statuesque figure and tosses it to the floor. His gaze does not leave me. I can feel it even as he disappears from my view.

Closing in from behind, his breathing grows more rapid in my ear as he presses his enormous length against me, teasing me relentlessly with his tip pressing against my entrance, his hand gripping my throat and his lips dominating mine.

There was complete silence - and then he plunges into my core and begins to thrust into me relentlessly. Pulling my hair back, I lose all train of thought as he closes the space between us. Our mouths only centimeters apart, anticipation radiating between us before he kisses me again.

I scream against his lips as he pounds into me. He lets go of my hair and places his strong hands on my hips, pushing down forcing me against the counter, further arching my back. His monstrous length ignited an explosion of euphoria and ravenous bliss that rendered me as nothing more than his to devour.

Untamed and clawing, two starved hearts pulse as one.

Each volatile unyielding thrust forces a pleasurable gasp from me, a languorous growl from him. That alone was intoxicating. With one strong hand on my hip and another coiled at my throat, he forces my head back to gaze into his dark voracious eyes before he dominates my lips once more. His tongue dances with mine.

He commands my body; coaxing me to orgasm at his will, drenching him with my desire.

Llewyn pulls out abruptly, and turns me around and hoists me above the counter. My legs instinctively wrap around him and pull him in. He gives a smug smirk, "I still feel there is too much fabric between us. There's still more of you to be laid bare."

He sets me down on my trembling feet and unties my hands, dropping the belt to the floor.

He grips the baggy shirt and rips it away from my body with ferocity and throws the remnants to the side. He steps back letting the somber blue glow of the moon peeking in cast a spotlight directly on me. He stares at me with blasphemous admiration.

"Holy fuck, you are beautiful, Lenora."

I suddenly feel shy but that subsides when I take in Llewyn in his full glory. His pale marble skin glowing against the blue shadows of moonlight. The irresistible sly smirk he wears when he knows he's gotten his way. The shine of danger in his eyes, the fear that runs cold in my veins - that only made me crave him more. Everything about him entices me.

"So are you."

He moves first, breaking the tension festering between us. Feasting on my lips first as he cups my breasts in one hand, teasing me with sharp nibbles and grazing his fangs against my ear and he pulls my hair back, exposing my neck. His eyes shine in the moonlight as he leans in, his lips curl at my skin as his protruding fangs graze them with a sharp kiss.

I wait for him to continue but he looks at me with frenzied eyes and quickly backs off.

"I'm sorry, Lenora. I forgot myself."

He turns and disappears down the hall, leaving me alone and lost in the shadows.

25

llewyn hellsinger

If I Had A Heart - Fever Ray

I am a monster. I tore into her like she was fresh meat on the slab. I knew what would've happened if we had touched. But all of that tension piled on after the library - and just seeing her there in the kitchen. I wanted her, but only the flesh.

At first.

It wasn't until her neck was exposed and I could pinpoint exactly where I would drain the blood from her body that I lost control.

That must never happen again.

Even if she asks for it. I haven't fed from a human in so long. Been purely on a blood bag diet since Serlanos' no feed order went into effect.

I am starved for fresh blood.

On the other side of that door is trouble. And it's knocking.

"Llewyn?" I hear her soft voice call on the other side of the door. She knocks again and then I hear her small footsteps walk into her bedroom. I sigh a deep breath of relief as I hear the sound of her bedroom door latching.

142

She must be so hurt and confused. I took off - I had just told her she was beautiful and swooped her off her feet and fucked her there in the kitchen. Leaving us both undone and unsatisfied.

I don't expect her to understand or to even forgive me. Especially when I was already apologizing at that moment for running out on her for the very man that has destroyed our lives.

I won't be surprised if she asks for a passage out of town. Away from here. Away from me.

Maybe that's for the best.

I have to protect her from me. She consented to the sex. She didn't consent to be a willing vassal. And she is no victim of mine.

I didn't think it would be this hard - I thought that I had more self control when it came to my bloodlust. But then the incident at the blood bank with Callum proved me wrong. The carnal mess that was left behind. Blood everywhere. The image is burnt into my brain. The only more horrifying thought is if that were Lenora's blood all over the wall.

I could never forgive myself if I let myself lose control with her.

I don't understand where this insatiable thirst came from. But I had to remedy it and fast. I knew who to call. The only person that could possibly understand my situation. And is slowly earning my trust, against all odds.

Cynfael.

The nightclub *CYNFUL* dazzled through the pouring rain, the marquee sign shone bright and blurry against the thick rain drops that pounced off my hooded head as I trudged to the front doors, digging my hands deep into my jacket pockets. The bouncer nodded me in and I was once more blinded by the red and black spotlights dancing throughout the club. Thick metal cages containing lustrous dancers that invited and seduced passerby. Couples gawk at me, on the hunt for a third and final. I was no ticket-prize nor a dollar slice to pass around, honey. I was here for one thing. Okay, maybe two things. First thing, blood. Second, an escape for Lenora.

I see Cynfael through the curtain leading to the Crow's Nest, a private sector for members only. Riskel, his biggest brute on the payroll, stands guard.

I freeze before I approach. Riskel furrows his eyebrows, as if to say 'what do you want?' Nothing that you would understand, but nor do I know how to explain. *I've taken in the hottest target of our kind's eye, fucked her and then almost fed from her.*

How am I going to explain to Cynfael what I've done? Normally I've had no trouble opening up to him as he's been there since we entered this country and assimilated to the American way of doing things. I confided my deepest secrets to Cynfael. But this one affects us all.

Will he understand how much faith I am putting into him to not go running to Serlanos? Serlanos pays informants well if there's someone unfaithful in his inner circle, even if it is the enemy.

I still hold true to my vow to protect her. I will see to it that she lives a long and happy life. Without the interference of vampires.

I don't think Cynfael will tell anyone - he will see this as a chance to take Serlanos down. Just as I did when the girl walked in at the wrong time. Maybe it was the right time. Maybe she served a greater purpose after all.

I had my fun - fantasy fulfilled.

I fucked a human over the edge of my counter.

Not just that, the most-wanted human in our world right now. Every vampire in the city has been out on the streets looking for her. Determined to earn Serlanos' goodwill and fortune. A fallacy at best.

I need blood. I am having a hard time thinking straight. The frenzy is buzzing.

In my head. Both of them.

I didn't finish. Fuck.

There's nothing worse than a vampire with blue balls. Which explains why I feel so ill. Every living organism I have left in my body is resting in my testicles right now.

I am supposed to go and ask Cynfael for help.

I don't think I have any option.

I approach Riskel, his nose flares in annoyance like I've been wasting his time already.

"I'd like to speak to Cynfael, please."

"He's not taking visitors right now." Leandro appears from behind the black curtain, less than pleased to see me here. A moan drifted from behind the curtain. A woman driven to tumultuous pleasure by the bite of a vampire.

"He may enter," Cynfael beckons me inside. Riskel and Leandro step aside and I pass through the black lace curtain and enter a dark room with black painted walls and dim lights. Black privacy curtains hung around an ornate daybed where a woman lay unconscious as Cynfael is bent over and drinking from her mercilessly.

He looks up, blood dripping from his lips, "Thirsty?"

"Ravenous," I croak through my deliriousness and indulge in my derangement.

Her blood was fresh and pulsed from her veins and into my mouth. Instantaneously I am frenzied at the taste of her. Unlike the donor bags that Callum and I ripped into at the blood bank. Those were cold and barely satisfying. Stored blood is nothing compared to taking from a fresh vein. And now the idea of how delicious Lenora's blood would taste and the feeling of her writhing in pleasure underneath me as I fuck her sweet, delicious brains out only teases me. The repercussions of blending feeding and pleasure are disastrous.

The vassal moans and writhes with euphoric pleasure until she is faint and quiet, but I don't stop. I wish this woman was Lenora.

"Careful, Llew. We don't kill willing vassals. Ariana still has more to give once she has some rest."

I fight against my instinct to drain her for what she's worth and pull my hungry lips away. I look down at the woman, delirious with blood loss. Cynfael hands me his red embroidered handkerchief to wipe away any residual blood.

"You look pale, Llew."

Ha. "More than usual?" "Yes. Surely, Serlanos pays his men well in blood if he can afford to part with so much the other day," Cynfael says, jumping to his point.

"I'm here to ask for your advice."

"Naturally."

"It's of an incredibly sensitive nature. It mustn't leave this room."

"Shall we go to more private quarters to speak?" Cynfael's interest has peaked, he loved a good intrigue.

I nod and he gestures to me to follow him back through the curtain. Riskel starts to follow up but Cynfael shakes his head. "I'm okay, Riskel. Private matters. We will be in my office. Do not let anyone disturb us."

Riskel eyes me sharply. I knew better than to try anything, nor would I. Cynfael has always been a personal ally of mine.

That was Callum's game.

Not mine.

Cynfael leads me up a set of stairs that I hadn't noticed before and down a long luxurious hallway. The walls wood panel and painted a sinful black with glitter-gold trim. An aroma of lavender and other spices fills the air and a faint whistle of classical playing in the distance could be heard.

What a bougie bastard. While Cynfael has rejected many parts of vampire society and the Cosa Nosferati, he cannot deny his love for the finer things.

Cynfael opens a door to an office that continues in the same fashion as the hallway. Black panel walls, vaulted ceilings with shelves filled with books I was certain weren't even real.

"You read?"

"One has to fill his time with something, Llewyn. Surely, you would know."

"You never struck me as the type."

"I am a vampire of many tastes. Now you didn't come here to interrogate me about my reading habits. What really brings you here?"

"I have a problem. It's a very sensitive nature."

"Any reason you couldn't go to your boss with this?"

There's a million and one.

"Yes. But I cannot give it until I am certain you won't go running to him."

"Llewy, you and I both know Serlanos is the last creature on earth I would run to. He's an unreasonable person to do business with let alone share one's secrets."

I do know. He only does business with him to keep the peace with the blood shortage. If it weren't for that - we would be at war. As if we haven't been fighting in the shadows already.

"Did you catch any heat from the diner incident? You bailed pretty quickly. I half expected you to stay to save face."

"I told Callum I would back him up, unless he started it."

"You placed your responsibility on a sure thing."

"I had other matters to attend to. Matters that now bring me here."

"Are you going to tell me or are you going to make me guess?"

"I fell in love with a human."

"Again?"

"I almost bit her."

"That just makes you a vampire. Not a good one considering you 'almost' fed from her."

"I don't want to drink from this human. Her life has been plagued by us long enough."

Cynfael's emerald eyes bulge from his head as he immediately realizes what I was saying.

"Are you saying what I think you're saying?" Cynfael sits down behind his desk. I can see it in his eyes how he's starting to possibly understand. Did he see who walked in that day or was he too busy goading Callum into starting an attack? Did he see us escape out the back door in a hail of gunfire?

"I need an escape for her. A way to get her out. Away from all of us."

"Show me," Cynfael demands.

"Show you?"

"Where are you keeping her?"

"Somewhere safe."

"Show me where. This is a test of trust, Llewyn. You got to have some faith in me. Have I ever let you down?"

No, he hasn't.

"If you tell me, I can help you. I cannot help you if you don't talk."

Okay. He makes a fair point. He needs to know. If he gets us out of here, I will devote my everlasting life to him. Soon my service will be his. I need to put some faith in Cynfael. He knows what his business is. And if he's going to help me, I have to prove I'm not yanking his chain.

"Tomorrow. I will bring you to her. You mustn't breathe a word of this to anyone. Or all of hell will break loose."

"You don't have to tell me twice, Llewyn. But may I ask, does this mean what I think it means?"

"If you do this for me, I am forever in your servitude, Cynfael."

"I have no use for servants, Llewy."

"Then what is it that you want from me?"

"It's not what I want from you. It's what I want *for* you."

"And what's that?"

"Happiness. Freedom. You see my men? I didn't hold a gun to their head and make them my bitch. They came to me, willingly. I am not a master nor am I whatever Serlanos is trying to be. I am just a vampire willing to tolerate others' ugliness, give them the space to be what they need to be. Dark or light. My grace has no conditions."

It sounds nice. Too nice, for a monster like me.

lenora holmwood

Living With Your Ghost - Communist Daughter

Silence. There wasn't a peep emanating from under his door to indicate Llewyn was conscious. I imagine him shutting himself inside a coffin, hiding away from the world. Does he even sleep in a coffin? I've never seen the inside of his room, he's always come to mine. Every part of me wants to know what Llewyn's bedroom looked like but that's a side of him I will let him unlock.

Was he even home? It's possible that he has left the penthouse. He's a master of slipping in and out unnoticed like a ghost. It's frightening at times, especially since he enjoys sneaking up on me.

I went to my room after he had abruptly left me in the kitchen, naked and with a bowl of unbaked brownies. I didn't quite know how to feel or react.

I felt no need for brownies, confusion and embarrassment had filled my stomach.

I go to take a shower to wash away what was. The ghostly feeling of his hands still lingers on me still lingers, his smell and kiss still bite at my skin and I want to savor it.

I doubt now I will ever get another chance.

So instead I just go to bed, as is.

I pull the silk sheets up over my bare skin and try to imagine he's in bed beside me, intertwined in his strong arms.

I wish that tonight had a different ending.

My ability to take myself to another place mentally has always baffled me - how real it seems. A coping mechanism I learned from years of imprisonment. It is easy to go mentally insane in such conditions.

I whisk myself away with thoughts of Llewyn. I can almost feel his body pressed up against mine, his fingers tracing the length of my body. His chilled breath on the back of my neck. The hum of pleasure playing on his lips echoing in my ear.

I craved more.

I wanted more.

I was never the good girl my father wanted me to be - I could act the part though. I had gone through the 'promise ring' phase and it lost its appeal real fast. It started with taking Andy Lebowski's virginity at his bat mitzvah and since then the idea of my sexuality being linked with my spirituality made no sense. The whole idea of virginity sounded too mythological to me. I never understood some men's fascination with taking a girl's v-card- other than being the first to ruin her for all of mankind.

And now having been locked away since I was sixteen by my deranged grandfather, parts of me that had been abandoned are now awoken in the most brutal way possible.

By someone who haunted me in my dreams, taunting me at my core, letting turmoil build only to deny me when I've barely had a taste. While he may be bloodthirsty for me, I thirst for him in ways that are illogical. He stopped himself from biting me. And I just want to throw myself back at him - tempting him to unleash the beast he's keeping at bay.

I am a flighty temptress. Dancing with death, a ballad of the macabre. Waiting for her vampire to finish what he's already started.

My eternal undoing.

I've never felt such a pull towards someone like I do with Llewyn. It's inexplicable. I still barely know him and yet I feel he's been a part of my life. Always. Before this life even.

It sounds mad. Insane. I know it as I think it.

I need to get out of here. Maybe leaving would be best. For the both of us. He never planned to keep me, did he? And I never said I'd stay.

He didn't ask me.

I wish he had. I feel the ache in my chest. I can't take more losses. I've already gotten attached and the idea of tearing myself away from him kills me.

I wanted to feel his lips on mine just one more time. I've never felt so alive or seen by anyone like he looked at me.

Tears prick my eyes and I feel them drop onto my pillow and I lay like this until emotional exhaustion takes over.

27

callum gyanstazi

My Name is Carnival - Jackson C. Frank

There he is. The stranger in plain sight. Walking like a ghost of the city's streets. Sulking in sadness. Or desperation. Smoking a cigarette. I pull the car up to the curb and roll down the window. He pretends not to see me, until I lay on my horn, spooking other passersby.

"Hey loser, get in," I bark out the window. He stalks over to the car.

"No, thanks. I want to walk," Llewyn blows smoke into the open window.

"I need to talk to you."

"Then talk."

I put the car in park and got out, standing level with him. Eye to eye. He looks dead and empty, a reflection of myself at times.

"What's with you man? Ever since you got back into the game, you haven't really been playing. You can't be that beat up about that human family you had. They would've been killed anyway. For just existing."

"Why is that? Why the fuck do they have to die? How long has it been since you yourself were once human? Or did you forget that part?"

"Jesus fuck, Llewyn. You're a vampire. Not only that, but you're in the hot seat right now. You've not delivered on your promise to bring in the

153

Holmwood girl and now you've let her slip through your fingers. Again. Serlanos needs her blood."

"I don't give a fuck what he needs, Callum."

"I don't want to take that back to him."

"I don't care what you do with it, Callum. I am tired."

"Our next meeting, it won't be so nice. I gave you a chance man and you're pissing it away."

"Good."

I watch him walk away, fury bursting like a flurry of bats fleeing from a cave. I followed him for a few blocks towards the center of town, but I was sure he made me so I turned and headed the opposite direction.

What an insubordinate fuck. I can't believe him right now. All he has to do is what he's asked. We've brought in hundreds of captives, blood bonds and mainly any willing victim that we wanted to fuck before we drained them dry. And he fails to bring in one girl.

It's like he's lost his spark. He looks more human than a vampire these days. Sometimes I question if the blood even took when we held him down and turned him. He was just some military brat at the time. Having made it back home through the first Great War. He was barely in his civies when we took him behind the alley. Ready to take his life only to make him a soldier of our kind.

Someone Serlanos could control.

I wanted a blood brother. Someone to take with me on adventures.

The family I never had was almost complete. I was left to rot in an orphanage until I was too old for anyone to want me.

That is until Serlanos picked me up. He took me under his wing. Became the father I never had.

But his acceptance was conditional. You do for him and he does for you. He can't do anything with an empty promise. Your soul is collateral.

Llewyn's soul is still at war.

I pull into a parking spot in front of the Homestead on Hinman, ignoring the no parking zone signs. Serlanos is known to frequent and push past security like swinging doors of a saloon. Serlanos is in the bar, entertaining a few of his clients at a large round table in the center of the room. Laughter. Cigars and money. All for what? What is the money going to? I recognize one of the men as Roderick, the attorney Serlanos recently turned to. He seems smug, a new look on his face. For a while he was an utter mess, dealing with the blood thirst, but since he's gotten used to it he's found his high ground.

Serlanos catches my eye as I approach the table. He can tell something is wrong.

"Excuse me, gentleman. I have to have a word with one of my men," he dismisses them gently.

Roderick looks down his long nose, like a crow's beak, hesitant to leave me with Serlanos. He's been buttering Serlanos up with lies about how he can bring him the Holmwood girl. He has control of the Holmwood Estate. That is his only upper hand. The only reason Serlanos had us turn him. To keep him close, otherwise he too would be dead. It would be too much risk to attempt to turn the next estate attorney to take on the Holmwood case.

Roderick has been paying the eastside dhampir clan to search high and low and as far as the Canadian border, if not past for signs of Lenora Holmwood, based on rumored sightings at bus stations and corner marts. Those rumors might be true, but if she hasn't been found by now -

Roderick moves to the bar, close enough to listen in with his newly enhanced hearing.

"Please, sit down. You look as if you've seen a ghost," Serlanos invites, gesturing to the seat next to him.

"I have. His name is Llewyn. I saw him leaving Cynfael's nightclub. Followed him for a few blocks."

"Did you speak to him?"

I nod.

"What did he say?" Serlanos asks, taking a timid sip of whiskey.

"Nothing you want to hear. Pretty much said you can shove it where the sun doesn't shine," I repeat over choking down my anger.

"I think your blood brother needs someone to watch over him. Stay close to him. Keep me updated. He's on his last chance to prove he's worthy of the Gyanstazi family. And I am losing patience."

"Heard, sir."

lenora holmwood

I Will Follow You Into the Dark - Daniela Andrade

Glass shatters against the wall - another beer bottle explosion assault carried out by Grandpa. His fury is fueled by malice and greed. His eyes grow red with hunger. His teeth sharp like a wolf, his master commanding him. Sneering from behind, Serlanos steps into the light. Blocking my path out of this hell hole. I can hear Theo's voice, from somewhere below. I look down. Limbs are scattered before me, my eyes follow the horrific trail to Theo's head. His eyes were shiny and fearful.

"You must get out, Nora. You promised you would get away."

I turn and see that Grandpa is revving a chainsaw, Theo's blood still hasn't been cleaned from its blades. Serlanos stands on the opposite side of the hall, his hand outstretched.

My hand trembles as it reaches out unwillingly to take his but it's stopped, another hand comes in and takes mine. I look up at its owner. Llewyn.

"Nora, darling. You're having a night terror."

I feel Llewyn's strong arms pull me against him, his soft hands caressing my tear stricken face. I feel chest heave with my tears and I finally catch my breath.

"It was so real. Like I was back there. In that apartment again. Trapped," I sob.

He tilts my chin up, but I don't dare meet his eyes. I feel embarrassed for him to see me like this.

"Look at me," he commands softly and I submit, my eyes welling up with fearful tears. " You will never have to go back there. Not if I can help it."

"And what of Serlanos? What about him?"

"He will have to pry you from my cold dead fingers."

I resist the urge to point out he's already technically dead.

"And you won't leave me again?"

"No." He says firmly.

"How do you know?" I need him to be certain of this. I don't know if I can take him abruptly leaving like that anymore. And if it were done by force, that's even more terrifying. Admitting that I needed him was saying more than both of us were ready for.

To say that I loved him would be crazy. *And true.*

"Because I've arranged a way out of here. For the both of us. We will go somewhere where we won't be apart. But you have to trust me."

This was all too surreal.

Where would we go that both of us would be safe? How can he guarantee that Serlanos would never find us. Llewyn is one of Serlanos top men. An underboss and hitman. Serlanos does not forgive disloyalty. He blew Grandpa's brains out once he found out I had escaped.

I cannot imagine the horrors that await for any one close to him that crosses him.

"How?"

"A friend of mine. Cynfael. He can smuggle us out. It's a risky plan."

"Another vampire?" I feel the hesitation in my voice. I wasn't sure if I wanted to know.

"Yes."

"Can you trust him?"

"I have no choice but to leave if we want to get out of here."

Just as I trust him, blindly so.

"Okay," I breathe and wipe away the last sting of tears.

He breathes a sigh of relief, letting his head fall to my lap. My fingers find their way into his long dark hair, twirling through his long silky strands.

"I'm sorry for leaving you like that. That was ungentlemanly of me. I should have explained myself. I -"

"You of all people don't have to explain yourself to me," I cut him off.

He stares at me, taken aback by my use of his own line.

"But you need to know that I wanted to bite you. There in the kitchen. I've wanted to since I first laid eyes on you. But I want you to give me permission first. Not when you're seduced by supernatural charm, or coerced in dire need of saving. And lately, I've been having a hard time controlling my thirst. So much so I am worried I might lose control around you. And I cannot have that happen."

I crawl into his lap and straddle him, caressing his face and looking deep in his stormy onyx eyes that speak such passion and loss.

"It won't. I trust you. With quite literally everything that I have. But please, don't ever leave me like that. I can handle the truth. I cannot handle not knowing if you're coming back. It is torture. You can talk to me. About anything."

He claims my lips and I am lost to him, swept up in his arms like a cloak of blissful darkness. I wrap my legs around him and pull him in closer. He pulls away from the kiss. "I'm crazy to think I was just going to let you go. The idea of being without you is just - I thought I could just stay away from you. But I can't. Not now. Not after I've only just tasted your lips."

"You're intoxicating to me. I've never been so entranced by anyone before."

"No one?"

I shake my head and hide a giggle.

"Not even Ryan Reynolds or Chris Hemsworth?"

"Who?"

"Right, sorry - I forgot. You've got some human stuff to catch up on."

"Human-stuff. I like that," I giggle.

"I like your laugh. I don't hear laughter very often. I'm glad I can make you laugh. Sometimes I feel like I am a real downer."

"I like you making me laugh. A vampire with a sense of humor. Who'd have thunk?"

"I have to ask - since we are sitting in a very intimate position and you're completely naked - the kitchen, that wasn't your first time was it?"

He sounds so nervous - as if the weight of ruining me for all of man and vampire kind was coming down hard on him.

"No. It wasn't."

"Oh, thank god," he presses his head into my bare breasts and breathes a deep sigh of relief. His eyes linger on the silver bullet pendant hanging around my neck.

"Where did you get this?" Llewyn asks.

"My father gave it to me shortly before he died. He told me it would one day save my neck."

"He might be right about that. It's pure silver. It stopped me from biting you. It was the sting of the silver that made me come to my senses," Llewyn admits bashfully.

"Interesting. May keep Serlanos and his fiends at bay."

"One can hope. Do you know where your father got it?"

"No idea. Dad kept us in the dark. It's to a point where I am not sure if I ever really knew the man. He had so many secrets. We never understood why Serlanos sent his soldiers over to our house or what they took from my father."

"Blood." He said firmly.

"Blood?" I ask that as if it's so surprising for a vampire. It just seems odd to me for a horde of vampires to shake down a human for blood. As if they couldn't just take a victim of their choosing. "Why blood? I thought vampires just kind of took blood from the victim of their choosing?"

"Most vampires do. We are different. We follow certain rules. Being a member of the Gyanstazi family involves a lot of expectations, especially as the underboss. The police commission is always breathing down our graves. We work in the shadows, trying not to make a spectacle of ourselves. Serlanos gives the word when we can feed from a fresh victim. For the most part, we live off of those who are willing or the blood that we hijack from the blood banks."

"How long have you been a vampire?"

"Since the end of the Great War."

"Serlanos was the one that turned you?"

"And Callum."

"Asshole."

"I'll tell him you said so. He'd be happy to know that coming from his intended bride."

I laugh nervously. "Please don't though. I don't want to give him the satisfaction he's even in my mind."

"I'm sure he would react well to that. Callum loves being rejected by women."

"Please don't, Llewyn. He's a monster." I beg, even with a hint of laughter in my voice. I meant it though.

"That, he is, my love."

I fucking love when he calls me that, his sultry english voice makes it sound like poetry. I have to stop myself from melting in his lap each time he speaks. I kiss him gently and whisper, "I'm going to go hop in the shower. My skin is crawling."

I hop up from his lap and he gives me a light spank. "Don't take too long. I plan on ruining you for all of mankind when you get out."

"I think you already started that in the kitchen." I say from the bathroom door.

"Well I didn't finish what I started. And you didn't get your brownies. That's two things."

I laugh and close the door and smile knowing I was with someone that was perfect for me.

29

leonidas holmwood

Party Poison - My Chemical Romance 1995

The Blood Donors Association hosts this fanciful banquet every year. A presentation to Chicago's Board of Health that there was further reason for funding our blood banks and the future of phlebotomy as a profession. Doctors, nurses and other medical personnel dressed in black tie and cocktail dresses gather in one room to try to schmooze each other into whatever ulterior motive they had hidden beneath lace panties and hushed tones inspired by the open bar.

Cocktail waiters halt before the stampede of sugar-crazed screaming children weaving between the tables. Privacy curtains for on site donations are hung and those who've yet to visit the bar stand in line eager to get their duty over with.

I shouldn't have told her. Rosalyn sits close to me as she barely holds it together. She was pale and nauseous with anxiety. She's had a bad feeling all day about tonight and fought me on coming out. But I insisted. It was important for our blood bank to have representation there. Especially from the boss. Being heads of the Department of Health, I had a duty here tonight.

"Stop your fussing, Rosalyn. You're wrinkling my sleeve. The children are having fun. There's music. Just relax and enjoy the evening."

I needed her to relax. I was the one on edge. The pressure was on me tonight. I had to address this whole room of people. Knowing that they were out there lurking amongst the crowd made me want to jump over the table and find the children and run, just like my wife was fitting to do.

I shouldn't have told her what happened the other night at the blood bank. I need one of us to be normal.

I scan the room for any sign of those fiendish beasts. The line for blood donations fluctuated. Participants stood in line showing each other their donation cards as if generosity is something to brag about. Their little cards give them some eligibility to brag. Little do they know they are just blood bags waiting to be fed to the beasts hiding in plain sight. How could they resist just willing victims here in the open giving blood?

They couldn't.

I spotted one that was there that night. He had his eyes on a petite blond that was batting her eyelashes at him as she stood in line to donate. God save her.

Charles McNally, vice president of the chair board, sneaks by our table, giving me the thumbs up that it is time. I glaze over him, my eyes not leaving the bloodsucking beast that has locked eyes with me, licking his lips as he stalks this poor woman to the curtain and beyond view.

I rise from my seat and kiss my wife, not saying a word of what I saw, and approach the stage as the honored guests take their seats after wrangling their children into their laps and silencing them.

The spotlight shines in my eye as I clear my throat. "Good evening honored guests, donors and patients. Thank you for joining us here tonight to celebrate our city's great achievements. This year alone we have collected 13 million units of blood from your generosity. That is enough blood to last us through the next great plague."

The crowd erupts into an obligatory applause. I was certain some of the audience were too drunk to care or even comprehend what I was saying. Anyone here is here for the money. And it was obvious.

"We, the Chicago Board of Health, cannot express our gratitude enough to you. For having such empathy to provide lifesaving measures for those who still strive for a better life experience. Hope. Kindness. Awareness. This is the legacy that we will leave for our children as we-"

The room is cloaked in sudden darkness as the power is cut and few of the emergency lights shutter on and a few scream before I can make any sense of what is happening. The sound of fabric ripping catches my fearful mind, and emerging from the crimson curtain is a crimson wet soaked hand with long sharp claws followed by its fearsome owner.

Serlanos Gyanstazi sneers at me, his sharp fangs extending. He believes I doubted he would show. But I never did. After learning of his true nature, I just feared the horror that would ensue in his presence. His reputation precedes him. A criminal monster. Making headlines but never caught. He's bought up most of the enterprises and rackets dominated by Capone in his days. Only recently has he taken an interest in blood banks. Probably because finding willing victims for himself and his horde to feed from is getting too tedious. It makes it easy to access when we keep the blood on hand. Hence his grim visit to my donation center last night.

Struck with fear, I step aside and let him take the microphone from my shaking hand.

Several screams in the crowd carry to the stage as Serlanos' servants flood the banquet hall, taking some of the audience hostage.

"Sorry for the intrusion," Serlanos sneers into the microphone. "I didn't intend for this to be a hostile takeover but Mr. Holmwood gave me no choice but to make it known tonight, as he refused to accept my offer last night."

Several gasps escaped those cowering below. Abhorrence of the actions taken on my behalf that led to this terrible moment.

"Doctor, nurses and other health care personnel, I welcome you to pledge your loyalty to me and no harm will be done to you or your patients." Serlanos steps down from the stage, walking the center path towards our honored guests table. "Patients, speak nothing of this night and you shall receive your treatment uninterrupted. I am Serlanos Gyanstazi. And I am the boss now. Those that refuse me well -"

The only sound that could be heard following was of bones crunching as those that were held hostage have their esophageal canal crushed, followed by the gurgling gush of blood as their throats are ripped open by the fangs of a horrendous monster. Terror drives the room. Tables tip over as guests attempt to outrun the bloodthirsty mob of vampires sending a mess of food and plates crashing to the floor. Children scream as they are carried away by their terror stricken mothers being chased by a snarling and drooling brute in a suit.

Dodging a few vampires that have made a few hedge fund executives their late night meal, I find Rosalyn and the children cowering in a dark corner.

"Come with me," I whisper, leading my fearful family through some private doors leading to the kitchens, hoping to find another exit out of this godforsaken place.

The kitchens were dark and quiet compared to the orchestra of violent screams and death gurgles that performed just outside the swinging doors. Hoping that no one follows us, we venture through the next set of swinging doors and into another banquet hall that was dark and unused.

Sheets covering the dining tables gave us enough cover in case anyone attempted to follow us. I find the door with the most light peaking through underneath. I assume that might be the quickest way to exit the building quickly. Hoping that there is not a vampire waiting for us on the other side.

The door opens into a white lit hall with windows running down looking out onto the Chicago Loop.

At the end of the hall— an emergency exit.

Clutching my one year old daughter Lenora to my chest and Theo on my wife's hip, Rosalyn and I bolt down the hall to the emergency exit and crash through it, sounding the alarms. Rosalyn freezes in fear, anticipating the worst.

We just signaled our location.

Every vampire in the building is bound to be flooding through those doors any moment now to chase us into the night.

"Run."

Heading for the car parked just down the street in the reserved event parking lot for Pendry, Rosalyn and I ran as our children screamed , feeling our fear through the way we held onto them for dear life. Squirming all the way to the car, I almost drop Lenora in the middle of the street as her tiny little elbow clocks me in the ribs, almost sending me to the ground. She is tiny but mighty. God I hope she keeps that.

Rosalyn doesn't let her breath return to normal until she's in the front seat, buckled in with the doors locked and the engine running.

The whole ride from the city I fought the urge to look over my shoulder as Rosalyn does. No one saw us leave so no one should be tailing us. I should be congratulating myself but I withhold from celebration until we are home with the deadbolt turned and my gun properly loaded and in arms.

The children whimper in the back, comforting each other as we enter north Chicago. Even as we pull onto Sheridan Avenue and into our driveway I still feel my body rigid with fear. I check our surroundings in the rearview mirror before we collect the children and seek refuge in our own home.

Rosalyn looks up and down the street as I fumble with the key to our front door and she nearly pushes me in as soon as it opens. As soon as we are inside, I turn and lock all three locks on our door, still not convinced it's enough.

And it wasn't.

I should have known something was wrong by the lack of sound from my wife and children settling into the house. I turn and find we are being held at gunpoint by Serlanos and three of his vicious soldiers, ready for more of what was served at the banquet.

"You thought you could stay one step ahead of me, but soon you're going to find that cooperating with me is going to work more in your favor than not, Holmwood. For instance, your beautiful family shouldn't have to suffer for your insolence," Serlanos sneers as he casts a predatory glower on my trembling family.

"And what is it that you require of me that would put my life and my family's life in such jeopardy?" I ask, trying to maintain my waning confidence.

"Blood. And lot's of it."

llewyn hellsinger

Too Sweet - Hozier

Lenora is in there, showering. Letting water pour over her curves and washing away the evidence of me on her. I'm out here waiting like a dumbass when I could be in there ruining her for all of mankind already.

The woman of my dreams. Hair black as a raven, lips as red as blood and skin so pale you'd think she was Death, herself. Femme fatale if there ever was one. She would be my undoing and I would willingly let her.

She is just as much of an alien to this world as I am. Just as fucked up and weird. Normal was never a part of this woman's dictionary. And she didn't need or want me to spell it out for her.

That was the beauty in her.

Lenora wasn't the good little girl that everyone made her out to be. The one that had to be sheltered from others and protected from man's unsavory touch. Was it any accident though that someone as unholy as me has been allowed to touch someone so pure?How is it that someone can be pure and yet has known only darkness and has felt the harsh kiss of mankind?

It's in her suffering and yet the profound way she's managed to only look forward in life.

The refusal to let it keep her down.

I wish I had that naturally. But instead I search for it in others - hoping that they can carry me out of the war zone that's been my life. Nothing but destruction has been in my wake - until she walked into my life.

I get to my feet and approach the door and gently open it, steam escaping as I sneak in.

What a vision she was standing under the waterfall-style shower, streams of waters outlining her small and curvy porcelain figure. She moves under the water like she's dancing for no one besides herself, a faint smile of bliss plays across her face. I can only hope she's thinking of me. She's not noticed I've even entered the bathroom.

I quietly slip my clothes off and set them aside. Her back is turned and her head tilted upwards as she rinses her long dark hair, I open the glass shower door and slide in. I stand there, taken aback once more. My hunger for her throbs in my cock. Even now I still can't refuse the thrill of the hunt. Only now my prey was much sweeter, precious even. I was feeding a beast that was ready for seconds and thirds.

My muscles tense and I feel my fangs sharpen with desire and blood-lust, I want nothing more than to sink them into that perfectly shaped arse of hers. I want to do things to her that she will never be able to wash away.

Instinct takes over as I advance on her. She gives a cute startled gasp as I press her up against the cold tile, and pin her delicate hands above her. I may have been too loose with the rules when I've said I don't read her mind. It's hard not to when I can hear her desires screaming for me to hear from the next room. She wants this.

I lean over her, her body bends to mine and fits together seamlessly. I feel the roundness of her voluptuous round ass press into me, torment-ing my arousal.

"Is this what you want?" I growl into her ear, teasing her with the tip of my throbbing cock, pressing into her opening, only to pull away abruptly as her excitement builds.

"Yes,"she rasps as I press a bit further. Her desire pooling at her entrance. I feel her torture as I pull away again.

"Are you sure?" I tease in her ear, biting a little.

"Yes," she whimpers.

I bury my teeming erection in her, plunging deep and mercilessly. Unleashing an onslaught on her whet quim. I hold her in place as she writhes under the weight of my thrusts, letting me ravage her from the inside out. She moves in sync with each thrust, her thighs and womanhood tightening around my girth.

Her knees begin to weaken under the weight of my assault.

She relinquishes a bemoaning gasp with each stroke, losing her mind to me, submitting to my touch.With my hands commanding at her waist I hold her up as I plunge deeper, bearing down on her small frame. She smiles through the cascade of soft bites and kisses I plant on her neck and bare shoulders. The sweet taste of her skin was savory, I could feel the blood pumping in her veins as I grazed her skin with my fangs.

She wriggles and moans with pleasure against me as I carry out my carnal and rancorous ravaging of her pussy. Delivering sharp slaps to her behind and pounding deeper and harder each time, gripping onto her hips and digging in with my sharp claw like nails. Her cries were now screams of pleasure.

"Jesus, fuck I'm not going to be able to walk when you're finished with me," she laughs breathlessly.

"You're right about that. I'm going to fuck your pretty little brains out," I leer into her ear, and give a seductive nibble.

"Good, that's what I was hoping for," she says with a playful squeal as I pull her hair back and bare into her with a deep growl and continue to pound into her mercilessly. Air escaped her lungs as I pin her flat against the cold tile, arms above her head.

"Don't stop," she whimpers beneath me. I feel her orgasm pulse around me, an unending surge wrapping around my arousal only coaxing me to feed the beast between us.

It's as if I've reached a whole other plane of existence, the other side where it's only me and Nora.

My craving for her has reached beyond addiction, and her cravings for more only matched mine.

We were dancing around the unspoken.

Two souls were matching as one. Inflaming each other, keeping an immortal light alive.

The water around us created a cascading oasis that only permitted us to exist, untainted and yet impure all at once.

Clean and pleasured, I wrap her in a towel,cradle her tired body in my arms and carry her out to the living room and plop her gently on the couch and hand her the remote. She's still learning how to use the smart TV. It's pretty cute how frustrated she gets when she gets stuck on the Home App. She doesn't bother to turn it on this time, instead she's watching me. I can feel her eyes on me as I try to remember what to do here.

"What are you doing?" she asks as I begin to search around the kitchen, the towel she's wearing falls a bit, revealing her perfect breasts.

"Making you brownies, like I promised." I have a hard time not staring.

"Hmmm. This almost seems too good to be true." You're telling me, I have a beautiful naked woman in my kitchen that I would gladly make brownies for any day.

"Is double double fudge from the box too good to be true?"

She nods eagerly from the couch, biting her lip. She's so fucking cute.

And still so alluring. I have half the nerve to pounce her right there on the couch. But she needs time to recuperate from our shower together.

She watches me from the couch as I pour the baking powder and crack the eggs into the bowl. I try to ignore her amorous stare. It's distracting. She underestimates my stamina, I could fuck her for a week straight and not feel a bit fatigued and she's testing those limits. But I don't want to wear her out.

She's just gained some part of her humanity back. I remember watching the grandfather chase the boys off his side of the street when he had caught one of the boys walking Lenora home from school, his arm around her shoulder. He wasn't about to let anyone hang around his granddaughter, for whether those reasons were pure or not we will never know. How long had it been before he started considering Serlanos' deal. Was he keeping her chaste for monetary value or did he at one point actually give a shit about her?

Every male in this woman's life has either been lost to her or betrayed her.

I am not going to be on that list.

I begin to mix the contents of the bowl and notice in my peripherals that she's moved from the couch. Out of sight.

Appearing behind me, I am startled as I feel her press her naked body against mine. Her breasts warm and supple against my skin. I want to feel them in my mouth.

Her hands trail down my bare chest, tracing the lines of my torso.

My back curls with chills as she plants soft kisses on my shoulder blades and digs her claws into my hips. Oh my flighty temptress.

"Oh, my sweet raven, you are a flighty temptress."

"Is that what I am? Your raven?" she coos seductively. She knows exactly what she's doing.

"I could leave you, nevermore."

"Someone's been brushing up on his Poe," she impresses me further as her hand reaches around, her fingers teasing at the base of my shaft.

"Gotta stay ahead of the classics," I grunt.

"You've been around for so long and you've not read everything yet?" She challenges me, knowing very well what it does to me. I feel myself harden in her grasp.

"I've been busy. Makes it hard to read all the time," I say as I concentrate on making a clean pour of the batter into the baking sheet as she continues to play. Her small soft hand takes my full length, her spindly fingers wrapping around like small vines around the base of a tree, starting off slowly she starts stroking me off. I feel her move down to her knees in front of me.

Nothing could prepare me for the serene bliss of being in her mouth, her perfect lips wrapped around the helm of my cock and taking me in deeper than I expected. *Dear god, where did she learn to do that?*

I am starting to think she doesn't want brownies nearly as much as she craves my dick and I didn't expect this. I've awoken a monster that I never want to contain.

I brace myself, grabbing a fistful of her hair and pressing into her mouth, her lips taut around my dick, her tongue torturing me simultaneously as she runs it up and down its length. I begin to thrust into this motion, riding the wave and only stop when I hear her gag and the tears begin to form. But as soon as I try to pull away she goes right back for it.

Okay then, madam.

"You can't seem to get enough, can you?"

She shakes her head and hums a 'mmhmm' against my cock which makes me weak in the knees. She giggles, lapping up the effect that she has on me. And I loved seeing what she would do when given control.

"What is it that you do exactly? For Serlanos, I mean? Like I've never seen you at the drops when Serlanos and his men came to our house," Lenora asks as I finally manage to get the brownies in the oven.

"Do you really want to know?" I hesitate in this as what I do isn't for the faint of heart. Would she look at me any different if I reveal to her that my job is much more than just raids and normal organized crime. It's not all what you see in the movies like the Godfather or Goodfellas. Sometimes it is.

Being the vampire underboss has its responsibilities, like a personal hit man for the don. The boss. The Capo di tutti capi as they would say. The ratto sanguigno as I would say.

I am the knife in the night. The cold chill on the back of the neck, there to remind you that whatever you're running from will come back.

She nods as she pulls a shirt over her head, covering herself (Dammit).

"I'm what one is called the underboss. I take care of those that try to skip out on a deal. A ghost assassin in the shadows."

"So you do kill people."

"Yes."

"How often?"

"More often than not."

"Do you feed from them then?"

"No. I don't feed from those that I am hired to kill for Serlanos, it's against our code."

"You have a code?"

"So to speak. And it's Callum's job to enforce it."

She's quiet. I know what she wants to ask, I see the guilt in her eyes for even thinking about it.

"I didn't kill your parents. I was attending other matters that day. But I cannot deny that I had some part in their demise. I found out they were trying to run and I passed that information onto Serlanos. I'm sorry, Lenora. If I could have stopped it, I would've."

She doesn't respond.

The oven beeps to signal preheat. I turn my back and put the brownies in the oven.

"I don't blame you. It's always been Serlanos. And his crew. But you're not like the rest of them. Given I am here, and not with him enduring whatever torture he has planned. You saved me and you literally didn't have to."

I breathe a deep sigh. I didn't realize I needed to hear that. Guilt is a fickle bitch. I've never felt right being even remotely connected to what Serlanos did to her parents. To her whole family. Robbing them of everything they had right after the funeral was cruel, even for Serlanos. He fed off of their suffering.

"Thank you for saying that. You really are too kind."

"I just tell it like I see it," she says with a genuine smile, leaning on the counter and reminding me of the other night when I had her bent over the surface. I shake those thoughts away. What has gotten into me? She has awoken something in me that cannot be contained. The way she looks at me with those big storm gray and blue eyes makes me feel as if she's seeing further into me than I can hide, unlocking doors that were long since locked and sealed shut.

"What would you like to do tonight, my dear."

"Maybe we catch up on some of that human-stuff you say I'm behind on," she dangles the remote in front of me. Just as I expected, I am the remote master. This feels weirdly normal.

As we lay on the couch and browsed the options on Netflix I saw her ooh and awe each time we passed anything that had to do with vampires.

"You know it's all fiction."

"I'll be the judge of that."

"Have you been taking comparison notes?"

"You won't like the results," she teases.

"Oh? Is that so," I climb on top of her, and pin her to the cushion with little effort. She giggles beneath me.

"First note though, you don't have hairy palms. That was one thing I could never get past when reading Dracula like no one was talking about it."

"The movie is even weirder."

"There's a movie."

"Yeah. You - you didn't know?"

"It wasn't necessarily something my father wanted to surround his family with. Most movies I watched with them and were PG. What I read was to my discretion, so I read more horror than I watched. And then for a while I didn't necessarily have a need to when I am living in one."

"Would you want to watch Dracula?" I ask a note of hope in my voice, tapping my finger tips together.

"Sure," she giggles.

"This is very surprising," I laugh as I flip through the streaming services to find Dracula.

"What do you mean?"

"I just didn't think that you would be interested in watching horror movies. I mean, wouldn't it be traumatizing?"

"It's easier to embrace the dark sometimes rather than run away from it. Pretending that something doesn't exist doesn't make it go away. It will catch up to you sometime."

This woman's insight and intelligence is beyond any mortal's I've come across.

No offense to my late wife Emily, but I feel as if I have met my match in every way.

leonidas holmwood

Look After You - Aaron Wright 1998

The screaming storm sirens break through the howling winds encircling the city, piercing the eardrums of those who were unlucky enough to be out on the street to receive its full blast.

Lenora covers her ears with her hands as I attempt to calm her. Storms have always been her greatest fear, keeping us up till all hours of the night since she was born.

The thunder rattles the old bones of the house, shaking dust and other debris from its hiding places.

Lenora buries her face as the wind screams past her bedroom window.

The rain patters heavily on the roof. A crack of lighting breaks through the night sky illuminating the dark room, Nora buries her face into my chest.

"It's okay, baby girl," I tell her as she buries herself deeper in my arms. .

I sit with her still, reminding myself there will be a time in which she will be too big to sit in my lap. I try to treasure these moments, as time is passing by faster each day. How long will it be till she is looking to someone else for protection?

Her cries and whimpers subside as she begins to drift off to sleep. Her breathing slows and her body becomes limp with slumber.

I very carefully move from under her tiny arm and pull the covers up and place a kiss on her head. I check the night light and close the blinds so the storm doesn't intrude on her sleep.

I close the door real slow, catching one more peak at my sleeping angel. Before it latches - a loud pounding at the door rattles the house more than the roaring thunder outside. Nora bolts upright in her bed - Rosalynd and Theo both fall into the hallway, fear cloaking both of them as they watch me descend the stairs.

There's only one reason someone would be knocking on the door at this hour. The relentless pounding on the door can only mean one thing.

Someone needs blood. And they need it now.

I open the front door and a dark horde of vampires, carrying one of their own screaming in pain, push past me into the front foyer. The creature's chest nearly blown to smithereens, the pale skin and tissue could not regenerate fast enough without the help of blood. The vampires carry him to the dining room table and keep him calm.

"What in God's name happened?" I ask Lycidas as he follows me to my office.

"We were ambushed. Some of Talon's soldiers followed us to the next location. Before we could even intercept the shipment, it was raining silver."

I open the bottom desk drawer to collect my phlebotomy bag and the small set of skeleton keys that dangle on a hook inside the drawer.

I turned to the classical built-in bookshelf and removed the leather-bound book hiding the keyhole in the wall. With a quick flip to the left the wall opens into a strongroom armed with the best in the vampire and monster hunting underworld, beyond which lies a steel vault. I turn the spindle and it lurches open revealing my blood drawing collection. Rows and rows of refrigerators and freezers containing various stores of lifeblood, plasma and the components needed to keep it from coagulating.

"Woah," Lycidas stands awestruck in the vault doorway.

"Tell no one about this. Act quickly, we need O- negative and a lot of it."

I hasten to the refrigerator of my freshest drawing. I have twelve bags. Lycidas grabs the travel cooler nearby and starts grabbing from the refrigerator next to me.

I see the vampire bite back the urge to just guzzle down a bag. Part of me feels for their kind. Whether they asked for this kind of life or not, it is not easy living off the blood of humans. I may throw him one, he was looking a little rough along with the others.

"Take one."

"What?"

"Take one. I mean it. You need it."

The vampire looks at me in shock as if I just handed him a silly straw along with it.

With his protruding fangs he rips into the bag and sucks it down like my daughter would her juicebox. Who can blame him? He's living on scraps that Serlanos throws at them, or whatever they can hunt in secret without making too much of a spectacle of themselves. Since Serlanos dominated the hospitals and blood banks, he's in full control of the city's drug supply. Tensions are high among the city's underworld creatures.

I will never forget the aftermath that occurred at the Hawthorne Blood Donor Banquet. I shudder just thinking about the blood shed splattered across the walls of the banquet hall. Valued investors had beads of rubies pooling beneath them as I stepped through the crowd and out the doors to my family waiting in terror.

It was then that I understood the true nature of these beasts and how far they will go to survive.

Lycidas has the cooler filled with as much blood, while I quickly slip in a more private and valuable store of samples. This poor creature is going to need more than just O-negative blood. Silver melts through vampire-like mercury at room temperature dissolving the reanimated tissue at a dangerous pace. The antimicrobial toxins flood the feigned immune system of a vampire.

Lycidas and I return to the parlor, the blood curdling screams permeating through the house. Rosalynd and Theo still stand at the top of the stairs watching from the shadows. I wish they wouldn't, they don't need to see this.

The vampire screaming in pain is being held in place as the three others hold him down. Lycidas preps the tourniquet as I prep the needle and tubing. I've done this so many times for donors and patients, that it felt like second nature.

The Cosa Nosferati have made plenty of visits since Serlanos has cornered my services.

The vampire was pale and had long dark shiny hair that curled and toiled at the ends. He gasped and rasped for air as the silver worked its way into the bloodstream and began attacking other parts. Lycidas holds his arm and wipes the vampire's sweaty forehead.

"It's going to be okay, Llew. Dr. Holmwood is going to fix you up."

The vampire nodded through his pain. I try not to look as I can see his tissue dissolve before my eyes. Reducing to nothing but a pile of ash and dust before me. As the needle presses into his vein, his eyes shoot open and dilate to three times their size as the crimson begins to feed into him from the tube. As the first blood bag begins to stabilize him, I fish the small vial from my vest pocket and pour the contents into the blood bag I was holding between my legs. No one questioned what I was doing, they let me do it. I could see the fear and horror on each of their faces.

Knowing if they were to die, this is how it would go.

Or worse like beheading and burning the pieces. According to a journal left behind by one of my predecessors, the vampire can feel every bit of it until they are reduced to ash.

The first bag dries up quickly and our pale faced friend is starting to show a sign of color. His rapid breathing has become more staggered as the disintegration begins to slow. I exchange the bags, feeling every eye on me as I do so. Every tepid breath being held as we watch the vampire on the table revitalize.

The blood flow continues and I continue to monitor the flow. I hardly notice as the group begins to relax.

The four vampires' attention was stolen by my daughter Nora who stood on the other side of the table, holding onto the thumb of our patient. Llewyn, with little strength that he's regained, holds her tiny little hand in his and closes his eyes. I ignore the small tear escaping from the corner of his eye.

The vampire Llewyn smiles at Nora who looks back at him with her big eyes and rosy cheeks. She is a great nursing assistant. So caring and gentle. She's able to see the good in everyone. Even the bloodthirsty creature on the table or the three surrounding her, watching in awe as this tiny innocent being attempts to comfort Llewyn. I've not seen this vampire often. Not as much as Callum who is pacing before the table seething with anxiety, or Lycidas and Norryx.

"You don't have to worry, Mr. Holmwood. We don't feast on children. It's unethical. Besides, this is too sweet. A child comforting a vampire."

All of the vampires start laughing and my daughter starts laughing and smiling along with them, feeling the excitement and recognition of being helpful.

"She's going to be a real heart stealer when she's older."

That's what I am afraid of.

As I watch the blood flow through the tube and into the arm of the vampire that held my daughter, part of me wonders if one day she will need protection from them.

llewyn hellsinger

How to Be Human - Amber Run

I left Lenora coffin-wrapped in the blankets in bed, I couldn't disturb her. She looked so peaceful. Yet leaving her, even for a moment, felt like ripping the fragile heartstrings in my hollow chest. I forced myself to close the door after leaving a note explaining where I was going on her bedside table.

Cynfael told me to meet him at the morgue down the street. The takeover over the death industry has made his corpse and organ trafficking racket an easy cover. Very few people care about the dead after they've gone to the coroner. It was easy to stage a funeral without a body for the bloodsucking mafia.

I exit the penthouse, checking my surroundings again.

Every part of me still feels I am being followed. Watch closely. Especially now that I've been publicly seen leaving Cynfael's nightclub. The choice words I had with Callum will surely come back with a fierce bite from Serlanos.

He doesn't take such insolence lightly.

I have the scars from the silver laced lashes Serlanos executed on me in the catacombs of the headquarters. Where he breaks in his new vampires.

I have been his favorite pet since he blooded me in that dark alley of the shadier part of London. Creating a beast he could control. A soldier that would obey.

No more. I hope I got the point across.

I was tired of living on the scraps that Serlanos threw us. I thought the take over of the hospital and plasma rackets would have kept us all fed without becoming a nuisance to the city.

As I walk, I feel my phone buzz in my pocket. I ignore it, keeping my head in the game.

It could be anyone. Serlanos or Callum. Possibly even Chief Warren.

First things first, Cynfael. He is awaiting my arrival. I hasten my pace as I fear someone is on my trail. Listen to your gut, it never lies.

Michigan Avenue was hustling with the usual stop-traffic, the general struggle of sharing the road with street-parked vehicles and kamikaze pedestrians darting out in their right of passage. The ghosts of the city's best architects are alive in the towering skyscrapers as the revival of their schools and styles are alive and new buildings are summoned by the day, ranging from Chicago School to Gothic revival. I always admired the buildings and the history that haunts them still, bringing tourists from every corner to come and catch a peak of what was once here before the Chicago Fire left it in ash and the plans to rebuild the echo of the White City.

I resist the urge to peer over my shoulder. There was no one that I would recognize now, Serlanos has expanded so far and wide across the city that if I were being followed, I wouldn't know who. Especially if they are able to shapeshift.

Cynfael waited for me in a parked SUV outside the Cook County Medical Examiner's Office. He was alone, just like he said he would be.

"Anyone follow you here?" Cynfael asks as I slip into the running vehicle.

I shake my head. "Not from what I've noticed."

"Good."

"So what are we doing here?"

"We are securing your passage out of here."

"What do you mean?"

"I have a shipment of body parts going out of state in two days. You and your human are going with them."

"Wait, you don't mean -"

"Yes I do. We fake both of your deaths. I will sort the paperwork and the coffins, you're over six feet right?" he says, pulling out a cigarette and lighting it.

"Cyn, why can't we just leave town?"

"Because vehicles are being stopped at roadblocks since your girl made a run for it and we don't know who will be manning those roadblocks. No one will question business as usual, not unless someone other than us two know we've been meeting."

Fuck. Callum knows. He saw me walk out of the club the other day. He knows and it is only a matter of time before he catches us. That is if we don't leave as soon as possible.

"No one else knows right?" Cynfael asks, catching the look of 'oh shit' on my face.

"How soon do you think we can get out of here?"

"The shipment arrives in two days, we unload the cargo and then load you and your girl in like sardines. Is your girl good with enclosed spaces?"

"She's going to have to be."

"And dead silent."

"Are you suggesting that I drug her?"

"It wouldn't be a bad idea. It's one way to avoid a shootout on the road in front of civilians."

He makes a good point.

"Can I talk to her first about it?"

"Sure, but there isn't much time. If we are going to do this, we have to decide now. Serlanos has been pulling out all the stops to find this girl. You've really dug your own grave, Llew. If you were going to defect like this you should've left town immediately."

He's right, I was dumb. And we got too comfortable.

Time to make an executive decision.

"Okay. Just tell me what to do, Cyn."

"Well right now, I need you to get ready to run because what I'm about to do is going to set off a lot of alarms,"Cynfael warns, puffing on his cigarette once more before shifting the car into drive.

"Should I have brought my mask in gloves for the occasion. I like to be prepared for crime, Cynfael. I am not dressed for the occasion."

"Don't be a smart ass. You should've known that we would be doing business while doing business. I am very efficient. Meet me back at the club? We need to hash out the details."

Cynfael stomps on the gas - the SUV goes sailing towards the front lobby of the building, colliding and bumping against other vehicles as Cynfael releases the wheel and prepares to tuck and roll.

"JUMP!"

I push on the door and do a barrel roll out and crash land between the rampaging vehicle and the parked car missing its bumper. I watch as the SUV bulldozes through the front lobby of the morgue creating an echoing boom that turns the heads of the public in all directions.

Alarms sounded and Cynfael and I exchanged looks. We flit away in a blur before a mortal eye could pinpoint either vampire at the scene of this chaos.

"Are you going to tell me why you drove the fucking car into the morgue or -" I ask Cynfael as we walk into his club, but am cut off by the parade of working girls gathered to suck up to Cynfael, desperate for his favor to be the victim of the day.

"Llewyn, business is not always clean in our world, you know that. I simply needed to send a message to the coroner. He's been resisting me and it's important that he receives that order. He will understand once he has to rebuild the walls knowing that nothing will keep me from getting my way."

"I understand you're the topdog of this racket but couldn't you just meet with the guy yourself?"

Cynfael stops and glares at me. I overstepped my bounds by suggesting how to conduct his business. A big pet peeve that drove him away from the syndicate to begin with. Too many rules and stubborn minds stuck with tradition. He was bombarded with unsolicited advice by those who refused to hear his own thoughts on how the modern vampire is to be kept fed and out of the limelight. Which is hard since many of them tend to make spectacles of themselves during No-Feed-Orders. He wanted to do things his way, since no one else would listen to him.

"Llew, while I appreciate your concern, you're the one in the shit seeking my help. I would appreciate it if you shut the fuck up and let me work."

I laugh - slightly relieved he didn't just kick me down the stairs as I climb up to the second floor to his office.

Sitting behind his large desk, he flips through a myriad of printed forms that screamed legal jargon that I didn't understand. Thankfully, Cynfael said he would take care of the paperwork. I just have to answer a few questions about myself and Lenora to make this plan plausible.

"So, to start, when were you born?"

I glare at him, as if he doesn't know that putting the real answer to that question would raise questions that even the coroner couldn't explain.

"I 'died' at thirty two so whatever thirty two years from now is," I furrow my eyebrows, already feeling a headache coming on.

"Happy birthday," Cynfael smiles as he writes down the dates in the tiny boxes.

This is going to be a long afternoon.

"Blood type?"

"Fuck off."

"When did you last eat?" Cynfael sets down the pen and goes to the mini fridge by the window.

It's been a few days. I've been rationing the blood I do have. I can go a couple days, but I get testy. And ravaging Lenora almost every chance we get to satisfy our lust for the other's flesh has been depleting my stamina. She brings out something carnal in me I cannot explain. The way her ass bounces up and down - stop. I am going to torture myself if I even think about her body.

"You cannot fuck away hunger, Llewyn. Trust me, I've tried," Cynfael says as he pours the blood bag into a whiskey glass and hands it to me and I gulp it down in mere seconds.

"Thank you," I say, setting the glass on the desk and wiping my lip.

"Llewyn, if you need more please, take some with you. I am fine. My vassals take good care of me."

Fresh blood always does it better. And while I am thankful for the blood offering, my reasons for ravaging Lenora's pussy incessantly is the only way to keep the dreams of drinking her blood at bay. The sexual tension takes over and I forget for a time that I need it. She absorbs all incessant needs other than that which is starved for her flesh and loving touch.

lenora holmwood

Man or A Monster - Sam Tinnesz

I awoke alone in the bed, wrapped in a blanket and found a note with a single rose on my bedside table. I pick up the ruby rose and breathe in the sweet floral aroma as I look at the note from Llewyn : *Be back soon, my love.* I lay back on the soft bed and breathe in the rose and soak in the amorous bliss. The things that a vampire makes me feel are unreal. With or without Llewyn touching me.

There are still many questions I have for him. Every night that I interrogate him for answers on where I fit into this world of bloodthirsty mobsters only brings up more questions that need answers. And when Llewyn isn't around my only tool is the library, which I admit will be difficult to leave behind. Llewyn has put so much effort into collecting these titles that I feel that there isn't enough time even being immortal to read them all.

Hopefully I will have some room when we leave to take some of them with us and start a new collection wherever we end up.

Having my mind already made up about what I was doing today, I decided to change up from the normal leggings and sweater ensemble I've been rocking for too long and reach for one of the pleated skirts and lace tights and paired it with a knit long sleeve top. It was nice to feel good about myself again. To look in the mirror and say 'that's me, lenora holmwood' and to not feel like such a spectacle to the public but rather a real person. For so long others have written my story for me. My own grandfather kept me prisoner in his own home for six years. Serlanos has been hunting me like cattle across the city, desperate to enslave me in some way I still don't understand.

And today I am going to find some answers. As I carry my coffee cup to the library, I pray that whatever I am looking for will be found within these shelves. The warmth of the library is intoxicating. I feel an immediate sense of relief the second I enter the room. A reprieve from the harsh realities of my life.

My stack of books haven't moved from their place by my chair. I've yet to have understood what components that make blood so desirable to vampires, trying to find what exactly could be so special about my blood. Llewyn mentioned that there are bloodlines of vampires. Families. Organizations. We barely scratched the surface of who's all involved.

"Aside from Serlanos, there's three other leaders. Cynfael who runs Southside, Talon the West and Ordelia is more downtown central," Llewyn explained as I took notes. He laughed at my dedication.

I was one step away from having a plot web built on my bedroom wall. I understand detectives now. They are a helpful visual.

Ordelia and Talon are a mystery to me.

Especially Ordelia. A female vampire. Or a succubi as some would call the female counterpart to the vampire. Most succubi survive off draining men of their life force and semen. Other legends tell about how succubi will use that semen to impregnate unsuspecting virgins. I picture Ordelia to be otherworldly and beautiful, destroying the hearts of men and women as she passes by. An elevated beauty that no mortal could resist.

"Ordelia runs most of the brothels in the downtown area. Her girls are primo," Llewyn explained.

"How often are women turned into vampires?"

"Not as often as you think. Many of the ones that exist today are by accident. Not all vampires are thorough when it comes to killing their victim."

"And what of Ordelia?"

"She was the first bonded to Serlanos."

I couldn't imagine ever willingly handing over my soul to that soulless fuck. Not in a million years would I bond with him in any way shape or form.

"Is she an ally to Serlanos?"

"No one is ever truly an ally in our kind. We all want something and are willing to do what we want to get it. We just have arrangements that keep us in line. Serlanos and Ordelia have an understanding. She provides the girls, he provides the space. If it weren't for their business they would be at each other's throats like the rest of us."

Ordelia was never in the spotlight. There are no photos of her online. Never on the television nor in the paper. She seemed to prefer it that way.

Every part of me wanted to meet her. She was such a mystery to me. A spectral phenomena or physical representation of femme fatale and I was here for it. I knew Llewyn could tell I was intrigued by her when her name was ever mentioned.

I flip through the existing stack but find nothing that tells me where these blood bond rituals originated from. I eyeball the sliding ladder that I've been dying to climb, suspecting the rarest of books must be at the tippy top. If I was hiding an important book, that's where I would put it, in hopes that any pursuer was afraid of climbing great heights.

Gripping the sides of the ladders with both hands I begin the climb and abandon the other titles down below for my search for something more. I've explored the strigoi of Romania and other vampire lore of the Carpathian mountains where good ol' Stoker based his award winning classic. I admit Stoker did his research for that work of art. The amount of old lore that I found familiar references to brought me right back to the idea of reading it all over again.

Which I know would drive Llewyn up the wall. It makes me wonder how much of Stoker's story was based in truth of lores and myths he got his hands on or if he himself had an encounter with a vampire himself. There are so many conspiracies on how Stoker got the idea for the novel.

And now knowing that vampires are very real make them all the more plausible.

I wish at times I had access to the internet to make my search faster, but I fear Llewyn wouldn't allow it for fear of bringing too much attention to our activity. Anyone could be tracking our signal. It could lead the enemy right here.

I don't know much about today's technology so I trusted him. I couldn't bear to be ripped away from this library. This comfortable life that I share in secret with Llewyn.

All is perfect in my world when we share an evening in these arm chairs together and share what we are reading, going on rants about why we love or hate it. He always has such insight to share when it comes to my struggle to comprehend the line between life and death.

It's indefinite.

One step at a time I climb the ladder to the top, focusing on not looking down. Despite my love for the library ladder, I have a severe fear of falling from great heights. And I knew the rarest of titles will be at the tippy top. I skim the titles as I ascend, seeing if anything screams 'I have all the answers'.

While none of the titles pertained to what I was looking for, they struck my interest but decided I could only carry down what I was after.

Priorities, Nora.

At the top I strike gold. *Bloodlines and Blood Wars of the Black Sea.* There were a few other titles following in line with that subject so I carefully tucked the four books under my arm and began the descent, still not looking down. Trusting my foot to find each step. I admire the architecture of the room as I climb down.

So much thought went into emulating gothic revival style. The elaborate woodwork that framed the vaulted windows meeting the matching ceiling at a steeple point. The dark oak wood paneling that wrapped the room together leaving enough space for the ornate furnishings which was the cherry on top to a dark academia dream. I never want to leave here.

I sense the bottom is near and my foot frantically searches for the floor, eager to feel a solid surface beneath them. But a hand at the small of my back stops me in place.

"Don't move."

Llewyn's sultry command has me locked in place on the ladder, only a few steps away from the bottom. He takes the books from me and I hear him dump them in the chair behind. He closes in on me from behind, his hand trails up my leg, disappearing up my skirt. He slips my panties down and tosses them aside on the floor in front of the roaring fireplace.

My heart is beating out of my chest. Desire is pooling between my legs.

Pressing me against the ladder, his hands grip my hips as he plants soft kisses up the back of my thighs sending sparks of pleasure through my body.

He gives firm *smack* to my exposed ass as he lifts the hem of the skirt. The sting ripples on my skin with seething pleasure. With one hand he parts my clenched trembling thighs and runs one finger up and down the lips of my begging pussy. I gasp each time he finger hits my clit, I throw my head back and he catches me from falling. Holding me in place as his finger works his way inside of me. I explode around him.

He knew what he was doing and he relished in it. Having me exposed and at his mercy. Resistance was not an option when it came to Llewyn's touch.

He switches to a circular pattern, immediately torturing me to my core. Teasing my entrance, he penetrates me with one finger for a mere second before pulling away. My knees are weak and my knuckles white from clutching the sides of the latter so tight. Pressing into the middle of my back he forces me to arch and stick my arse out further.

"Take a step up," he orders, whispering into my ear and then trails kisses down my neck ending on a tiny nibble. I do as he says. "Keep your back arched. Stay just like that."

He grasps my hips, digging his claws into my skin as he spreads my thighs, releasing the heat pooling at my center and leans in, his tongue at my quivering entrance, trailing down and penetrating. He consumes me, hungry for fuckery. Devouring me in every way possible. Pinning me to the ladder as each stroke of his tongue intensifies against the folds of my sex.

My orgasm building, one of many to follow in a storm of bliss.

"Jesus, fuck," the words slip my lips, giving Llewyn all the validation that he needs to continue.

I feel him smile as he flicks his tongue across my clit, robbing me of all sense of reality.

My body convulses under his hold on me. I throw my head back and let out a deep moan as his tongue carries me away. He drinks up my arousal, his face soaked with my never ending desire for him to ruin me for all others.

He consumes me in all ways, nearly lifting me off the ladder to delve deeper, he does not abandon the talents that his long fingers tease at my entrance.

Torturing my center with his slithering tongue, he feasts on every orgasm my body serves him. Lapping up every quiver of my thighs. His fingers pulse in and out, benumbing every nerve ending as he gradually increases speed. He can command my body to come at will. It's as if he's keeping a tally of how often he strikes that cord that unleashes a symphony of moans and cries of pleasure, hoping he can turn those into screams.

The ladder creaks beneath me, feeling the force of his hold on me. My whole body jolts against the wood as he slips a second finger inside of me.He bites my bare skin *hard*, giving a small taste of what his fangs would feel like, only leaving me craving more.

He pulls away, and towers over me. The shadow of his daunting figure haunts the light casting against the bookcase, growing as monstrous as his arousal against the back of my thighs. Gripping my thigh, he lifts my leg and with his great throbbing length, pushes into me - the moment his girth rips into me, I let out a staggered gasp and grip the ladder tight, unprepared for the full bodied pounding. His full length plunged deep, hard and unrelentingly fast. No human could match this stamina. An onslaught of multiple orgasms took over and I surrendered to them.

Grasping a fistful of hair, he pulls my head back, his sharp fangs extending and threatening pleasure as he grazes them against my exposed skin as he kisses my neck. He presses into me at his full length, my knees are weak, his hand reaches around and finds my clit with gentle ease. Madness ensues within me as he plays with my arousal, pressing into me, and then pulling out fast. Repeating this movement only tortures me further.

"It's so lovely fucking you just like this. A delicacy to devour," his voice low in my ear, like a haunting whisper, coaxing me into an oblivion of pleasure. He loved the control and how willingly I surrendered to him, his touch, his everything. And I loved the way loving him threatened danger.

I relish it.

I find no comfort in stability, only chaos. I've known nothing else but facades of what that is like. Being with Llewyn is like finding balance. I'd let him consume me if it didn't cost him his sanity. There's a toxic part of me that wants to tempt him but not enough to follow through. He made his boundary clear.

The fantasy is worth out-living.

I can't respond, and he loves that he has rendered me speechless, leaving my eyes to tell him I am wanting more. Abruptly, Llewyn pulls out and rips me from the ladder. With a swift swoop and turn, he heaves me up and over his hips, my legs wrap around him and he carries us to the empty armchair.

His strong hand at my throat as our lips collide at once, his tongue parts my lips and his tongue dances with mine. His nails dig into my skin as he sits down in the leather arm chair that's been asking to be christened. Settling me over him, the tip of his erection teasing at my entrance once more. I grip his shirt, expecting him to continue the sensuous attack on my pussy.

"I want to see all of you." He breathes against my lips as he rips the skirt off at the zipper and tosses it aside. His fingers trace my collar bone and down to the front button on my blouse before gripping both sides and tearing it apart and letting it fall off of me. An alluring smile plays on his perfectly handsome face as he takes me in, the pale yellow light from the window casting a spotlight on us. The way he admires me is overwhelming, he grips my wrist to keep me from hiding or shying away from his gaze.

"What did I say about hiding yourself from me?" he asks aloud as he takes me in. His gaze has a hold on me, hypnotic and unwavering.

"Don't," I repeat back, smiling. The authority in his voice only drew out my arousal further. I liked testing his limits. And I liked when he got bossy.

"Good girl," he snarls as he claims my lips in his, biting my lip and sucking it in as he lowers me down on his hard throbbing cock. My chest tightens as he enters me again, gripping the chair for dear life. *Holy fuck, he is thick.* Every time we have fucked, it takes me by surprise.

He releases a deep sigh of relief, feeling the depth of his penetration and the tightness of the inner walls of my inner sanctum closing in around him. Gripping my throat with one hand for control, he began to thrust upwards, bouncing me slowly, sliding in and out, gradually increasing speed before the momentum did all the work. He reveled in carrying me over his cock, watching me riding out each burst of pleasure like a tidal wave at full peak. His claws digging into my backside, the sting of them drawing blood only heightened my arousal, soaking him through and through. I could feel it collecting underneath me on his trousers that have been unzipped enough just to unsheath him.

"This juicy ass is going to be the death of me, my dear," he moans as he spanks me again. He buries his face into my neck, nipping and biting. His strong hands cup my exposed breasts and pull me forward, taking a nipple between his lips.

I lost my goddamn mind as he plays, pulling and sucking as he ravages me in luxury. However, being on top gave me an advantage. I begin to take some control back. His eyes widened with surprise, wondering what I was about to do as I slowed the pace and grip his shirt at the collar. His stormy and sultry eyes roll to the back of his head as I begin to take it slow as I grind and roll my hips, creating a mutual frenzy between us.

"Two can play this game, sir," I whisper into his lips as I suck in his bottom lip and give him a taste of my own bite. Something in doing this activated something more feral than I anticipated. I could feel every vein in his cock throb within me as I tighten around him hard and then release as I grind on him.

I unleash a carnal frenzy in both of us as I ride him into oblivion. Grunting and growling, he tenses up, showing he is close to release.

"There's my little monster. You're just as feral as I am. Serlanos has no clue. Nor does he deserve a taste of you," he laughs through his grunts as I let out an involuntary scream as a flurry of orgasms take over and he regains the upper hand again. He loves control and I love giving it to him. None of my past experiences understood my need for dominance in the way Llewyn does. How to worship a woman and yet ravage her at the same time. He read my body as if there was an invisible map only made visible to him.

With one hand he grips my throat and snarls, "Let's show them what he's missing." He picks me up with such ease, and without pulling out he carries us over to the tall curtained window. Llewyn pulls the drawstring opening the curtain and lets the bright yellow light break through the winter frosted window. Its source: searchlights on helicopters, employed on Serlanos' payroll to find me and bring me in. His need to flaunt me only turned me on more. Making a mockery of Serlanos, showing him that what he wants so bad is being ravaged by his underboss.

I can't tell who is turned on more by this.

Standing in full view of the window, Llewyn fucks me midair. Pounding into me hard I cannot control my screams. He looks into my eyes, watching as every brain cell melts away from existence with each thrust into me. His cock is going to tear me apart. The other danger of vampires is getting fucked to death, thats another note to make.

"Show him what he can't have. Because there's no fucking way I am letting you go."

He turns me around, and pushes back into me hard, his reentry creating a new cascade of orgasms as he folds me nearly in half at the thighs, exposing our incandescent fuckery to the world as the searchlight shines almost directly into our window.

Lowering me to the ground, he repositions me with my back arched and almost on all fours as he proceeds to ram into me, leaving me no chance to prepare for the next storm of erotic ecstasy.

The things I would let this vampire do to me has no end. I wanted him to fuck me with every inch of him that my tortured sex would allow. Whatever he's awoken in me can never be tamed again.

Pushing down, further arching my back, he begins plunging into me jackhammer style. The weight behind him only intensified the feral pounding he delivered. He grunts and moans as I scream and clutch at the rug in front of me as I experience the most intense orgasm just as he releases into me, his thrusts however were unrelenting.

"I'm not fucking done making sure you've been completely satisfied," he says bending low and pressing deep into me, until he was sure the rhythm of my orgasm pulsing around him had completely dissipated.

Ravaged and breathless, he releases me and pulls out and slumps to the floor next to me.

The afterglow illuminated the room, outshining that of the search lights outside.

"Jesus fuck," I say, bewilderment evident in my voice.

"I don't think Jesus would fuck you like that, my dear."

"Are you calling Jesus vanilla?" I giggle.

"No, but he's the last person I would credit for what I just did to you," he says, inspecting the damage his nails had done to my backside. Streaks of blood combed my bare skin trailing from the source.

"I'll be sure to send a 'thank you' card in the mail then."

"I'm sorry about that," he gestures to the marks on my skin.

I sit up and lean in close, " I'm not."

Llewyn caresses my face and presses his lips to mine so gently. The duality of this man is imaginary. Men like him only exist in books.

"I am sorry that I distracted you, you seemed like you were on a mission."

"I was. How dare you distract me?"

"I'm sorry. It will probably happen again though."

"I hope so."

34

callum gyanstazi

The Pit - Silversun Pickups

The sun bursts between the buildings and bounces off the canal bringing a beaming ray of light through my windshield, blinding me. I have to move if I am going to get a proper view. I've been staking out Cynfael's club all night now, waiting for Llewyn to return to Cynful so I can trace him from there.

Llewyn has been elusive. I know he's not out of town like he has been making it seem.

He's here in the city, I can feel it. Avoiding us all and consorting with the enemy.

But he hasn't shown in days since the last time I caught him leaving the club. At this rate, I am not going to catch him on the road. I need to be up higher, gain a vantage point. I debate walking over to the building across the way. But it seemed like an effort for nothing.

My car shakes as something lands on top shaking its entirety. Nails scrape and claw on the roof unleashing an unpleasant screech.. I look to my left and in the passenger seat sits Norryx, the slithering snake sitting there proud of his skill to rattle my nerves. In the back seat, Lycidas kicks his feet up.

203

"Goddammit, I wish you two wouldn't do that."

Norryx and Lycidas cackle like hyenas, "Lighten up, Callum. Speaking of light, the sun's out. Maybe it's time to take a break. He's not coming."

"Give it time."

"Sure, waste your time. Just like we did with every lead Llewyn gave us. Zilch. Lenora Holmwood is a ghost in the wind. I checked security cameras at other bus stations. She was at the bus station on Davis. But from there, nothing."

Norryx and Lycidas both looked well fed, having just returned from another raid of a blood bank in Indiana. It seems they too have fallen into the trap of the jobs. The blood lust is taking over.

" I see you two are looking well."

"Blood raid went well," he gloated, pulling a flask of blood from his coat pocket and passing it to me.

"Thank fuck, I am dying here."

"Drink up, we pulled some extra for ourselves. This waiting around for new leads to blood banks is getting old."

"Tell me about it, at least you're not hunting down the person that's supposed to be hunting the salvation to our problems." "Take a break. Something will turn up - you're not going to learn anything by sitting here boiling in the sun."

"Roderick has been talking up a big game."

"Roderick is full of shit."

"He said your pay is ready. He's been waiting for you to come pick it up. Maybe he has some leads from his horde of dhampirs."

Maybe Norryx the serpent has a point.

I walk past the receptionist desk, his mousy bespectacled secretary wide eyed as always when she sees me. She doesn't bother to tell me not to go in there. She barely even speaks as she stiffly buzzes me in the secured door.

I cannot imagine what it's like to work for a monster like Roderick. Ever since Serlanos turned him, he's become more of an arrogant ass before, as if he didn't already have an over inflated ego already.

Roderick sits in his leather bound chair, the office walls having been newly painted a modern gray with accent walls. The wide bay window was now covered with black out curtains. Roderick has made up for the lack of sunlight with new ornate lighting and decor.

"Callum. I am sure you're here about your pay. I can assure you it's all here, you don't need to count it again."

Roderick is a contemptuous dick. He loves the fact that he's had the time to cozy up to Serlanos while I've been out chasing ghosts. The cash I couldn't give a shit about, it was the blood I was after. My stock is as dry as my throat. I can feel it clench for the tiniest taste of iron left in my mouth.

"Yeah, yeah I'm sure it is. But I am here on different matters. I hear you've been talking up a good game to boss-man. What gives, man? A month ago you would've rather spat on our kind than enter in our game."

"Adaptation is key to survival, Callum. Surely, you've learned that by now."

"I hear you got dhampirs all over the Canadian border. Any leads?"

"What do you think?" He raises an eyebrow at me.

"Thought so." He's all talk.

"And you came all the way just to interrogate me about what we both know."

"And what do we both know?

"There's a reason why we aren't finding her. Someone is hiding her, someone who knows how to hide in plain sight."

He means Llewyn.

"Llewyn wouldn't betray Serlanos like that. He couldn't. Where would he hide her?"

"Your blood brother has been consorting with mortals and others of the like. He's not to be trusted. The fact that Serlanos is having you tail him is a sign. Why else would he be caught doing business with Cynfael? Why else do you think he abandoned you at the diner, Callum? He's abandoning you. And worst of all, once Serlanos gets his hands on the Holmwood girl, he promised her first rytes to me. And to think you've been fighting for that all along," Roderick sneered, a malicious smile playing on his face. I want to smack it off of him so bad. But I promised I'd be on my best behavior.

"Shut the fuck up. You're never going to touch her as long as you still walk this plane. She was promised to me. And only me."

"Have you ever asked yourself why Serlanos is so fixated on her." Aside from her being breathtakingly beautiful, yes.

He's blood crazy. Has been since and has been squeamish about sharing. Despite the copious amounts of blood we have stolen from hospitals, blood banks and black market retailers, we are still short of what we are due. For all that I do. And now Roderick has the nerve to tell me Serlanos has promised Lenora to him.

"For the first rytes. Her blood will allow a gateway for immortality for all that taste it. In his eyes, he's completing the family"

"Do you know why that is?"

"Um, er"

"Have you not done your reading, boy? Tsk tsk. Well it only figures, considering you were brought up in questionable conditions. Go back to the lore."

"Dracula?"

"Don't be smart - that's fiction. The mythology, the lore. The stories of old and what shaped Dracula. The myths that explain the many truths of our kind."

"You've lost me."

Roderick sighs before explaining, "According to the legend of Draxius Khor, consummating the first rytes involves a crucial procedure in which both parties drink from each other. The blood exchanged strengthens the union. For Ms. Holmwood, the blood exchange would ultimately turn her or kill her if she is not strong enough. For us, well her virgin blood would make a vampire impervious. No silver bullet would keep us in our graves. Decapitation would be ineffective, reversible even. Invincible. What need for blood would Serlanos have if he were to claim that power. What would he need from you?"

He's not wrong about that. Would he have a need for any of us if he didn't need blood? The same way we do. It's not like we can all consummate first blood rytes on the same human. She belongs to one and only one.

Serlanos is stubborn. Set in his ways.

"Any more questions?" Roderick says impatiently.

"Yes. Where the fuck is my money and my blood, Roderick. And I swear on Khors blood that if you cut me short I will impale you in the dungeons myself. You remember the dungeons right?"

Roderick ignores my threat and throws a duffle bag at me.

"Get the fuck out."

35

lenora holmwood

Dark Paradise - Lana Del Rey

Llewyn pours us both a glass after I cleaned up from him ravaging me beyond existence. I felt him in my joints, the marks of pleasure on my body twinged with a reminder of how much I wanted that again.

But now it was time to focus. Or so I thought.

I find myself zoning out, my focus bouncing from the books on the table to playing with the bullet pendant on the chain around my neck. My constant fidget toy. I try not to let myself get distracted by the alluring vampire sitting beside me.

I catch him smiling to himself as I adjust myself comfortably in my chair, pleased with his work of ravaging my body.

"So Cosa Nosferati, that's based on the Cosa Nostra, right?" I say, breaking the silence.

"Yes, it was our adaptation when we infiltrated the original outfits."

"It translates to *offensive things,* if I'm not mistaken," I go on.

"That's fitting. We do some pretty offensive things."

"I can think of a few offensive things we've done in the last hour."

"Darling, those weren't offensive things. What we did was positively sinful," he says with a sharp seductive smile. I felt my arousal stir again like a restless monster butI have to get it together and focus.

I settle into my chair, Llewyn is still watching me from the corner of his eye. I smooth out my new clothes which are baggy and comfortable. Maybe he'll be less likely to ravage me again if I wore something less form fitting, but that was doubtful. Llewyn would probably still try even if I was wearing a garbage bag.

The way he admires me with his eyes alone was overwhelming, and he did not like when I shied away from his adoration. 'You deserve to be admired, Lenora."

Even if it's from one person, who's attention I cared for the most, it was still overwhelming at times. I know he knows when he's being too nice to me. I am not used to it, even though I find myself being what he calls 'too kind' to him. Neither one of us are used to this. Being with someone who actually gave a damn and listened.

The only people I've been surrounded by are those who wanted to take something from me and my family or those who said that they cared but only wanted the publicity of being associated with someone who was involved in organized crime. The fanaticism that some have with true crime these days extend over the line of inappropriate. Even as I lay on the ground, completely malnourished and struggling outside the subway, people wanted to get their two minutes of video footage that eventually made it to the news. If Llewyn had it his way, he would've marched down to the station and bled out the anchor who had the balls to show a victim on camera like that.

Llewyn is distracted by something on his phone while I survey my reading options that Llewyn had stacked neatly on the table next to my glass of wine. I had no idea where to start. Sometimes I wish I had some untraceable database that would just allow me all the answers, including the one on how to defeat Serlanos once and for all. But to kill him meant to get close to him and I had no desire to do that.

Llewyn's phone was more advanced than the one I had before going into hiding. Grandpa discarded our phones, fearful we were being tracked by Serlanos and his men. Grandpa swore he saw them outside the gate, watching. Following us back and forth from school.

And they probably were.

In the beginning, I truly believed he meant to keep us safe from him. But Serlanos did what Serlanos does, he bulldozes through people to get what he wants. Leaves them with no choice but to turn to him because they have nothing left.

Grandpa didn't want us talking to the press or anyone concerning the investigation into our parents death. Smart phones were barely a thing then. It's now 2016 and technology was nearly unrecognizable to me. The phone I had was the first of many to follow in its design, a touch screen.

I was hesitant to use a phone. I feared that with one click of a button I would accidentally alert Serlanos and his men right here. It wasn't worth the risk. Besides, I enjoy the sentiment of gathering research from a book. I feel like a true scholar seeking through old texts that probably haven't even touched the surface of the world wide web. Is it truly possible for a database to know everything about everything? How can it be trusted?

I can feel Llewyn's stare as I struggle to choose from the titles on the table. "What are you looking for?"

"Answers." I hear his eyes roll at my vague response.

"Did I render you incapable of expanding on your thoughts? I'll be more careful next time."

"Not at all. And you know what I'm looking for. Whatever makes my blood so valuable to Serlanos."

"Have you considered that maybe he's just a creepy prick that found a target he could completely control?"

Yes, I have. But there is something more.

"Yes, that is a factor into this, but you and I both know there's more to this."

Llewyn hesitated before giving a recommendation, scanning the options.

"Check out *Bloodlines and Blood Wars of the Black Sea.*"

Llewyn knows. I know he does, otherwise why else would he point this book out. Is the answer for both of our fates in this book? Or just mine?

I know he won't just tell me. He wants me to figure it out for myself.

Telling me would only be too easy. Besides he likes to watch me mentally squirm just as much as he likes me writhing beneath him.

Being the underboss of the Gyanstazi family has to give some privilege to sensitive information pertaining to the family business. The value of my blood falls into that category in my opinion.

"What's in here that's so important?" I am testing him. Will he give me anything more than what he has?

"Read and you'll see, " he smirks.

"What! No tropes or book blurb? You've obviously read it, so give me an honest review," I demand playfully.

"Well for a little horror freak like you, there's blood, there's gore and vampire lore. Also a bitter sweet love story of two star crossed lovers separated by death."

"Okay, you had me in the blood and gore."

"Just read and we will talk when you are ready."

Sometimes I wonder if I will ever find the answers I am looking for or just more questions that need answering. Taking more time than we may have here before we have to escape.

I flip open to the first page, not holding my breath on finding the answers that I need. I sip my wine and focus.

1818 - In a small village outside of what is known as Romania, the plague struck, taking the lives of half the villages' population. The village physician, Draxius Khor was at his wits end, losing all hope of reprieve from this cursed plague. Where there was sickness, a deeper evil lurked in the shadows ready to unleash the full force of its wrath.

Determined not to lose another child to the plague, Khor sought alternative measures that went against most of everything he believed in. But desperate cases called for desperate measures. He knows other professionals that have been denounced and ridiculed for using such atrocities in their practice, suggesting that traditional medicine extends beyond what we understand of the natural world.

In his desperate search for a remedy for the rapidly spreading disease, word of his quest spread to the next village over to the controversial Zephira. Having kept the village plague free, she earned the respect of the King's men and was permitted to practice so long as she didn't cross over into more taboo forms of magic and the occult: blood magic. Believed that plague was spread through blood and the existence of witches raising paranoia, the Batrans, or elders, were determined to keep hysteria at bay. But there were always some that were determined to give Zephira some grief.

Attending to the injuries and maladies of the commoners brought Zephira trouble at times from those who still believed she'd had been burned at the stake by now. False accusations of witchcraft and attempted framing were no stranger at Zephira's doorstep. Every one of them squashed out like a bug.

The rumors and shame did not keep those in desperate need, beyond doctor's expertise, from knocking at Zephira's door, ready to greet death.

While her practices were controversial, they were effective. Keeping those who would've perished alive and well, and the village happy. King Solomon's soldiers were willing to overlook this so long as she didn't break her promise to King Solomon.

Hearing of the village doctor's quest for remedy, Zephira began thinking of the power that her knowledge of blood magic and Khor's openness and expertise combined would bring. Zephirah sought Khor out and made an offer he couldn't refuse. Seeing her effectiveness in keeping the plague away from her village, Khor was convinced of her ability and didn't hesitate to join in a pact to cross the line together. Zephira believed that they could create the cure, the antidote to end all disease. Making mankind indestructible with just one sip.

In the name of Zalmoxis, the Dacian God of Life and Death, Immortality and War, the two of them would create the elixir of life.

It is lost in translation as to how exactly Dr. Khor and Zephira achieved this. Many accounts from villagers say sacrificial rituals were performed at dusk in the nearby woods separating the villages. Virgins or animals, it was unclear what shrieked in the night as it took its last breath, All to serve the greater good.

With the rumors spreading of the sacrifices and the sudden disappearances of young women and farm animals, Solomon's men were forced to take action. Suspecting that Zephira had crossed over long ago, the soldiers followed her to Khor's crumbling practice, following the disappearance of two women in the woods.

Not allowing another scream to crush the eardrums of those surrounding the workshop, soldiers break down the door and find inside atrocities that were beyond any horror imaginable.

Shreds of flesh and muscle tissue hung from the ceiling rafters of the basement like intricately woven persian tapestries, the liquidated remains of corpses congealed on the floor as thick as molasses beneath the soldiers' feet. Many of them were too ill to remain there to arrest Dr. Khor and Zephira as they lay in their recent sacrifices blood and bones, consuming what was left like carnal animals. Stomaching their disgust, Zephira and Dr. Khor was arrested and brought in on charges that were listed as most reprehensible. Held by the belief that consuming the blood of their sacrifices would give them immortal powers, the two of them were deemed mad.

Both were committed to the seminary for toxic blood syndrome, or hemochromatosis, where there is too much iron in the body. This can lead to severe organ damage.

Still in the belief that he had achieved what he had been sent out to do, Draxius Khor is on his deathbed, dying of organ failure. His wife, Ionela, despite the shame that followed her and husband, stood at his bedside as he took his last breath 'I will be back, my love. Forever will be ours.'

I sit back in my seat, letting this legend process in my mind.

"That was a tragic love story," I say finally to let Llewyn know I was ready to talk. "Is there anymore? It feels a bit finished."

But Llewyn's attention was drawn to his phone. I could not decipher the look on his face. A mix of anguish and fear furrows his brow. "I'm sorry, what? I was reading something on my phone."

"Everything okay?"

"Yeah, just a work thing."

He says that a lot. I know it's because he doesn't like to remind me that he's in direct contact with Serlanos. Considering the trauma that ensued the last time a phone call had interrupted our time in the library. Even though we spoke about it, I know he doesn't want to sour the mood.

I can't say I blame him. Sometimes even still I am embarrassed that I reacted that way. So I don't press further.

"So Draxius Khor. Did he come back like he said?"

"What do you think?"

"I think-"

We are interrupted by the familiar fervent vibrations of Llewyn's phone, beckoning him for duty.

"I am sorry, I-" Llewyn stutters, his eyes darting between the phone and me, hanging onto all the thoughts ready to pour out of me.

"It's okay," I stop him, and take his free trembling hand in mine. "Duty calls."

He sulks in his seat and stares at the phone before answering.

"I'll be right there," was all that he said before hanging up. I didn't catch a glance at who it was, but I figured it was probably better I didn't know. It wasn't my business.

Llewyn stands, still holding my hand and draws it to his mouth and presses his lips to it.

"I am so sorry. We will continue this when I return. I shall not be long," he says before leaning down and taking my lips into his. Every time he kisses me feels like the first and last time. The same gasp of air gets trapped in my lungs as if he has stolen another inch of my life with his kiss.

Leaving me star-dazed, I watch as he strides out of the room with his waist coat over his shoulder.

llewyn hellsinger

Come Follow Me Down - George Taylor

What the fuck could Chief Commisioner Warren want from me? I've done a good job of staying out of his way, hardly ever have we had personal beef, despite what he suspects of me. What I do for Serlanos is an otherworldly horror that he cannot seem to get a reign on, so he's been more civil.

I know he's trying to get on my good side.

But he's pissing me off with the way he's blowing up my phone.

He's been trying to find an in on Serlanos' game for years since the Blood Donor's Banquet massacre, but little does he know it is so much bigger than that. Bigger than his mortal little brain can fathom.

It's not just Serlanos' way, it's all of us. Every vampire family has its own code that they follow, their own oath, but all agree on one thing: our secrecy is key to survival.

We can only survive in the shadows, and Chief Warren is focusing his gigantic-big-dick-search light right on our business. The Gyanstazi family has been a spectacle to the city since we rose to power. We had an agreement, make him Chief Commissioner and he won't see our faces in the news. We won't cause him trouble unless he gives us shit, and Serlanos has made a point of making him an asset. Requiring most of the police forces sources to find and bring in Lenora Holmwood has been financially exhaustive. And all of us are feeling it in decreasing weight of each duffle bag we collect from Roderick.

He called me down to the station. Saying he had something I would want to see.

And when it came to Chief Warren, I wasn't willing to take any chances.

If I could, I would serve Serlanos to him on a silver platter, but that would ultimately destroy me and then Lenora.

This isn't just about me either.

It's about her, it's always been about her. Ever since I felt that tiny hand on my face when I lay there on the kitchen table cold as ice while Dr. Holmwood administered blood into my undead veins, reviving what was left.

Fated together, perhaps. I've followed her as much as she's fallen into my lap by accident, and on purpose. And now that I have her, safe and secure for now, I cannot risk that.

Whatever Warren has to show me, it's about her.

The station is bustling with overworked and disgruntled, officers man-handling cuffed degenerates calling bullshit on their charges. The pen is packed with many contenders for Serlanos' recruitment, he's always look-ing for those who've got nothing to lose and a lot of rage. Makes for a good soldier, possibly even captain.

Chief Warren stands in front of his office door, arms crossed and impa-tient.

The room hardly notices my presence until I walk through the bullpen to meet Warren, who does not say two words and gestures to me to follow him into his office. Closing the door and locking it was not enough privacy, he closed the shades too. His cool demeanor wears thin and now he's shaking at the knees, realizing he's just locked himself in a small dark room with a vampire who was more than capable of making anything look like an accident, even in a police station.

"My my, it must be important for you to go to this effort all for me," I jab.

"Don't flatter yourself, Llewyn. I wouldn't have called you unless it was of a dire nature."

"Then tell me so I can depart sooner and let you collect your senses. I can see you shaking, you don't want me here just as much as I don't want to be here."

Warren circles to his desk and sits, breathing in deep to calm himself before proceeding.

"Ordinarily I would be going to Serlanos with this information but I thought you'd like a chance at it first."

Turning the computer screen on his desk for me to see is what I feared most.

A camera still image of Lenora going into the diner the morning of the swap. I froze, unable to hide the fact that any color remaining in my pale face had drained to sheet white.

"This was taking only moments before police arrived, however we see no record of her leaving. She wasn't among the bodies we recovered from the aftermath. Our coroner has double checked all samples of the deceased remnants against the DNA we have on file for Ms. Holmwood. None of them match. Would you care to explain this?"

What should I do? I'm literally caught. He and I both know that I disappeared from the scene when police arrived. I have never been caught, but the cameras show that I was there. In plain sight. Nothing was supposed to happen, so why should I have worried about being seen on camera. I was just a man there doing business with my clients, at least that's what it looked like to the rest of the world.

It was the one time I've been caught on camera. The most damning evidence as well. Fuck modern technology. I wish Serlanos left me in the penalty box for eternity at times. It was peaceful despite the protruding spikes forcing their way into my back, the reminder of my wrongdoing.

Warren isn't stupid. He's put two and two together and if this gets back to Serlanos, we are fucked.

"Llewyn, just tell me, where is she? You and I both know that Serlanos is going to rain down hell on us all if this gets out. The pressure on my squad and the whole police department has been astronomical. And since her disappearance from the hospital, I've been tracking her down on my own. She needs to be free, Llewyn."

"She will be. And so will I."

"Where is she?" Warren demands once more.

"She's safe, and that's all you need to know."

"Llewyn don't be an idiot. You and I both know we can only hide from Serlanos Gyanstazi for so long. He will find out. Not from me, but from anyone else who has access to these files. Anyone of these fuckers out here would sell this information to get the cash and the pressure off our backs. Our families' lives are at stake here."

"I have a plan."

"Well I hope it works because there's not a way out of town, above ground or under. Serlanos has my men and his men paroling the perimeter of the city. The only way out of here is in a body bag."

Good, because that's the plan. But I don't tell him that. He's toeing the line of friend and enemy and I have just openly admitted that I know where Lenora Holmwood is to a Gyanstazi informant, the most lethal one we have. And I can see the burning urge in him to do the right thing. His job.

But the photo frame of his smiling family stares back at me, reminding me of what's at stake. I see my face in the frame, reminding me of what I too have lost, a wife and child. How I would have done anything to save them from the fate which had befallen them. A fate in which I brought on them.

I could not subject Chief Warren or his family to that torture no more could I submit Lenora to the torture of being bound to Serlanos for all of eternity.

"I just need more time."

"I cannot guarantee that, Llewyn."

He's right, and it was stupid of me to ask.

"Thank you for calling. I will be going now."

I stand.

lenora holmwood

Blood//Water - Grandson

I awake with a start— half expecting Llewyn to be there beside me, as he is always most nights. But he didn't come to bed. The clock reads 4am in flashing red lights matching the ones bleeding into the large window. I hit the button on the remote, lowering the darkening curtains, hoping that I could just fall back asleep. But it's too late, my mind is already awake and spurring with questions.

The somber grim glow of the light of dusk filled the room with a familiar loneliness. The one that crawls in when you least expect it, reminding you that when it comes down to it, you're all you got.

Although I do have Llewyn, when he is here.

Where is Llewyn? Did Llewyn even come home at all? He didn't say when he'd be back. Just that he'd be back soon, leaving right when I had so many more questions than I did answers. I reread the tale of Draxius Khor over and over again to see if I had missed anything but yet nothing could calm my eager mind until Llewyn returns to allow me to thought-dump all over him.

He didn't say what he was doing, however I have learned not to ask. When he is called by the boss, he has to go. No questions asked.

It's how the wives of the mob operated. The less they knew the better.

It's better that way. I trust that Llewyn will tell me what needs to be known. And that is when we need to pack up and hightail it out of here.

The lore beyond that small excerpt is unclear and unfinished, like someone was ripped away from its pages with their feathered quill in hand. Their last words scribbled and ending on a smear on the page, it's unfinished. It can't end on a cliffhanger like that!

Is there more to the story that we are missing? Has Llewyn found it or am I to go on another scavenger hunt that ends with him fucking my brains out on the library floor? Not that I minded that at all, but I crave answers more than I crave spicy vampire sex. Which is a thought I never thought would have crossed my mind in a million years but here we are.

I flip over to my other side and close my eyes to submit myself back to sleep, hoping that the promise of Llewyn being there when I awake to talk about everything will lull one back to sleep. But I found myself just thinking about Llewyn earlier in the library. Remembering the way he moved me and bent me to his will, possessing every nerve ending in my body with his touch and invoking his mastery over me with his entombing kiss. His lips capture my breath and his hands embrace my soul in ways that no mortal could evoke from me.

At least not in my experience.

Any high school boy that claims that they have the ability to fuck good has nothing on 200 year old vampire. Llewyn has repeatedly proven to me that every sexual encounter I've had prior to falling into his arms has been complete nonsense.

I don't know if it's his immortal powers of being a vampire that has me hooked, but I never want this spell to be broken. There's a part of me that feels that all along he was meant to be by my side, and me by his. In flesh and in spirit.

I was never much for religion, more so consider myself spiritual. I may not be sure of there being a god or a savior but I do believe that we are all somehow connected. That two souls can be tied together by fate.

Llewyn I feel as if I've known my whole life. He knows me without me telling him things, Understands to be gentle, but I am in no way fragile. He doesn't tell me answers to things not because he doesn't think I am not smart enough to understand, but because I am more than intelligent enough to find the answer. I think he gets turned on watching me figure it out.

He has an academia kink and I am more than willing to oblige that.

Although the amount of clothes I am going through due to him tearing them off of me is getting a bit overwhelming.

Sleep moves in and takes hold— but abruptly ripped back awake at the sound of a crashing sound. I jolt upright in bed. Frozen in place.

Has someone broken in or is that Llewyn?

I fly out of bed and throw on my robe and grab the iron cast candelabra from the dresser, drawing it high and ready to swing on any intruder that dares cross over our threshold. If Llewyn can't be here to defend our fortress then I must.

I tiptoe out into the dark hallway, the mirror's reflection of my ridiculous defense against danger has me feeling doubtful I will make it, but it's the best I've got. Approaching the kitchen I see the light to the stove was left on with a tea kettle set atop. The fridge door wide open casting its dim yellow light on Llewyn who has sunk to the floor, in a blood-starved daze. He was paler than normal and weak.

I've never seen him like this.

I drop my weapon and pull Llewyn into my lap. A half empty blood bag falls from his hands.

"It's—it's not enough. It's not enough," he struggles against his hunger. Anxiety flows through my body as my decision is already made up.

"Sh sh sh. It's okay. Take mine," I say as I roll up the sleeve of my robe, but he stops me.

"No—I can't. You don't know what you're asking of me, Nora."

"But if you don't you'll die. And I cannot do this without you," I say firmly. He looked at me with sorrowful eyes, knowing I was right. This blood shortage is really taking a toll on Llewyn, and being as he was close to breaking free of Serlanos's control, he would be losing a steady blood supply.

"But what if I don't stop," he sputters, tears in his eyes.

"You will. I trust that you have the strength to stop."

Llewyn's storm grey eyes are filled with internal dread and remorse. I knew he never wanted it to come to this, but I would have done it without him asking. He did say it was my choice to give consent. He's sunk his dick into me, so if he's worried about breaking Serlanos's claim on me we are well past that. This is no longer about my curiosity and fulfilling a weird emo girl fantasy. It was about survival. It's always been about survival. And I cannot survive without him.

I offer my wrist to him again but he puts his hand up to refuse once more.

"No, not like this."

With the little energy he has gained from the blood he drained from the blood bag dripping on the floor, he sits up and pushes me back to the floor, maneuvering himself on top of me as I slowly lay my head back on the kitchen floor and stare back up the blood-starved vampire hovering over me, ready to feed. My breath is staggered, and everything begins to slow around us as his eyes narrow in on me.

I know I said I trust him to stop, but what if he doesn't? What if he loses himself to the blood lust? But all thought stops as my eyes lock with his and the idea of losing him in any capacity becomes too much to bear. It is worth the risk. He leans in slowly and low, his breath deep and anxious as he hovers over my quivering lips.

"Are you sure, Nora?" He asks just one more time.

"Yes, my love."

With a cold hand stroking my face he draws me in and his lips entomb mine, fully and completely without escape. He presses his body into mine, pulling the robe away, exposing my bare skin.

"Well this is a nice surprise," he smiles as he brushes the hair away from my neck. He leans in slowly, letting the tension draw taut. My heart drums louder as he lowers his head to my neck, his aquiline nose brushing my jaw. Trapped in breathless anticipation, but he tortures me further by brushing his soft lips against my skin, trailing kisses down the length of my neck and down my chest. His perilous tongue is heedless as he explores my mouth like one would an enchanted labyrinth. Leaving no part of me abandoned, he rolls my nipples between his lips, plucking and pulls and drawing out a moan from me with a sensual bite and then releasing. Pushing himself between my legs, he violently tears his belt off and unsheaths himself and positions himself at my entrance.

"I seem to be distracted by another hunger, my dear."

"It'd be a shame to leave both unsatisfied."

"That it would," he said with a hint of a growl in his voice that had my pussy throbbing for him. And he knew that with the way his thick tip teased at my entrance pressing into me.

Everything stills around us. The only sound, our heavy breath as he lowers close to my ear, knowing what was about to transcend both of us.

"This is going to hurt, only for a moment," he growls into my ear, his bloodlust taking control.

Dead silence permeated the air and was shattered by my enthralled gasp as Llewyn sinks his teeth into my flesh. A stinging sensation followed by pure ecstasy flooded my veins as he drank from me, the pull from his mouth enclosing my skin was intoxicating. I succumbed to oblivion as he penetrated my body, my inner walls tightening around him ready for immediate release. Wrapping my legs around him, I pull him in with my legs, the weight of him against me only intensifying my undying orgasm.

"Oh my—fuck," I moan, fingers digging into Llewyn's back.

"There's my little monster," he breaths into my ear, and laps up a dribble of blood dripping down my neck. "Your blood is a delicacy, my love. Sweeter than the finest wine. Paired nicely with the sounds of you enjoying my cock."

Llewyn pounds into me hard as he continues to lick at my neck, kissing the bite marks before sinking his sharp fangs in, the sting summoning a black parade of pleasure to march through me, commanding me to come with each stroke of his cock. My eyes roll to the back of my head and my thighs quiver with each thrust. He relinquishes his bite, my eyes widen as my arms are pinned above my head with one strong clawed hand.

Blood drips down his languid lips and he wipes it away with his thumb before licking it off.

"Satisfied?" I tease.

He smiles before answering, the seductive curve of his lips has me tightening around his wide girth that throbbed inside me. "When it comes to you, I am only getting started."

"I'm not going to be able to walk later am I?" I giggle as he tightens his grip on my small wrists.

He shakes his head, "I'm afraid not, my dear. But I will gladly carry you to where you need to go."

He buries his face into my breast, kissing and lightly biting as he carries on a fevered plunder on my sex. Each graze of a protruding fang against my skin sends me through another ring of pleasure driven oblivion. He reveled in how much biting aroused me, unlocking a new way to provoke every nerve ending in my body at his disposal only encouraged his onslaught of nips and nibbles against my flesh.

And nothing could prepare me for the way he feasted my breasts, capturing my nipple in his mouth and letting his tongue imprison me in a tomb of undying bliss. Ethereal pleasure poisoned me as he sunk his teeth in around my areola and gently sucked as his tongue tortured me further, his cock impaling me. His spare hand gripping my hips, his nails digging into my skin which only heightens my arousal. He lets out a guttural sigh as my orgasm pulses around him. He bares his protruding fangs as he is about to finish, growling sensually. My god, there was no hope in resisting this man.

I am madly in love with this beast.

Naked, trembling, and wet with blood and satisfaction we lay there in the carnal mess on the floor.

"Fuck I went to hard, I am so sorry," Llewyn says tending to the deep puncture wound on my neck.

I sit up as he presses a paper towel to the cut.

"I'm not."

"We cannot make a habit of that. It's dangerous. I could have killed you," he reminds me, even though his satisfied smile still plays on his face like a broken record.

While I know he was right, I've never felt closer to him in that moment. I'd let him feed from me for eternity. It didn't hurt, in fact I hardly noticed. I hope slipping into death is just as peaceful as making love to Llewyn.

"I only did it because you were going to die. I know that's a boundary and we crossed it—"

"We have a habit of bending the rules, my dear."

"Maybe there are some rules worth breaking."

He claims my mouth once more, picking me up off the floor and sets me on the counter.

"Not at the cost of losing you," he whispers against my lips. "No matter how fucking delicious you are."

38

callum gyanstazi

Carousel - Melanie Martinez

Blood squelches through my lips as I savor the raw game and juices in my mouth, letting the flavor linger on my palette. The slaughtered stray cow that was my dinner lay in the grass beside me as I lay back and let the fresh blood revitalize this hollow shell.

For a few brief moments, I remember what it feels like to be alive again, like a brief high with a hard crash to earth.

I hear Lycidas and Norryx grunt as they tear into another cow nearby. Their fangs gnash and smack as they feed. 'The wolves got them' the farmers will think. Or coyotes. No one will think three vampires stopped for a raw beef midnight picnic in the middle of the meadow.

This blood shortage bites ass.

Very rarely did we ever have to resort to hunting lost farm animals. It was mainly during No Feed Orders sent down from the powers above Serlanos that we resorted to hunting in the woods outside of town like blood-thirsty savages rather than the comfort of a city alleyway. The Blood Syndicate controlled how much was stolen, a sizable amount across the nation would draw attention to our kind, which makes life difficult for Serlanos and his blood racket. He's bought the silence of most by extra payments in the shipments he intercepts at the hospitals and blood banks.

Feeding on animals wasn't the same as feeding from a live vassal, but it kept the syndicate from breathing down our necks and Commissioner Chief Warner off our backs and in good favor. I wonder how long that will last now as the public is out for justice for the diner massacre. He is looking for any reason to blow the whistle and expose our kind. Keeping in his good favor is in our best interest.

The Blood Syndicate does not make a habit of forgiving those who make spectacles of themselves in front of mortals. Moving in secrecy is key to our survival. I guess that's why adopting the mafia lifestyle suited Serlanos so much when we arrived in Chicago. He was able to be in the spotlight and let the rumors of his atrocities chase away any competitors or enemies ballsy enough to challenge him. Those who knew the true horror of his nature weren't around to speak of it.

Rule of thumb: If you're going to take down a mob boss, make sure you can kill him.

Serlanos learned from the best. As crime moved to the internet, finding a useful racket for vampires like us to corner and thrive proved to be difficult.

Cynfael and Ordelia had their paths in the sex industry. Talon was still a mystery to all of us. Always hiding in the shadows of society. He dabbled in a bit of everything. Being 900 years old will come with a scroll about a mile and an infinity long of talents and skills he's acquired in surviving in a mortal dominant world. All we needed to know about Talon was that he was not a force to be reckoned with and he earned his throne in the Blood Syndicate.

Serlanos attempted to sway the election vote for governor, but Talon stood in his way. Talon let him have Chief Warner, even though his loyalty to Serlanos and the whole Gyanstazi clan was needle-point thin, hoping that would keep Serlanos in line.

But nothing can stop Serlanos. He always gets his way.

His influence spreads deeper than the underworld.

I wanted to be him, I thought as I watched the young boy laugh and scream with excitement as his mum and dad fawned over him as they rode the carousel together. Kensington Park was bustling with families out for a stroll. Perfect targets for pickpocketing.

I have to bring something back to the boys at the workhouse tonight. We've been living on scraps that Mother throws to us.

The boy's giggles create a rage inside me that I've never felt.

Jealousy.

It dances before me and laughs in my face. Everything I've ever wanted. A loving mother and father.

Reminding me that I am an orphan.

A nobody. A ward of the state. As I am reminded by my all-intent-and-purpose Mother, the overseer of the workhouse. Fourteen other boys are crowded in the same room as me, lined up in rows in little boxes each labeled with a number. Our arrival date and our eighteenth birthday. Some of them are made up as some birthdates are unknown.

I've had sixteen years to make my fortune and hear I am pickpocketing at the park. Rubbish. Some boys like me have found a mentor by now. Someone to take them under their wing when they leave the workhouse.

I have no one. Just me and the boys I look after.

"You're all scum, the lot of you," Mother would sneer at us as she blew the candles out at night. "If the Good Lord didn't take pity on you, no one would."

Charming woman.

No one felt the loving embrace of the workhouse Mother. She had nothing loving to embrace. Not like the boy's mother on the carousel.

The father in his bold top hat and handsome custom tailored suit beams at them proudly. He knows what he has.

He has what every poor fuck like me in London wants: Stability. Family. Love

The little boy has no idea how lucky he really is. And every part of me seethed with the need to show him. And then rip it all away.

I don't handle jealous feelings well. I'm a notorious pickpocket and I am not afraid to brawl with anyone who dares to pick a fight with me. Cost-mongers on the street cower when I walk the streets, ready to collect what I am owed. If they hold out on me.

The moment I decide that I want something is the moment the poor sucker has already lost it. However, I'm not perfect.

The beadle and I have taken many by-the-ear strolls down Leedle Street to face reprimand at the hands of the workhouse mother. Her stern sour face was hardly a welcoming sight as the tall door to the parish groaned open a crack. Her cold glare falls on me with disdain for my very existence. She's never surprised, just more disappointed. As if there was ever any hope from me. Or she takes it personally as her ability as a caregiver, which she should.

I've been a pain in her tightly wound arse since the moment I was dumped on her doorstep, leaving no note of explanation for my origin nor an apology for burdening the already burdened parish matron.

She reminds me of this each time I am escorted home. So I am here in Kensington Park, honing my skills.

I am much older than the boy giggling on the carousel. By his age I learned so much more about the world and its cruelties, it's amazing how innocent he's been kept. How naive. I feel the strong urge to give him a taste of the real world. What it's like to be abandoned and unwanted.

I watched the family disembark the carousel after the tenth ride that day.

"One more ride before I close down for the evening, Mrs. Hellsinger?" the carousel operator asks. They are regulars, they've been here before if he is to know their name.

"No, thank you, sir. It is well passed supper and this little tyke needs to get washed up. See you next week?"

"I will be here!" the operator calls as the small boy runs ahead of his mother and father.

"Llewyn, wait for Mummy please," the boy's mother calls as she chases after him. The boy's father laughs as he strolls down the path after his wife. The father swoops in and throws the small boy over his shoulder, he is still laughing hysterically.

As I venture out of the bushes to follow my intended prey, I lock eyes with the carousel operator. His eyes dug into mine, threatening to send me to my grave if I were to touch a hair on that boy's head.

He knows my game, I was certain he had snitched to the constable and the beadle - so I don't test those limits and take off in another direction.

It was very clear that I could have a whole lot less. But I am unwilling to let anyone try to take what I do have from me.

"Callum, wake up dude," Lycidas shakes me awake. We are still in the field. The flies are circling the dead cow carcass, rendering it soiled. Norryx yawns and stretches telling me we all fell into a small blood-coma.

"Come on, get up. We gotta get back to town. We've been gone for a while. We left Dalton in charge and I don't know how long he can handle watching the newborns during this no-feed-order.

That's where all the blood is going. Why have we been shortened in our payments for our undying servitude to Serlanos' desires?

No feed orders were brutal for all of us, but especially newborns. They are rationed extra during these times as living off animal blood doesn't begin to satisfy their thirst. While blood bags aren't the freshest— it's human and that's what mattered.

I wipe my chin of blood and drool , as if it would make a difference— I am a bloody mess. I feasted like an animal. Blood stains dribble down the front of my vest and tie. Picking up my dress coat draped over the crumbling wooden fence that lines the perimeter of the property, I try to hide my shirt. I look across the horizon and can nearly pinpoint the dairy farm that provided us with our meal tonight.

"By Khors Blood, thank you for granting this feast tonight," I murmur under my breath before following Lycidas and Norryx back to the car that is parked on the dirt road at the bottom of the hill.

The drive back to headquarters was quiet. Roderick's words played on repeat in my head. What would Serlanos need from me once he has Lenora Holmwood? He may have promised her to me before. But he's been making alot of empty promises these days. He gains one lost soul just as he loses another. *How long will we all og riding his carousel before we learn it leads to nothing?*

As we enter the museum district, I watch the tourists galavant across the street. I hear their blood pump with excitement, smelling sweet with bridled glee. I wonder if I will ever have that chance at feeling that again. Alive, like that family on the carousel.

Maybe Lenora Holmwood is my chance at that.

39

lenora holmwood

Somewhere Only We Know - Lily Allen

I awake, nestled in his strong arms in bed, the covers draped over us. His long dark hair falls over me, tickling my nose. I giggle and he pulls me in closer and kisses my neck.

"You've been asleep for a while."

"I like to sleep. It's nice."

"Any bad dreams?" he strokes my cheek, my skin tingles at his touch.

"Nope, not this time."

"Good," he tilts me forward and kisses me deeply, the fullness of his kiss enveloping my lips entirely. Tingles erupt and pass through my body from head to toes. I don't know if I will ever get used to this feeling.

He breaks the kiss and I turn over to face him.

"I have a meeting today to arrange our leaving," he says.

I sit up in bed.

"How soon is this happening?"

"With some luck by tomorrow we will be out of Chicago. Headed north somewhere."

I sigh with relief.

236

It's finally happening. Llewyn has made what I thought to be impossible happen.

"I'm going to go put some coffee on," he kisses me on the forehead and leaves the room.

It's been so blissful here, it's strange to think we are just leaving. Abandoning the wonderful library that he has cultivated. I've only scratched the surface.

I hear Llewyn, humming in the kitchen as he makes coffee and I put on my sweatpants and throw my hair in a bun and join him.

"I frothed the milk this time, so hopefully you like it," he places the steaming foamy mug in front of me and the heavy wafts of the magic bean sauce tickles my nose with warmth and welcome.

"This is heavenly, thank you. So when's your meeting?"

"In an hour. I will be back right after and we will go from there."

This feels so dangerous, yet exciting.

"And we're staying together?"

He stops and comes around the counter and takes my hand. "I'm not going anywhere without you. I'm not letting you out of my sight. You are my life now. I hope that's clear by now."

Shivers scroll up my spine as he pulls me in and his lips settle over mine, claiming me as his. I revel in the feeling of his lips enveloping mine fully, his hand caressing my neck making me want to melt right there.

He breaks the kiss. "I have to go get ready. Drink your coffee. There should be eggs and bacon in the fridge."

The moment he mentioned bacon I realized how famished I am. Allowing myself to feel hunger is still a strange feeling. Luckily, Llewyn has been understanding and tells me to eat as little or as much as I want. He wasn't keeping tabs on me. Having food available was such a strange concept to me now.

As a child, Mother kept the fridge stocked like we were going to bunker down for the apocalypse. I am sure that woman went to the store everyday. Llewyn let me order grocery delivery considering he didn't eat and I knew what I wanted most of the time. He was willing to try what I cooked and it was nice to have someone to cook for other than myself.

The savory smell of bacon had me drooling over the pan. I watch as the white pieces of fat fry, pop and sizzle to the appropriate amount of crispiness.

"That smells delicious," a voice I didn't recognize startles me from behind.

I drop the spatula and turn around.

An alarmingly alluring man I didn't recognize stood before me, his arms resting on the counter, as if he'd been watching, waiting for sometime. That's something about vampires that I don't know if I will ever get used to.

leonidas holmwood

Vampires Will Never Hurt You - My Chemical Romance

The next day, I call my wife at home, where she sits agonizing in fear, knowing that what we have to do next won't be easy. Bad things happen to those who try to flee from Serlanos's wrath. We've seen it firsthand. And Rosalynd has watched the aftermath on the news.

But I made preparations for us. A friend of a friend who has a way about making people vanish. It will require quick acting on our part. No contact. No goodbyes. Just go.

"I need you to gather any important papers, documents and the key under the dresser. Take them to Roderick's office. He will know what to do with them. We will meet at the matinee showing at the Victory Gardens. There I will collect you and the children from school. We must leave no trace of us, Rosalynd. Do you understand?"

Her voice quivers over the phone as she replies with a faint yes. It defeats me hearing her so frightened. Knowing that this will put our whole family at risk.

I dash for my phone and make the call that everything has been set into motion and then collect my briefcase and the box locked away in the safe beneath the floorboards. Inside a pistol, loaded with a silver bullet.

It's kill or be killed now. And I am going for the kill. I want to kill this hold this monster has over me and my family. For too long we've lived in fear of them haunting our doorstep one last time. Coming to collect what they so desperately need. What they would kill me and my family for and step over our dead bodies after draining them for all that they're worth.

The least I can do is make sure my family is safe and taken care of. If anything is to happen to me and my wife, the children will be cared for. They will be safe with my parents. They've dealt with Serlanos and his type before.

I make an excuse for my boss who can read the worry on my face but doesn't ask too many questions. I hang my lab coat and exit the building with the security officers watching me walk off into the distance.

I take the L to the theater and contemplate my options here but find that I have none left. I dug us into a hole.

I have blood debts that I have no possible way of paying.

I stand outside the grand marquee of the Victory Gardens theater, staring at the time. The disgruntled ticketbooth operator grows impatient with me as I stand just far away enough to require his attention but not enough to offer his service.

This used to be a place of joy for our family at one point. On Friday nights after school we would travel down here for an evening on the town. See a movie and then meander over to the Barnes & Noble to peruse the aisles. Lenora, my teenage daughter, would be caught in the classics, lamenting over a new edition of Edgar Allan Poe or Dracula while Theo would be fluttering through the comic books at warped speed.

I wish they could be here with me, for one last film in the dark together. But I fear for them to be caught out in public, near me. Any association with me at this point is a death wish. The conversations that would ensue after the credits rolled made me feel grateful to have an insightful and open-minded family. Theo, brave and boisterous, like a true knight. And Lenora, kind and innocent, yet so knowledgeable of the dark. My wife, Rosalynd, is saintly and says her prayers, giving hope to our future.

They are everything in this world to me, and I must protect them.

As I sit in the theater and wait for Rosalynd to arrive, I watch a father and daughter enter and take their seats near the front. I am reminded of the moments I had alone with my daughter. She caught me alone in the office, sorting through the family safe when I came across the most precious heirloom I could pass onto someone. A silver bullet, encrusted with a wire metal bat with garnet jewels set in the wings. The bullet was soldered to a gold plated chain.

"Come here," I ask her, and she obeys. "Turn."

I place the chain around her neck and she turns to face me, her beautiful pallid features glow a pinkish hue and her big storm gray eyes shine with admiration as they had when she was a young child. She was daddy's girl.

"How do I look?"

"Perfection, my dear. Don't ever let it leave you, it might save your neck."

I feel a tear in my eye and wipe it away as my wife takes her seat next to me. She's stiff as a board and it wasn't from bracing the cold and wind outside.

"Everything went as planned. I got the documents from Roderick like you asked." She whispers to me as she hands me a file. I flip through it just to be sure. Everything was here. I tuck the file in my briefcase stashed at my feet.

"Hopefully he didn't ask too many questions?" I take her hand and kiss it, reassuring her that everything is now set. It's time for the next step in our escape plan.

"Just the usual. Asked if I was in trouble. I didn't say anything. I just gave him the documents and said that he knew what to do with them and then left."

"Good woman. Thank you," I sigh and pull her in for a kiss.

Little did I know, it'd be our last.

41

callum gyanstazi

Cubicles - My Chemical Romance

Chicago PD Chief Warren has been a reliable resource for the most part-however, I know he's in many pockets of dangerous people. And he resents being on Serlanos' payroll, considering the countless times he's attempted to bring us in - which we've proven pointless. I don't know who else he's tipped off out of spite. Anyone that has a coin to trade for information. How do I know Llewyn or Cynfael aren't one of them? There's a reason we've never seen him in cuffs. I just hope I get there first. I have to hope that this will lead me somewhere closer to finding Lenora Holmwood.

My future wife. I am going to have so much fun tearing her apart and showing her how it is at the top of the food chain.

I cannot keep disappointing Serlanos.

He's like a father to me. Without him I would be nothing. I would have died as a poor orphan back in the 19th century. That hell hole of an orphanage did no one any favors.

The police station is in an uproar as the Vorcolai has caused a riot, they're hands are tied up in a bloody mess brought on by what they think is a blood crazed cannibal. Which they wouldn't be completely off the point. They are known for eating their children.

The officers on duty were swamped with the aftermath of paper work and processing those that had witnessed the massacre that had taken place that they hardly noticed me slip in the building.

Officer Oliver Harker waved me through as one of the arrestees threw his chair at a glass barricade and it bounces back and hits him in the face. That plexiglass works wonders.

This town is getting out of hand. All at the hands of our kind. And worse.

The more we invite in, the more trouble we seem to have. But the mortal police just believe that there's a bad batch of bath salts circulating.

That or fentanyl. The drug racket is mostly cornered by the western outfits.

"You got your hands full here, don't you."

"I don't want to talk about it. You have no idea," Harker snapped, his eyes digging into me, as if it were solely my doing. He was usually more even tempered but by the way Warren glares through the blinds of his office door tells me the pressure is real and my welcome in the building is only tolerated for so long.

It was my kind that bothered him. We're the reason why he's swimming in paperwork each day. and up most nights covering up a newborns savage dismemberment of a homeless man. Afternoons covering our tracks with the media by blaming the bizarre face-eating behavior on bad batches of fentanyl or bath salts.

"Yeah, yeah. I know. Just show me the video."

"Alright. Well there was a robbery at the bank across the street later that day, so going through the footage, we see that Ms. Holmwood entered the building at roughly 6:52 am. She doesn't exit. And she wasn't in any of the body bags collected from the scene. So what gives?

Indeed, I see the frighteningly stunning mortal enter the diner - but we never saw her.

"Can I have a copy of this?"

"Sorry, I can't do that— police investigation. It's still active."

"Fine. But you owe me one."

"I think I just paid it, thanks. Now get out."

Charming fellow.

I leave the Police Plaza fuming. Anger and betrayal mix with malice inside me. I cannot believe it. I didn't want Roderick of all people to be right about Llewyn. But how else did she escape?

It can only be explained that she has been hidden and with the help of the very person I thought I could count on to not fuck up.

Llewyn has always kept me on the straight and narrow. He's well disciplined. A military brat.

Followed orders well - to a point.

Now it's like I don't even know him.

After the lip he gave me the other day on the street I can only go into this with my guard up.

It may not end well. Mostly for him.

And Cynfael has been helping him. Why else would he be seen leaving the club?

Cynfael is the most skilled trafficker in the city. He can source what you want and when you want it. He's tempted me several times during one of our dry spells.

My phone buzzes in my pocket.

Fuck, it's Serlanos. He wants an update. It almost seems like it's by the hour.

He is losing his patience.

"Any news? I heard there was a lead."

"I am going to check it out. I will call if it works out."

"Call soon, I expect results, Callum," he hangs up before I can respond 'yessir.'

I couldn't tell him. I had to see with my own eyes.

Give Llewyn one last chance to explain himself.

What he's done. What he's planning to do.

How could he?

We're supposed to be blood brothers.

I dial Norryx as I step off the elevator of the police plaza.

"What's the situation?" he says, picking up after the first ring.

"Keep tabs on Cynfael. We find him, we will find Llewyn. We find him, we find the girl."

"Copy that boss."

After ten minutes of pacing outside and inhaling a cigarette, I dash to my vehicle. I was too impatient to wait for an update.

With luck I will find Llewyn myself.

I hope I am wrong.

42

llewyn hellsinger

Emily - My Chemical Romance

Fuck fuck fuck. I am an idiot. I should have moved us the moment Chief Warren called me in. Lucky for me, Cynfael got there to warn me. Now I just need to collect a few personal items and get back to Lenora before Callum or someone else finds my hideout.

How did I not see this coming? With technology advancing - it's harder for humans to hide, let alone anyone who's trying to capture some supernatural being seen fleeing the building.

Serlanos has his hooks in Chicago PD, just as Cynfael has his connections.

The question is, who's got a bigger pocket? We can only hope that we are one step ahead of our foes. The ones that so desperately want to rip Nora away from me.

I should have seen this coming. Chief Warren could only hold on to that information for so long.

Warren has been our inside guy for so long we've gotten to see him rise to police commissioner. Lately his hands have been tied since the diner incident.

I take Lenora's hands in mine, the fear is plastered all over her face. "My love, listen closely. I need you to go pack what you can. We leave tonight. I will be right back. I promise," I kiss her forcefully, as if it were our last. Her small hands clutch onto me, afraid to let go. She hates when I leave her.

I can only imagine every worried thought going through her head.

Everything is happening so fast. Sure we knew we were leaving today, but not like this.

"Cynfael. Please watch her for me." I don't take my eyes off of her, clutching her hands for dear life. She looks at me like it's the first time and the last.

"Don't worry, scout. I got it from here. You're lucky I got here when I did," Cynfael assures me, twirling his gun in the air.

"Yeah, no shit."

I let go of her hands and tear myself away and hurry out the door, down the emergency exit and out the side door to the sidewalk.

I just have to get to the safety deposit box and get back to my love. For too long she has been trapped like a songbird in a cage, and now we have a slim shot of escaping, unscathed and without a trail.

I turned the corner, checking my shoulder to make sure I wasn't being followed.

I've been careless. So much so that Cynfael was able to find us. Who else would pick up my trail?

I arrive at the dinghy post office box where my few precious personal items lay for many years now in a safety deposit box. The few items I was able to smuggle with me were from another lifetime. Unstirred until now.

I look into the dusty tin security box. The onyx and garnet ring still lay there - the same one that my late wife wore.

I pulled it out of the pile of ash long after the fire had fizzled out and stuffed it in my pocket like it was nothing.

Walked away, already having moved on.

It still sparkles just as it did as I stared at it at the bar, heartbroken and shell shocked. Drinking myself into oblivion. No other woman that has worn this ring has made me feel as alive as Lenora does.

Even before becoming an undead soldier.

I want Lenora to wear it. It belongs to her and I am almost certain it always has.

Once we are safe, I will make her mine.

She won't be taken away from me like the others.

43

lenora holmwood

Laura - Bat For Lashes

While I don't have much, I want to bring what I can. I don't know where we are going. So it makes it hard to know what to bring. Warm clothes versus not warm clothes? I don't have a mix. It's winter here in Chicago. A foot or more of snow has gathered at the bottom of our skyrise. Time to start with the essentials. I dug through clothes that Llewyn had graciously ordered for me. I packed what I could, picking between the plaid skirts I had ordered. I couldn't take them all. Which is unfortunate because some of them are really fucking cute.

The idea of leaving here to never return was strange to me. While I may have spent all of about a month here, it seems so long ago that Llewyn rescued me and brought me here, promising me a safe haven from the world below.

I start getting excited about the prospect of life on the run with Llewyn. Dangerous. I am looking at it as a new start for both of us.

We can both be free.

Digging through the closet, the old satchel my brother had packed falls to the floor. I pick it up and stuff the few essentials I have inside— at the bottom of the satchel, the bus ticket, an old notebook that he used to pour over in the middle of the night, and a hoodie.

All that I had left of Theo.

"We're getting out, Theo. It may not be the way we planned. But it's happening."

I wipe away the tears of relief and gather myself.

We still have a ways to go.

We will celebrate later.

Picking up the notebook, some pages fell out of the binding.

My heart drops like a guillotine as I immediately recognize the writing, my father's. My fingers tremble as I pick up the folded pieces of paper with our names scrawled on the front of them. The ink and paper worn and faded from Theo reading it over and over, keeping them close for no one else to see. Theo was so quiet and secretive, all sure to protect me. But why didn't he share these with me? As I unfold the pages, three separate pieces of paper come apart. One addressed to both Theo and me and the other two were for each of us. My father's final words to us, hidden in the pages of his work notebook. He kept this close to him wherever he went. Theo spent nights watching over me and reading this by the moonlight. I always knew about it but he never let me get close enough to acknowledge the notebook's existence.

There has to be something inherently important that couldn't go on the record. Perhaps maybe, just maybe the answer to what I've been looking for all along. What is it about my blood that made Serlanos want to claim me in front of the whole Blood Syndicate as his to create a covenant with? I don't want to get my hopes up, as it could just be a heartfelt goodbye from a father who was about to meet his demise. But I doubt that. The pages were hidden in a notebook that no one else but us knew about, and I am sure he wants it to stay this way. He wanted us to find this.

I take a deep breath before I read the first word on the page.

My dear children,

Theo and Lenora, I never in my life imagined a scenario in which I would need to use these words, but, if you are reading this then I am dead. And you are now more vulnerable than you were before. It is my fault, completely. And I truly apologize. I don't forgive myself, even beyond the grave and until the end of time.

I have to explain first how we got here. I wasn't given much choice, but had I had one, I would have gotten us out of here the second Serlanos Gyanstazi darkened our doorstep with his shadow.

I am sure you know by now, or at least I hope, that Serlanos and his men are indeed what popular culture would call a vampire. However through my research I realized they were more powerful than we want to believe. That's why I must urge you both to keep this letter and my notebook for your eyes only. In the wrong hands, it could mean so much worse for the future of humanity itself.

I wish I could have said no, but I was given no option. Serlanos had sought me out himself, knowing the work that I do with genetic testing. He had bought out every other cryogenic lab and plasma donation center after he bought out every hospital. Those who did not wish to comply with his demands either fled or disappeared. I didn't get enough warning, but I should have known.

Lenora, my darling, there is a reason for him wanting your blood. I was a blind fool to have not seen it before. I was careless and he had gotten ahold of a sample, tested it and then confronted me when suspicions of my holding out on him became known. Had I not paid the blood debt, you would have been taken from me.

With me gone, he has surely replaced me with someone more willing to do what I couldn't. And hopefully that never comes to fruition so long as you are never claimed by him. Keep the pendant I gave you close, always, as it may save your neck, for -

I am torn away from the answers I have been so desperate for by the sharp sting of a cold clawed hand with a strong grasp on my arm, the searing pain forcing me to drop the pages at my feet as I am dragged out of the walking wardrobe.

The aggressor shoves me to the ground and I turn to find a vampire I recognize: Callum Gyanstazi, seething with a mixture of emotions I can decipher. Somewhere between victory and spiteful rage.

"You, my dear, have been a great pain in the ass to track down. And here you are holed up with my dear brother Llewyn, playing house mouse for him. Tell me, Ms. Holmwood, did you remember while he was fucking you that you belong to Serlanos?

Of course I remember, and I don't acknowledge it. How can I, a mere mortal, be expected to adhere to the ridiculous nature and demands of vampire society? Especially one as barbaric as the one which Serlanos plays mob boss in.

"How—how did you get in here?" I stutter, scooting away as Callum backs me against the wall.

"I have my ways. Llewyn was a bloody idiot for leaving you behind in Cynfael's care. Besides, did you honestly believe that Llewyn could keep you safe here forever? If Cynfael can find you, surely I can," Callum sneers at me. " And I must admit, this isn't how I imagined our meeting, had you come quietly before I may have been a bit nicer about this. But you've outrun my patience."

I can imagine Callum's rage. Here he finds me in Llewyn's penthouse, while I am sure he has been working like a dog to search for me as soon as Serlanos had exhausted all of the city's resources at his disposal. The search for me has become certainly strenuous financially, Llewyn said there were cuts in their pay, and increased the longer Lenora remained on the run. The idea of me costing Serlanos loads of money just to fail at finding me ignited a small spark of joy. Good, I hope finding my ass is expensive. This fucker has ravaged my life. He has offended me at a great personal cost at the expense of my family and my freedom and I intend to repay the favor.

"I couldn't care less if you're nice or not, you're a beast just like Serlanos," I spit in his face. He doesn't flinch. But his lip curls with malice.

He leans down, wiping the saliva from his stone carved face, a blade of white blond hair hangs in his face as he draws close to mine and raises a hand to my tear beaten face.

"You don't even know half of it, Ms. Holmwood. Once Serlanos is done breaking you of Llewyn, you and I are going to have some fun," he growled.

"You wish," I stutter through my fear. I cannot let him know he has an affect on me. How my disgust is equally exasperated by my attraction to him. Despite his beastly qualities, he was built to be a sun-kissed Hollister model, with white bleached shaggy hair and pale blue eyes to match. It was a shame he was so horrid.

"Not a wish, princess, a command. That you will soon get used to," Callum retorts, dragging a cold finger across my face, wiping away the tears of my reality being shattered once more. "Now get up. Serlanos shall not wait another moment longer. And I am eager to pay a proper good-bye to Cynfael before we go."

I hate being called princess but even more so now the words have passed over his poisoned lips as he mocked me and my fear. Growing impatient, Callum grabs my arm and forces me to my feet. I resisted as he attempted to steer me towards the door.

I didn't want to know what a proper goodbye to Cynfael would be, coming from Callum and knowing their history. I was almost collateral damage in their last exchange at the diner. But I fear I may have no choice.

I attempt to break his grasp on my wrist, but he is too strong. His death-grip is turning my hand blue, his nails drawing blood with such ease as if my skin were made of paper mache. Being a being of dark abilities has its advantages like incredible strength. I can feel Llewyn hold back when we are intimate, fearing he may break me with each thrust.

Twisting my arm behind me a sharp numbing pain extinguished any control I had over my body. I feel his cold breath in my ear as his annoyance flares against my skin. How easy it would be for him to just take me for his own now. It's what he wants, I can see it in his eyes through the reflection of the dressing mirror. How long has he waited for this moment exactly?

"We can either do this the easy way, or the hard way, Ms. Holmwood. Are you going to fight me or am I going to have to give you a taste of what will come later?"

I have no desire to make things easy for him, however, I don't want to know any sooner what he has planned for me. I am lucky he hasn't feasted on me right here.

Why should he respect the claim Serlanos has made on me when Llewyn hasn't? What is stopping him from feasting on me as he ravages me from the inside out?

The idea of anyone else besides Llewyn touching me made my stomach revolt and my skin feels spoiled under his touch. I have no breath to breathe a word of resistance and submit to his control for my sake.

"That's my princess,"Callum coos, feeling my resistance faltering under his hold on me. I cringed at the feeling of his skin against mine.

I fucking hate him. I hate everything about him and what he stands for. He has caused just as much damage as Serlanos has, being the aggressor knocking on our door, there to enforce Serlanos' demands for blood. Serlanos has wanted my blood, but for how long my father did not say? What did he learn and what is in this pendant that is so valuable?

I fear that I may find out sooner than expected, and not in a good way. I just pray that Llewyn finds the notebook and the letter and can stop Serlanos before he accomplishes what my father refused to do for him. I don't think Callum saw the notebook on the floor, and hopefully he doesn't go snooping for it.

Even as I fall into the enemies hands, I must keep my father's word. He has done everything he could, even in death to keep me safe. He refused to hand me over to Serlanos, as any good father would. Yet, somehow he got ahold of my blood. I cannot bring myself to be mad at either Dad nor Llewyn, and least of all Theo.

They've all tried to save me, all at their peril.

Now, I have to save myself.

44

callum gyanstazi

Sing - My Chemical Romance

Getting into the penthouse and finding the girl alone was one thing— getting past Cynfael is another. With one hand with full control, I direct her towards the door with little effort as she is frozen with fear. She knows I am stronger than her.

I admit, it was quite alarming to find me in your room when you were falsely promised safety in the hands of a vampire. Who'd have thought Llewyn would've been so stupid to promise something like that?

Seriously dude. Come on. We're vampires. It is what we fucking do.

It's like he's not learned his lesson.

Now because he wanted to keep the one human we needed for survival as a pet I have to figure out how to get us both out of here. And I am not about to scale the building like some Frankenstein monster climbing the building with a damsel over his shoulder.

I want Cynfael to see me— that I've won. Whatever Serlanos has planned for this girl will pay off tenfold, he's told me in private many times now.

I want Cynfael to sit in ruin.

Realize that in the end, we were always going to win - we didn't have to do it his way when we arrived in the States. Serlanos knew— and Cynfael shouldn't have left.

Sure he may be able to get all of the willing victims he wants with the sex clubs and whatever other rackets he's involved with.

But nothing will compare to what the first rytes will do for us— power beyond any feeble minded mortal's imagination.

She squirms beneath me - attempting to speak, more than likely to beg for her life.

"The more you resist me the more difficult you're going to make eternity together. I will ensure it," I sneer into her ear, gripping her face.

We exit into the long vaulted hall— the skylight breaking through with the afternoon sun, illuminating my path to victory. I feel her feet push against me, stalling.

"Don't worry, sweetheart. I got something special planned for good ole Cyn. We're old friends. Don't ruin this for me."

I peer around the corner— Cynfael is closely inspecting a dark abstract vase on the console table, questioning Llewyn's taste in decor, which I have to agree is monotone and bleak.

Cynfael is also a creature of questionable taste. It's what humans might call bougie. I don't know, I heard some kid on a skateboard in passing say it on my walk the other night. Humans are all nonsense these days. Even their offspring.

His back is turned— making the perfect opportunity for a grand surprise entrance— making it two for two now. I creep around the corner— dragging the girl with me, she clings to my arm, bearing down all her weight to slow me down.

"Hello, Callum. It's nice of you to join us tonight. Please be gentle with the girl. She's fragile." Cynfael greets me, unphased and still focused on the vase.

Dammit.

Every fucking time.

"How did you know?"

"I saw you following me, asshole. Not to mention, the girl's reflection in the vase gave you away. I've not known her long, but she doesn't walk like that."

Fucking hell. The girl was slowing me down.

"I see you've recovered very little of your pride since the last time we met— I can assure you this will not help you gain anymore."

"Think again, fucker," I say, the hand on the hilt of my gun. Before he could put the vase down, I pull the silver-bullet-loaded-gun and just as I pull the trigger, the girl sinks her human canines into the hand covering her mouth.

Cynfael is hit in the leg and goes down. The silver sizzles and pops as his skin tears away at the opening of the gun shot. The screams that came from him were more than satisfying.

Considering how he left me to the wolves the last time we met this was the least he deserved.

I felt the girl recoil in my clutches as I watched with great pleasure as he writhes in pain.

"How does it feel? To know that you're going to lose, Cynfael. All these years of rebellion against the Cosa Nosferati will be for naught."

"It-It doesn't have to be this way, Ca-Callum," Cyn struggles.

"Oh, but it does. If you hadn't walked away you could be a part of this too," I kiss Lenora on the cheek who cringes at my touch. Ouch— I can't be that horrible. We'll work on that later.

"D-don't. You don't know what you're doing. Serlanos has promised you all a lot of bullshit. And you're going to get bitten in the ass if you keep up with him. He only serves himself. If you don't see that by now, Callum, then I don't know how to help you."

I stand over him. "I don't want your help. You're wrong. You've always been wrong. Ever since we came here you've been wrong. About me, about Serlanos, about Llewyn."

Cynfael laughs, blue blood splutters from his mouth. "I've been right about you from the beginning. You're a little arrogant brat with Daddy issues. Beyond repair."

The silver has worked its way into his frigid blood stream, rotting him from the inside out. I find a tie nearby, and gag my poor damsel so she doesn't try to bite me again.

"Have fun rotting in hell," I throw Lenora over my shoulder and carry her out as Cynfael begins to waste away to nothing, laughing.

On the elevator, I make the call to Serlanos.

"I've got her."

"Good. Bring her back to headquarters. The Blood moon is rising, it is time."

"What about Llewyn?"

"Don't worry about him. I will deal with him in my own way."

Ms. Holmwood squirms and screams against her restraints. I smirk, her efforts were cute.

"That's right darling. I'm afraid to extinguish any dream of running away with the charming and mysterious Llewyn. He lied to you about so many things. It's really quite cruel."

Silence blanketed the park as wealthy families left for their warm homes, leaving the dribble of society to find shelter and the dark and cold. I didn't come back with much after following that poor drunk bastard. He had spent his last pence on a mug and was walking himself back to his wife, who was surely going to laugh and leave him the moment she finds he got mugged by a street rat.

I go back to the park, hoping to find some straggler with a penny that will buy me and the boys some bread at least to split after Mother blows out the candle, just as she extinguishes hope and joy so easily. The pathways are empty and as I approach the carousel I am immediately haunted by the little boy's laughter, his mother's smiles and his father's admiration for the both of them.

Fuck. Am I really that much of a lost boy? Is it just that simple?

I wouldn't be such a little shit if I just had that. The life I have does not allow for pleasantries and simple kindness. Nothing in my life is sugarcoated.

I've never known a mother's kiss nor a father's embrace.

And that is what kills me the most.

A wheezing cough from behind breaks my stream of lamenting thoughts. The carousel operator sits on the bench nearby, watching me intently as he gathers his breath.

Unnerved, I begin to walk away.

"That was a pathetic attempt boy," the carousel operator gruffed at me.

I stopped in my tracks. "Oh yeah, and what do you know about pickpocketing, old man."

"Enough to know you're not going to get anywhere with hiding in the bushes. Do you think any man gets what he wants waiting on the sidelines?"

I shake my head. He was right, hiding in the bushes was childish.

"If you want something in this life, you gotta take it like it's already yours."

"I'm doing what I can, alright!" I wasn't looking for a lecture, especially from some jackass that operates on the fringe already. In the backdrop, and invisible.

I already felt shit for having nothing to bring back to the perishing parish boys.

"And what if you had someone to show you how to do it right, boy?" the man barked from the bench as I turn away, sick of him already. He already ruined what might've been the biggest steal of my life.

But something told me to stay. I turned my heel back to him. "I hope you don't mean you."

The man lets the insult slide and his face crawls into a sinister sneer.

"Of course, I mean me. Who else is going to take the time on a runt like you?"

No one.

"Who are you?"

"Serlanos. Serlanos Gyanstazi. Welcome to your new life, boy," Serlanos' hawk golden eyes shine, and his smile widens, his extending fangs sharp and ready to kill.

lenora holmwood

Secrets & Lies - Ruelle

I choke on the gag as I am dragged out of the penthouse building and out to the dark streets and shoved into the SUV where I am met with two other vampires, drooling with bloodthirst and malice.

Lycidas and Norryx sit on either side of me, closing in. Drooling and snapping their fangs at me menacingly. Both of them are trying to intimidate me, make me fear for my life as if they live off of it, but I couldn't give them the satisfaction even as I feel myself cringe as I bump elbows with them. They sense my discomfort immediately and lean into it.

"To think you were right there in the diner the whole time we could have had a small snack," the one on the left with slick black hair named Lycidas sneered into my ear, one hand gripping the back of my neck. I cringe at his touch, his nails dig into my skin and I help against the gag.

"What a pretty morsel you are," the other one named Norryx mirrors Lycidas. Leaning in sneering into my ear. I could hear him viciously lick his lips.

"Settle down, boys. You'll get your fair share later," Callum says from the driver's seat. He tilts the rearview mirror so my eyes reflect back at him. I can see him smile from the back of his head. I don't let him see the fear in my eyes. But I can't help but feel the choke hold of tears build up in my throat. I feel nauseous and my head is spinning.

I close my eyes and try to take deep breaths through my gag.

He will come for me. Llewyn will rescue me.

But rescuing me would mean a death trap for him. I could not sentence him to whatever torment and punishment Serlanos had planned for him.

The SUV pulls into the lower level parking garage of the Chicago Art Institute. Callum flashes the security badge and we are waved in no question.

Callum opens the door to the car and I am unloaded from the vehicle. Callum removes the gag.

"Scream and I will bleed you dry right on the spot. Don't test me," he growls, leaning in close.

I nod and then escorted, surrounded by vampires on all sides into the building, with Callum leading the way.

Every part of me wants to run but I stay put. I have to wait for the right time. I have to trust that Llewyn will find me.

I have to trust that Cynfael will be okay. Llewyn returned in time to save him.

I have to trust that I will be okay.

I am led down a series of hallways lined with large flat boxes— concealing priceless frames and possibly some renowned works. Large towing carts were packed with boxes marked fragile.

Callum takes us down winding halls and then out to the main lobby that was dimly lit by the security lights.

The gift shop was closed and empty. The lights were out and there was no line wrapping around the entirety of the store. I remember following Dad around until he found the precise replica of the best art piece in the exhibit we saw that day. It was strange being here after hours. Without him.

I had been here so often on day trips with Father and Theo, and field trips with school. I picture a younger me standing in line in the gift shop, watching as I pass by. It felt so surreal now, like another life that has been painted in my memory.

Only to be left at that.

I choke down tears mixed with fear and anger.

Callum let us through another set of doors and down some stairs.

Lycidas exchanged snide looks with Norryx. Callum strides proudly like he's brought in a prized cattle from the fair.

I ignore them all. I pretend they're not there as I walk to my doom.

We descend the stairs for what seems like miles beneath the museum. Far enough that I felt closer to hell now than heaven.

"If you behave, perhaps we will have you moved to a more appropriate suite fitted for a submissive bride," Callum insinuates, but nothing could convince me to be nice to him.

We reach the bottom and Callum stops in front of a padlocked door that looked as if it had been there for centuries.

Inside, a cold dark room, devoid of any mercy. Corners dense with cobwebs and crumbling pieces of the wall. Undecipherable scribbles in dried blood decorated the sharp jagged dungeon walls. I was surprised to not find any instruments of torture. But there was no need for a horde of vampires that could feed from the fear of their prisoners without even touching them. Llewyn's description of their various abilities still gives me chills. It always spooked me when he shifted into the shadows only to appear behind me. He made up for it by a sweet kiss on the cheek before disappearing again.

I stand there and stare into the abyss. Callum shoves me in and locks the door as I crash to the stone cold floor. I hear his maniacal laugh echo down the corridor as he walks away.

I'd rather die in this dungeon than be an obedient and submissive wife.

Falling to the floor in the dark corner, I let loose the sobs of fear I've been choking down as soon as he was out of earshot.

What if Llewyn doesn't come for me?

I wake as the door to the cell is wrenched open, my eyes blurring with tears and restless sleep still hanging over me. A large dark shadow blocks any light bleeding in from the dungeon hall.

"I am sorry it took so long for us to come together, Ms. Holmwood. I apologize for the lack of hospitality my men have shown you."

Serlanos Gyanstazi towered over me. His eyes were shiny with greed and desire. Like I remember from our last meeting, and our first. My waking nightmare is now reality.

"It's not like hospitality is a part of a vampire's nature," I responded coolly, refusing his outstretched hand to help me to my feet. I stand on my own.

"You certainly have a sharp tongue on you. I'd like to see what it can do," Serlanos says, closing in.

"Never will I ever dare to touch you willingly," I stuttered, my confidence wavering in his intimidating presence as he drew in closer. He grabs me by the neck and with little effort presses me against the wall with great force. I feel the life force drain from my body under his hold, my resistance weakens.

"You don't get to say no to me— not anymore," he says, his deranged eyes tearing into mine, his grip on my neck tightening.

"Pl-please," I begged against the struggling gasps escaping my windpipe, tears forming in my eyes.

"Remember, your blood and your flesh are mine, Ms. Holmwood. And under the Blood Moon tomorrow the Blood Rytes will be enacted and together you and I will ascend to greatness. You will not steal this from me."

He releases his choke hold on me and then leaves the room before whispering instructions to one of his henchmen waiting outside the door.

I retreat to the back corner of the dark and cavernous dungeon cell. I'd rather spend eternity here than a moment as Serlanos' wife. The idea of consummating anything or ascending anywhere with the man that has destroyed my whole family turns my stomach inside out. Dry heaving sobs take over, my whole body convulsing as it struggles to gather itself.

Why did Llewyn have to leave? What was so important that he had to part himself from me? We should have left the moment Cynfael slunk into our apartment. We were vulnerable the second he found us.

I want to be furious at him, but who's to say we wouldn't have been caught somewhere on the road? I cannot torture myself with what if's. But what is torturing is not knowing what is. Like what the fuck is in the rest of Dad's letter.

What kills me even more is not knowing the rest of Dad's letter. The fact that everyone but me knows the significance of my blood. The big secret. It's been nagging at the back of my head.

And now it would consume me. Maybe quite literally.

Why didn't Theo tell me about the letters? I cannot fault him entirely, but had I known, I'd maybe have made better choices. Serlanos got ahold of my blood at some point and knows the power that it holds. Believes that our union will help us ascend to an indestructible life. Was the legend of Draxius Khor true? Or is all of this one big hoax.

While consuming blood may prolong the life of a vampire, it doesn't give them any special power beyond survival, from what Llewyn has described.

A conspiracy theory built upon legend and lore? It's hard to know what's real these days.

The other question that I've been dreading to acknowledge is: was Llewyn the one that collected my blood?

I am now very aware that he has been watching over me most of my life. Always hiding in the shadows. The faint gentle hand that caressed my face in the night when I was having terrors. The angel watched from afar when we moved to the apartment building. He was there when I was found outside the subway station. I don't want to believe that he had any part of this, but by his own admission, he was involved with my parents' horrific murder display.

46

llewyn hellsinger

Soldier - Fleurie & Tommee Profitt

The door is wide open when I return to the penthouse—I freeze and pull my gun, ready to slaughter any one who comes within range.

Cynfael wouldn't be this careless to leave the front door open. I gave him strict orders to keep this place under lockdown. I don't know who followed him.

I push the door open further and creep in, slowly and cautiously.

Just beyond the sofa on the floor I see a finely tailored black shoe and the hem of custom fit pants.

Cynfael.

"Is that you, Llew?" I hear him sputter from behind the couch.

"Yeah it's me, Cyn." I walk around the couch, and see the mess that is my friend on the floor. "Well I can say, you've looked worse before."

Cynfael laughs, dead tissue falling from his face as he continues to decay. "Get me some blood and we can share this laugh later. Callum's got your girl."

"Fucking hell. What happened?" I dash to the fridge of my fully stocked fridge of blood bags and open one up and pour into a plastic cup.

"Fuckhead came in fully loaded, popped me in the leg, threw the girl over his shoulder and then left. She bit him though, so it kind of saved me."

That's my girl.

"Drink up, buddy. I'm going to need you to call in reinforcements. We're going after the Gyanstazi family." I felt the ferocity roaring beneath my chest as I spoke.

It's finally happening. I've officially defected from Serlanos and his family of vipers.

I lifted Cynfael up, he was so frail and parched. Devoid of life. I tilted the cup to his lips and he slowly drank, looking me in the eyes as he did. Flesh and bone begin to reform before my eyes and a hint of color in his skin.

"O-Negative?"

"Of course."

"Thank fuck, that's good shit. Hand me my phone, it's on the counter."

I retrieve it for him and he quickly dials his underboss— Riskel.

"I'll send you the location. Get here as quickly as you can. Serlanos is going down tonight."

The call ends.

"Do you know where the cockroach is hiding?" Cynfael spits up as he talks.

"Absa-fucking-lutely. Now quit talking, you need to save your energy if you're planning to be of any use tonight. Or better yet, you should sit this one out."

"Not a chance, Llew. Callum is going down. Tonight. By the way, I noticed your girlfriend is wearing the Nosferati symbol on a silver bullet. Was that a gift?" He waggled his eyebrows at me, but I ignored that. Cynfael never knows when to be serious, it was part of his charm, even as he lies here with silver eating away at him.

"It came from her father, she told me."

"Is it pure silver?"

"I think so, why?"

"Just find it strange that our emblem would be on something we could never touch. And how you've managed to touch her while wearing it is beyond me. Maybe that might save her from Serlanos biting into her."

It better or I will never forgive myself if something happened to her.

lenora holmwood

Color of Blood - Chelsea Wolfe

It didn't take long for one of Serlanos' henchmen to come fetch me from the dungeon. The turn of the lock clacking open startled me as I had been on edge, listening for the approach of my demise. Lycidas wrenches the iron door open and slithers in with the dim light of the torch outside.

I stand up, still pressed up against the corner wall of the cavernous dungeon chamber, leaving no room for him to appear in the shadows behind me.

"Follow me," Lycidas commands. "I am to take you to your new living quarters. There you will be dressed in the favor of your bridegroom's choosing, for the *rituri de sânge* . A masquerade ball is a longstanding tradition in the Blood Rytes ceremony, however we don't have the time as the blood moon is nigh. There in the Crimson Hall, Serlanos will present you to the entire vampire society as his familiar, his property, his bond. If you behave, he may be willing to forgive your past transgressions. However, I wouldn't count on it," Lycidas adds sneeringly as he leads me towards the dark and treacherous stairwell.

"I don't want his forgiveness. I meant everything I said," I retort.

"It does not bode well for those that refuse him," Lycidas snaps, turning on me, his eyes dilating with rage and narrowing in on the subtle bruising on my neck, evidence of Llewyn having tasted the forbidden fruit. "Do you wish to see what becomes of those who give in to their insolence!"

Jealousy erupts inside of him. The only thing keeping Lycidas from sinking his fangs into me is Serlanos' claim on me, the same claim that held Llewyn accountable if he fucked or fed from me.

Gripping my wrist with such violent fervor, he drags me in the opposite direction of the stairwell towards the fire lit chamber at the end of the hall, past the dungeon in which I was imprisoned. His long silver hair whipping in the air as we fly towards the next room at such speed I thought we'd catch fire. The large chamber, where a faint glow of red that could only make me believe we've reached the mouth of hell glowed with violent radiance that I shielded my eyes from the soot and ash billowing from the enormous incinerator roaring to life in the middle of the room. I fought back against the vampire dragging me there. But nothing could save me from witnessing this awful sight that loomed over us.

Gripping a fistful of hair, Lycidas holds my head up, forcing me to see the blood-curdling horror before my watering eyes. Piles upon piles of corpses at different rates of decomposition stacked on each other like a shish kebab with a large spike piercing them through and through. The spike towers high to the ceiling, coated in blood, and tangled in a mess of organs and torn limbs braided together. The corpses at the bottom were nearly unrecognizable. Only pieces of their clothing, if wearing any, were left. Torn scraps of dresses and shoes from various periods of history.

A monumental timeline of vampiric rejection.

"This is what happens to those that turn their backs on the Cosa Nosferati. I would hate to see your beautiful figure at the top."

My stomach revolts as I choke on my sobs. He does not wait before dragging me back down the hall, returning on our original path to my demise.

Shame and fear spiraled through me as I led back up the treacherous staircase to an upper level of the lair. My insides corroded with remorse for the women who died in the face of choosing between an eternity with Serlanos or impalement. My stomach became a hollow pit of despair.

Lycidas stops at the landing five floors up from the dungeon, and looking down over the railing, the stairs went further than that. The underworld itself.

This floor had long halls, decorated with tapestries, lit by the small glow from ornate lamps hung on the walls and long rugs darting in every direction the path led.

Lycidas opens the doors to a lavish bed chamber. Furnished with the finest in IKEA for vampires, it must be the GOTIKA line. A large canopy bed sits in the center of the room facing a large dressing mirror and dark oak dressing table. Behind a curtain on the far side of the room leads to a lavish bathroom with an stone tub and a grand fountainhead carved in the likeness of the goddess Medusa, the snakes from her hair coiling around the edge of the tub with her mouth open as the spout.

Lycidas gives me the grand tour with little emotion in his voice. He sounded tired, knowing how much more is to be done.

"You will remain here until the ceremony. Ordelia and her girls will help you prepare in fashion more suitable to *his* taste."

Lycidas leaves me, closing and locking the door behind him. My chest heaves but not with as much fear as I had in the tombs. My surroundings, while just dismal, are more appealing than a cold rotting cave dug in the underground of Chicago.

It's like Serlanos built a whole castle underground, surpassing the tunnels once used by Capone himself.

The Blood Rytes have begun.

Masqued balls and lavish parties to start the celebration. Serlanos declared my blood as his and now it was time for him to make good on that declaration in front of the entire Blood Syndicate. Facing a room full of bloodthirsty vampires that would feed from me were it not for Serlanos' claim on me only made my blood run cold. I feel a shiver and rub my arms, hoping to find a blanket to cover up with.

But looking down at myself, I felt my skin crawl with the dirt and blood smeared on my skin. The bruises left by freakishly strong vampires restraining me to bring me here. Defensive wounds from kicking the shit out of Callum as he violently manhandled me in the penthouse.

The last thing I wanted to do is soil the one bit of comfort in this cold crypt. That stone bathtub looked like an escape that I could use right now.

The water squirted and spat from the large carved spout as I turned on the faucet. I sit on the edge of the tub and pour in the bath potions that were left on the vanity.

For a moment I get lost in the spiraling swirls of different colored soaps bubbling together in the tub. Disassociation. Sometimes it's necessary when one is thrust into a waking nightmare. One that they've spent their lifetime escaping.

The tub was steaming with hot water.

I shed the scraps of my clothes, dropping them to the floor.

Exposed. Vulnerable.

But I stepped into the tub anyway and let the water consume me.

The bubbles wrap around me, welcoming me in. I lay back against the tub wall and let the bubbles build around me, taking in my surroundings.

The bathroom, while dark, was calming. Quiet. Peaceful. Allowing me a moment to gather my thoughts without interruption.

Numbness took over, physically and emotionally, a sign that dissociation was settling in like a familiar creature of the night.

I was trapped, with no certain escape planned, and somehow I felt fine.

That's probably just the shock of my situation.

There's a part of me, however, certain that I was going to somehow escape.

I've escaped Serlanos before, I can do it again.

It's a matter of choosing my moment. It's me versus a horde of vicious vampires that want to drain me of my blood or use me as their personal fuck toy.

I had to act fast. Think ahead of their own game.

Someone is coming soon to dress me for this masqued ball that is consequently also my wedding party. The chance for Serlanos to claim me before the whole syndicate. To prove that he could get whatever he wanted, whenever.

I could use this to my advantage.

As the bubbles grow around me, my body becomes more relaxed. The essential oils or whatever was in these bath potions were massaging, licking my body, easing my aching bones. I am falling deeper into a relaxed state.

Lenora.

A voice calls me in deeper, inviting me to completely let go of all inhibitions. I am at my most vulnerable and yet I didn't care. The room could be on fire but I couldn't give one fuck right now.

The water works its way between my legs and immediately I am aroused. I let the water carry me away somewhere far from here mentally.

Washing over my body in waves, the water took a more corporeal form. Sensual curves pressed against mine as if the water had taken on a feminine shape, holding me against her as she washes my body with her own. Soft kisses trickle down my neck, relaxing the tense muscles and aches from being tossed around, and then I feel two hands cup the side of my face.

I open my eyes and before me is the most ethereal beauty, with long flowing silver hair and skin as pale and bright as the moon. Her bright red painted lips poised for seduction. Her bright yellow eyes fluttered with lustrous admiration as they took in my awe. Her curves fit in with my own and she stood at eye level with me.

This could only be Ordelia.

"I've waited a long time to meet you, Lenora Holmwood," my name sounds like a spell on her lips. "To meet the mortal that Serlanos has claimed for his path to ascension." She starts circling behind me, her fingers trailing across my bare skin. Her touch is sensual and debilitating as she envelopes me under her spell. She circles back in front of me and draws me in close. Her wet naked body pressed up against mine. Mutual desire percolates between us.

Our lips almost touching, she whispers, "And I have to beg you to forgive me for indulging myself, but I just have to know how you taste. Before *he* ruins you."

Ordelia entombs my lips with her own, parting my lips with her tongue, she consumes me. Her manicured hands play with me, pulling at my nipples and then trace the curvature of my body, tormenting me, finding their way to my pooling center. She plucks at my torment, her delicate fingers trace my entrance, her desire transfixed on every gasping breath I release at her expense as she teases me. She does not abandon any part of her command over me. With her white fangs, she delves into my neck, near where Llewyn fed before and the familiar sting benumbs my whole body as she punctures through my skin.

I feel the pull of my blood against her lips as she drinks from me. Ordelia drank my desire as she entwined herself with me. My orgasm builds as she feasts on my blood, her hands imprison me in a trap of ethereal bliss, as she pulses two fingers in and out of me.

The release was uncontainable, and did not relent for even a moment. Ordelia delights in what easy prey I was and how I wordlessly submitted to her indulgence.

And the truth was in that I was under her spell the moment she whispered my name like a siren calling out to sea.

I unravel around her finger as she ravishes me, sating our desires at once.

Relinquishing her lips from neck, she laps up the dribbles of blood before using her own saliva to heal the wound. Dizzy from blood loss and bliss, Ordelia takes over the rest of the washing, letting me sit back against the back of the tub as she washes my body.

"I remember the night he ruined me. I vowed to never let it happen again and yet here I am, preparing you for the same pointless ceremony. I take good care of my girls, Lenora. And if you will let me, I can take care of you too. An immortal life does not have to be completely miserable, not if you let it."

My hair cascaded down my shoulder, curled and pinned precisely. Ordelia's fingers ran through my hair as she gently dressed me as I stared into the mirror, benumbed to everything that had happened up to this point. Picking up the silver bullet pendant from the dressing table, she places it on me, despite the burns it engraved on her fingers.

"Never take this off again," she whispers in my ear before kissing my cheek, reawakening the warm feeling she cast on me before.

I've kissed girls before. My first kiss with a girl occurred late at night at church after a youth group, before God and the few choir boys that were looking in, giggling and ready to run off to tell one of the elders.

I remember how the world slowed around us as she made the first move, after weeks of friendship and skipping confirmation class to explore some part of the church's basement.

That was my first step into becoming a 'bad lesbian influence' as the mother of the girl called me. Mom and Dad didn't humor any hate towards me, we stopped going to church soon after. Not that it was a big deal at that time. Going to church felt too strenuous.

Theo and I were at an age in which we could choose for ourselves. I just think Mom was tired of spending Sundays convincing us to go to church when she herself barely wanted to go. Soon Sundays became a day at home to lounge around and do homework. Dad stopped going with us to church long before this, and Mom caught the brunt of the whispers about his business from the elderly ladies in the congregation. The ones who once praised my father for his work now shot scolding stares across the pews as the offering plate was passed around.

Now I understand though, it wasn't because of me we stopped going. It was Dad. I don't think he could face the shame of working with a devil like Serlanos.

I never did hear from that girl again. Rumor was she moved away. Ordelia's girls quietly attended to my make up and nails, the curl of jealousy playing on their lips as they provide forced praise.

"He will absolutely melt when he sees you," the one tending to my nails would say each time I sniffled as if it's a comforting thought to have someone like Serlanos find you attractive.

"Ladies, this is Lenora Holmwood. She will be your ladyship. We will follow her command as she will be one with Serlanos. And his will is law. Treat her with the respect that she deserves, as tonight she faces the same sacrifice we made so long ago. We will be her guide and her greatest confidantes in all terms of affairs associated with the Gyanstazi family. If she asks you to do something, you do it."

The other vampiresses nodded in obedience but none of them meant it. I could see it in their envious red eyes. What makes her so special?

I wish someone would fucking tell me.

48

callum gyanstazi

Cemetery Drive - My Chemical Romance

I pace the crimson draped stone halls outside Serlanos' private chambers waiting for him to call me in and grant me his official blessing for the first rites ceremony at dawn. To consummate the turning of flesh to ash, to brand the mark of the first that was cursed to roam the earth forever. It would be the greatest honor. And Serlanos promised it to me. Long before the hunt for Lenora Holmwood began.

And Serlanos doesn't go back on his word.

The bride in waiting was moved to a more superior suite to dress for the ceremony. She was still sullen and withdrawn when I retrieved her from her cell and escorted her to the grandest chamber suite the catacombs had to offer. The walls of this place screamed with the burden of housing the undead; and she feared joining them.

The door to Serlanos chamber peels open and I am beckoned in by his dhampir attendant.

Serlanos stands gallantly before a full size mirror that sits in the middle of the archaic chamber room. Suited in a crimson long-tailed devil coat, embroiled with black lace paisley patterns, he looked like Red Death in-

280

carnate. "Callum, I am glad you're here tonight is a big night, my boy. The night everything changes for us. Tell me, how do I look?"

"Over dramatic at best."

"Hmm. Fashion was never your thing. However, tonight you must look the part."

He throws a suit-bag and unzips it to find one identical to his inside. The suit I am to wed Ms. Holmwood.

"Go get dressed. And check in to see if my bride is being given the best treatment. I don't want her in foul spirits on our wedding night."

Dead weight filled my hollow nerves. What did he just say?

"Wait—your bride? But you promised her to me: I brought her in when no one else could. Not even Llewyn, your lost cause project," my blood hot with rage against my chilled skin.

"Plans change, Callum . Considering her blood value. I'm going to need her for more than a good fuck and bloodletting."

Rage twitched under my skin- my mouth dry with betrayal.

I can't tell which is worse; Serlanos' betrayal or Llewyn's. I can't fucking trust anyone in this lair.

"But you promised that I would get to be the one to actually marry her. You only made the claim to-"

"Tough shit," he spits sharply each syllable like a strict pluck of a flat violin string.

"I brought her in, this is bull shit Serlanos."

"And you will be rewarded for your services,"Serlanos says, vainly straightening the lace kerchief at his neck.

I've heard enough. Whatever his reasoning, his words meant nothing to me anymore. I storm out before any more lies can spew from his mouth.

Lenora seemed disgusted at the prospect of being wed to me.I can only imagine how sickened and horrified when she learned she'd be officially bonding with Serlanos himself. She was more than just a bond, bought and sold. I should have known that he was claiming her as his all along when Roderick began boasting to the others that Serlanos had promised him first rytes.

Speaking of the creepy asshole, he's lurking outside the corridor leading to Lenora's chambers. Coveting what's just beyond his reach. What was never his to begin with.

Nor mine.

"What are you doing here?" I spit a thim.

"I'm sure you heard the boss's news," Roderick sounded disgruntled. Just as the rest of us. We only believed that he was claiming her for the family, for all of us. Not for some sort of blood ritual. All of his other wives he's shared, what is so different with Lenora? He couldn't actually believe that he could have an actual marriage with her, could he?

I don't respond. Everyone's heard, I was last on the list. I'm not going to let Serlanos stop me. I continue onward, doing what Roderick was too afraid to do. Take what's his. And she was never his.

She was promised to be mine.

I enter the dressing chambers to see the bride dripping in black and crimson threaded together with gold. She was a vision that would mark the death of any man that cast eyes on her beauty.

Serlanos doesn't deserve this perfect creature.

Nor does Roderick.

And what of Llewyn?

Two of Ordelia's sluts fuss over Lenora who wears a ghastly expression. Staring at herself as the black lace veil is placed on her head, her long cascading hair covered with shades of death.

"Get out." I order the two strigas who hiss and snarl as they shudder past me; leaving us alone. Lenora stiffens like a wild deer entering flight-or-fight from a wild predator as I approach"

"How can I help you?"she demands, twirling her hair.

"You look absolutely stunning," I feel my dick throb against my leg. The dress she wore would be on the floor in a matter of seconds if it were up to me.

"Thank you," she responds timidly, waiting for me to have something else to say. But all thought leaves my mind and rage takes over knowing that this beautiful creature is going to be Serlanos' new fuck toy.

I advance on her, she freezes as I approach, shuddering as I raise a hand to her porcelain face.

"You were supposed to be mine," I lament outloud, not caring that she knows how much I wanted this to be real, even though I knew deep down it never would be.

"I don't think I am supposed to be anyones," she whispers nervously as I lean in closer.

"Maybe you're right," I say as my lips crash against hers, my eyes sting with the feeling of knowing what will never be. She doesn't resist, and not because she felt the same regret. I know she bares no feelings for me. But because she too needed to know who she was meant for. I read Llewyn's name on her lips.

They were always his from the begining.

Breaking the kiss, I whisper a word to her I never thought I would speak.

"Run."

49

lenora holmwood

Heaven Help Us - My Chemical Romance

The long hem of the beautiful crimson bridal gown floats behind me as I dash down the hallowed halls of the underground vampire lair, hopeful there wasn't an enemy lurking in the shadows around the corner.

Jagged pieces of bone protrude from the crumbling clay tunnel walls threatening to tear or snag, pulling me back into the cryptic lair with no plans of letting me go. How long would it be before someone noticed I had escaped? I pick up the hem of my dress and quicken my pace, but cautiously dodge a sharp piece of rock that protrudes from the wall like a threatening fang. Skeletal hand fragments reach out as if to grab and keep me here.

I reach the stairwell and begin the ascent from hell. When I was moved from the dungeon to the bed chambers I didn't keep count of how many floors up that we traveled but I was grateful I wasn't starting the climb from the bottom. I peaked over the railing and could hear the faint echo of tortured screams from below. I shudder away from the edge and focus on my footing on the rigid steps, praying I will never haunt these walls with presence again.

284

The dress snags and catches on the barbed edges, each time I fear a fanged fiend has caught me in his claws, and let out a deep sigh each time it's just a skeletal fragment or a stone cut just at the right angle. I need to ditch the dress. It's slowing me down.

The top is near, a bright halo of light cast itself at the rough archway opening I came through. Just beyond that an emergency exit.

I just need to keep pushing forward.

I hope Llewyn comes or finds me before someone else does. I couldn't wait for him to rescue me-I saw my chance and took it. I just want to find him and get as far from here as possible. somewhere only we know. I just hope we find each other. Before it's too late.

Nearing the top, the stairs become impossibly steep and are partially deteriorated. I cling to the railing and hoist myself past the crumbling masonry. The black heels I am wearing are killing me. I step carefully up to the landing but find the back heel of my shoe is tightly wedged in a crack of the masonry. If they weren't buckled at the ankles would ditch them and make a run for it barefoot. I tug and pull, almost losing my footing and tumbling backward down the stone stairs to my death. But I catch myself on the decaying bone-tied railing.

Just as I feel my foot loosen from the stone stair crevice, I feel a dark looming shadow cast over me.

I am not alone.

"Tsk, tsk. What do we have here? A damsel in distress?"

I freeze in place.

My malefic bridegroom stands over me, wearing an expression that is somewhere between enraged and smugly triumphant that he was the one that caught me.

He kneels down and grasps my foot at the ankle and removes it from its stone tomb with such ease it was nearly embarrassing. He looks me dead in the eye, his hand drifting upward toward the hem of my dress.

"You do have quite an aptitude for escape. You may have eluded my men, but you will no longer slip through my grasp. And after tonight, you will be bound to me forever. In flesh and blood."

With little to no effort, Serlanos lifts me over his shoulder and begins the descent back into hell.

I kick and scream and thrash my body, hoping the inertia would send us both tumbling down the stairs.

"The more you fight this my dear, the harder our union is going to be," he sneers.

His grip on me is strong, his claws dug into some exposed thigh as the hem of the dress rides up. I wince and cry out, in pain and hopelessness. The cold sting of my blood dripping down my leg only reminds me of my failure.

I had the chance and I took it to run. And I still got caught.

I've let myself down.

I promised myself I would no longer be a prisoner to anyone.

Not Grandpa, not Llewyn, and especially not Serlanos.

llewyn hellsinger

Kill All Your Friends - My Chemical Romance

Riskel arrives at the Penthouse with a stone face, showing no signs of panic, and immediately begins tending to Cynfael. Even as he's patching Cynfael up, who still was insisting he was good to go. Loyal and unwavering to the core. Several of Cynfael's other henchmen filed into the room, locked and loaded for a good fight. Leandro, a short stocky vampire with dark greased back hair, sizes me up as he enters the room. Immediately feeling challenged by my presence.

Faine and Payne, twin brothers that coil together like slithering snakes, followed in behind, full of blood-crazed energy.

"Jesus, boss, the fucker got you good," Leandro says, kneeling down close, but Riskel pushes him out of the way.

Half of Cynfael's left leg was still regenerating and he could barely stand. Regeneration is a painful process for a vampire to endure. The stretching and pulling of the tendons and ligaments as new tissue forms at a rapid pace and sews itself back together. I can barely begin to watch as Riskel poured a mysterious mixture from a flask on the wound, speeding up the process grotesquely.

"So what's the plan?" Faine asks, licking his lips ready for action. The looks on some of them say that they've been waiting for this for a long time. Tensions have been high for far too long, waiting for the last thread to break into a war. A blood war. Facing the largest blood shortage in decades, we vampires are forced to claim what's left by silver and fire. Using our own kinds' greatest weapon against each other. Serlanos has made enough empty promises to the entire syndicate.

Promising an end to our undying thirst. Paving a way to an indestructible, immortal life. All a bunch of hooey from that damn old bastard that claimed he found the path to immortality by drinking only the purest in blood.

"We're going to be invading the Gyanstazi chapter of the Cosa Nosferatis headquarters. Since you don't hold residence there, you won't be able to enter without a guardian. Since I am public enemy number one in their eyes, I won't be able to get us in there without a little bloodshed."

"What is our mission?" Leandro demands, as if he needed more of a reason to go kill off the most powerful underworld boss in Chicago.

"To find and rescue Lenora Holmwood."

"The girl that Serlanos has been after this whole time? Why? He's got her. The search is ove-"

"Because I am in love with her. And I said so."

"So what, you're the boss now just because you defected from your family. No way, I -"

"Leandro, you will listen to him! Does it look like I can lead you in a love-driven rampage right now?" Cynfael cuts him off. "Riskel, is the mobile armory fully stocked?"

Riskel grunts in confirmation as he binds Cynfaels leg with medical gauze to catch any green seepage. Like a beast, Riskel picks Cynfael up like a ragdoll and carries him to the elevator and down to the running vehicle.

In the back of the SUV, an armory of silver loaded firearms of various calibers. Some had scopes and other equipment. I enjoy a handgun but the rifle seemed tempting.

"Pick your poison, Llewy," Payne gleefully stands over to watch my amazement at their collection of vampire hunting gear. *Oh I intend to.*

"Do you know where we are going exactly? That place is a maze from what I remember," Cynfael yells from the front seat as he messes with the on-screen gps.

"Yes. But we must be fast. Serlanos has expanded his part of the nest to the underground tunnels that spread throughout the city so he can travel quickly. If they've moved from the nest, they could be anywhere. Even in parts outside of the city."

"Where is the nest located?"

"Below the Art Institute. The catacombs."

"And how are we going to get there without him or his henchman noticing?"

"You'll see. Make a right here on Broadway and park." Riskel follows my instructions with no hesitation.

Just to the left a block down was the Dark Parlor, one of Serlanos's favorite hangouts.

"The Dark Parlor? Really?" Leandro scoffs as he climbs out and observes our target entry point.

"Yup. There's a secret entrance to the tunnels. These tunnels were once used during prohibition. But since vampires infiltrated the mortal outfits they've been used for underground travel for the syndicate."

"I know about the damn tunnels, I just didn't think that Serlanos would frequent somewhere as flamboyant as the Dark Parlor," Leandro laughs to himself.

Cynfael, damn his soul, clamors out of the back seat, his left leg struggles and wobbles beneath him as he puts his weight on it.

"I'm a little stiff, but I can do this," he attempts through his whimpers.

"Are you sure?" We will need a getaway vehicle once we have Nora. Someone to keep a lookout in case any of Serlanos's men are coming."

Cynfael looked at me with the saddest of eyes, like a small child that was told they were going to miss out on festivities and games.

But his expression matured and he accepted it.

"You're right. But if you see Callum, please tell him I said—oh god, no that sounds so lame still if I have you say it."

"Gee thanks and here I thought my delivery of 'Fuck You' was beyond reproach."

"No, it's just that I want the payback to come from me directly. It just won't mean as much coming from you. I just want the fucker to really know how I feel."

I place a comforting hand on Cynfael's shoulder.

"And you will have that moment. I promise you. But now is not that time."

Cynfael sulked but he understood, seeing as he can barely stand without holding onto me or the side of the car.

"Please come back. I'd hate to hear that you've fallen back into his web of lies. Getting you out the first time was no easy task."

I kiss Cynfael on the forehead. He has no idea how thankful I am for him helping me believe for just a moment that I could be free.

"When we return we are getting out of here like a bat out of hell."

"That's my boy. Now go get your human."

Riskel nodded at Cynfael who got back in the car and locked the doors. Anticipating an ambush.

Pane and Faine are up in the latest of vampire hunting weapons, including silver throwing stars and automatic crossbows.

"Goddamn, whose monster hunter rig did you rob? Van Helsing's?"

I've never seen weaponry like this before.

"Close to it. Best in the vampire hunting market. I mean what better way to kill a vampire than go to the ones that do it for a living?" Leandro has the look of a gleeful young boy with a new toy in his hands.

I laugh in agreement. "That's great and all but maybe something a bit more discreet. We don't want to look too obvious going into the bar, no repeats of the diner incident. Some would think we are there to torch the place. We want in and out. No casualties if we can help it. We aren't here to start another turf war - however that is what will follow if we succeed. We must find Nora and leave as quickly as possible."

"And if we are caught?"

"Let it rain."

We file through the black swinging door and are met with the comforting aromas of pipe tobacco and all the glamor of a rum-running establishment. Low-lit and lofi vibes only. Dark souls of the underground crawl out of the grimiest of corners to meet here.

It's not a place for mortals. Dhampirs convene at the bar, whispering to themselves as we pass. They recognize me, glaring or admiring in awe.

Knowing that I am here and not with my normal crew, that bound to turn some heads. I would not be surprised if there were spies here, updating Serlanos on my every move. Which is why we must move quickly and entertain nothing from those that might want to start a brawl to delay us.

The bouncers do not question our presence as I march us past to the far back of the lounge, however the attention of others in the room was distilled by our presence. We disappear behind the black curtain separating the private rooms and the main lounge.

At the far back of the long hall was a stone statue of a book upon an altar.

"What are you doing? I thought that the entrance was in the basement?" Leandro complains. He's resisting my leadership. I can feel the animosity in his voice.

"One of them is." I approach the altar and examine it. On the threshold of the altar was an ornate sundial. I turn the dial two clicks to the left, lining up the horizon to sunset. The mantel lurches and groans before shifting forward to reveal an opening with a tight stone staircase leading into unknown darkness.

"After you," I gestured to Leandro towards the stairs who was growing impatient with my command already. I could tell he didn't completely trust me, nor could I blame him. I am leading him right into enemy territory and was at one point Serlanos' most trusted ally.

But with what I've done already, I am a traitor. But the others don't know that. For all they know this could be an ambush and I am a double crosser. How else do I prove to them that I am not?

Riskel is watching me closely. I was certain that if anything were to go wrong he would break me beyond regeneration. There can be no fuck ups. Everyone that has come in with me into this dark crypt will come back out with me, plus one.

The one. My one.

I must find her.

lenora holmwood

Horizon -Aldous Harding

Serlanos supervises from the sidelines as his undead servants work anxiously to repair the torn hem in my dress from my failed escape attempt. I wear a look of contempt, my ankle shackled by a chain to a ring in the ground. Serlanos dangled the key, standing afar taunting me with it. Just out of reach. My freedom is hanging on by a string.

I refuse to look at him. I can't, not without crying or wanting to scream and neither are going to help me right now. I can't give him the satisfaction that he has any sort of effect on me. He's been trying to win my affections, and will continue to fail miserably. Nothing could possess me to admire the man in any capacity. The embarrassment of being caught and then carried over his shoulder has yet to have worn off. A devilish smile spreads across his face as he can see the tears that beg to form in my eyes. I am cloaked in hopelessness. He holds the key to my freedom and he will never let me go.

Not until he's taken all that I have left to give. And he deserves none of it. I feel bile form in my mouth at the thought of him even touching my body. The way he undressed me with his eyes and feasted upon me like some slab of meat.

"Chin up, my love. Soon we will be wed and will be able to consummate our union."

"I would hardly call this a willful union, sir. I thought you needed a willing vassal to complete a blood bonding ritual."

"And what do you know of dark magic, my sweet?"

"I read, so enough."

His face falls into a less than patient expression. "As long as you do as you are told, it will be an amicable one. And maybe I will make sure my soldiers go easy on you when I am finished with you."

"And what is it that you so desperately need from me? Haven't you taken enough already?" my voice trembles as I feel the ferocity of my words escaping my lips. I want to cry. I am so angry.

He advances closer and fiercely grabs my face in his cold, dead hands, forcing a contemptuous kiss, his lips demanding submission upon touch, his tongue pierces like a scythe, ripping and parting my lips and dominating, leaving no room for resistance even though I had tried. His sharpened fangs begged for a sample as he bites my lip, relishing in my pain as I wince. He pulls my lip in, drawing blood and leaving his one of many marks.

He breaks away and stares into my tear ridden eyes, stroking my cheek. "Not even close."

The black veil is placed and covers the pain of his kiss on my lips, and my pride, as I am led by Serlanos in arm down a dark tunnel towards my doom.

The jagged tunnel walls begin to close in on me just as Serlanos' hold on my arm tightens, his long nails digging in deep, I can feel the sting of blood rising to the surface as he breaks the skin with little effort. I winced and blinked back tears that I was already choking on.

My lip still throbbed with the sting of his venomous kiss. My stomach twisted in knots.

"The Blood Syndicate are awaiting us, my dear. It is time for us to declare our vows. You look ravishing."

I vow to shit on everything you love or even remotely enjoy. I remain silent. I have no response. Nothing that will help me now.

Dread spreads like a plague and consumes me. I want to collapse but the firm hold on my arm keeps me on my feet and pressing forward. Llewyn tried his best to explain the ritual to me as his archives were unclear on the details, the ingredients needed, or how many sacrifices one needed to create a blood bond. Bonded in blood and flesh, which was more than I wanted to bare to this man who has taken everything and left nothing in return. Not even to his most loyal subjects. He starves them with promises of eternal power and invincibility.

But how does he plan to achieve that with me? Am I to feed them for all of eternity? Be a slave to a nest of blood thirsty and merciless beasts that have no regard for human life? Or even become one of them?

In the hall waiting for us, vampires adorned in their finest waistcoats and tailored vests or draped in lavish black lace gowns. Their faces hidden by intricately designed masques, ready for a celebration of the millenia. The glow of superiority and violence emanated from them as they all curtsy and bow as Serlanos and I enter the corridor and silently follow us as we begin down the long path, to which Serlanos took it upon himself to entertain us with

"Through our union, you will be granted every power that I have. You will be seen as equal with the Cosa Nosferati. You and I will be one, fused together by our blood. A bond that will follow us beyond the grave. Beyond oblivion. But with that will come responsibility."

"I think you've got the wrong girl, Mr. Gyanstazi."

"No, I haven't. And it's Lord Gyanstazi from here onward," he corrected me. I resisted rolling my eyes. *Serious, Lord?* " I've been waiting for you for a while now. Ever since I set eyes on you. Your father tried to bargain for your safety. Knowing what your blood can do. He tried to pay that debt."

"What is so special about my blood compared to the others?" I demand to know. I was tired of this guessing game of what he wanted from me.

Whether it's my soul, body, or blood he will have none of them.

"Your father never told you?" Serlanos stops in his tracks and looks at me with disbelief. "Oh darling, aren't you a naive treat?"

"Are you going to enlighten me?" I can feel a mix of impatient fury and terror in my voice.

"I would much rather show you," the malice in his response turns my blood to ice.

Every part of me tells me to fight and run, but his grasp on me is too strong. I was surrounded by bloodthirsty vampires that drooled and snarled at me each time I looked over my shoulder at them. If it weren't for Serlanos, I'd be at their mercy. I avoided their eye contact as we paraded down the hall towards the stairwell heading downwards towards hell. The screams grew louder as we descended back to the dungeons.

"I have spent years searching for someone like you, Lenora Holmwood. Beautiful, smart, and with a strong bloodline. And now you're about to become Lady Gyanstazi, which comes with responsibility. Unlike my previous wives, you will stay by my side. You will have equal my power and respect from the Blood Syndicate. My claim on you offers protection that is punishable by death if violated. I'd like to show you what happens to those who touch you without my permission."

Please Llewyn, do not come. I know he can read my thoughts. If he is anywhere close, please let him be listening. I need him alive. I need there to be hope. I don't know how this will end but knowing he's out there somewhere gives me comfort.

"What makes my blood so strong? You've yet to enlighten me."

"Seeing as we have a great distance to go, I will fill you in. Are you familiar with the legend of Draxius Khor?"

"Of course, but what does that have to do with me?" I am really tired of him not getting to the point. It's that smuggish tone in his voice that tells me he does it deliberately, to appear charming. The vampire charm he had was wearing thin and I doubt marrying me will give him back that spark, nor consuming my blood.

"Everything, my dear. He was the original vampire to have ascended. Following his mortal death, he rose again, only to search for his wife and his loyal familiar, Zephirah," he goes on, the sinister female vampire in the cloak beside Serlanos smiles as if he's getting to her favorite part in a bedtime story.

"The one who led him to the answer. Now he had to spread the good word to his family. His wife, Ioanela Balauru, was of noble blood and her father, Lord Theodor Baluru resented her union with Draxius from the start. Finding his practices obscene and deemed evil amidst the rise of the vampire hysteria in Romania. After her husband's death, reports of his appearance haunted his poor wife into madness where she was later committed for hallucinations claiming that her husband was calling her to join him. After the first night she was found pale and near death with two pricks on her neck. And by morning she was cold with the kiss of death."

"So he did succeed."

"Had you not finished your reading, dear girl?" He said with a touch of arrogance in his voice, as if he gives off the impression of a well-read person.

"My copy of the legend was unfinished."

"Very well, it is not your fault for not knowing. Yes, he did succeed and then some, paving the way for us now. You are about to be very well endowed indeed, carrying on the legacy for bloodlines to come."

"He had children. What became of them? Surely he did not leave them behind."

"They were taken by Loanela's father, as soon as she was committed to the seminary with a sickness similar to her beloveds. For their protection, much like your own grandfather did, took them in and hid them away from the world, moving farther than Khor's empire could reach. And that my dear is where you come in. I have traced his roots back and forth, finding the line that led to the incompleteness of the Khor Dynasty. And it led me back to you."

To me? I may not know much about my family tree but I am pretty sure Dad would have mentioned I am related to some vampire lord from Transylvania, right? I did heritage projects in schools and Dad mentioned we had eastern European roots but wasn't specific. I knew about as far as my grandparents and that was it. Our family was small and close knit, but not too close.

"How can you be so certain?"

"A sample of your blood fell into my hands. None of this was by accident. Our union will complete the covenant that Draxius Khor set out to do. And your blood will make our dynasty strong. As we will create more vampires, an army of beasts that are indestructible. Securing our place at the top of the food chain.We will live forever."

The missing piece of the puzzle that everyone but me has finished. Dad knew as did Theo, and yet somehow I was left out. It was as simple as telling me my birth story. All of Serlanos' hopes are drawn on a legend. A myth. Sure Khor found the path to immortality in becoming a vampire, but how is it that consuming more blood could make one more powerful, that unless it possesses some otherworldly magic ability? I am still unclear how magic truly fits into this world. There were a lot of truths and untruths that Llewyn could neither confirm nor deny. I don't know if this was due to him not knowing or under the belief that keeping this information from me would protect me.

I don't understand this shielding of information considering all my family has preached my whole life about how knowledge was power. Dad didn't question my activities outside of school because I carried a 4.0 GPA and was on the debate team and literally fulfilled the role of perfect daughter. Why wouldn't Dad want to empower his children that were being head hunted by a power hungry vampire? And how did Serlanos get my blood?

I am quiet. I don't press further as knowing more won't save me from what is about to come. Yet all of these thoughts gnawed away at me as we descended further back towards the dungeon, closer to the screaming. I don't want to see what horrors lie beyond what I've already seen.

We reach the very bottom, screams of terror permeate Serlanos pushes me through the chamber towards a heavy door, the chamber next to the one with the shish-kebab corpses and heavy stench of decaying flesh, my stomach revolts and turns and I resist the urge to vomit.

The chamber room housed another large locked door that was adorned with gothic carvings and the Cosa Nosferati emblem as the locking mechanism.

"It truly is terrible down here, isn't it?" Serlanos notes as he pulls out the keys to the locked door. Screams emulate from inside, beckoning us to stay away, or help whatever poor creature is in there.

"You designed it that way, sire," one of the vampires in the escort party pointed out.

"Ah yes, it has the effect I was going for."

"Terror, doom and hopelessness? Yep, you nailed it," my mouth speaks before I could restrain my intrusive thoughts.

Serlanos lets that comment slide, but I have a feeling my humor is not going to be appreciated here as much as it was with Llewyn.

"You will find, Ms. Holmwood, that with the power that I hold, it will do well in your favor to respect me," Serlanos reminds me.

"Respect is earned, not granted. And therefore you will have none of mine."

"I think you will find that you will be changing your attitude once you see what's behind this door," he declared, turning the lock and pulling the door open.

The door opened casting the only light in the chamber on the center of the room where a bleeding, bare chested Callum kneels, chained to the floor. He'd healed from the stab wound I delivered to him in my attempt to escape, but that was nothing compared to the open lashes on his chest and back. Two of Serlanos' burliest henchmen hoist Callum to his feet as Serlanos approaches him. Looking down his crooked nose, Serlanos meets Callum's fear stricken eyes. His pride diminished along with his smug and arrogant mug.

"You know why I have to punish you, right, Callum?" Serlanos commands Callum to answer, but Callum refuses. "Answer me!"

"I let he-her go. I am sorry-I" Callum starts to whimper as one of the demented beasts behind him cracks the whip. He winces in fear.

"No, no, not that. Although that was bad, you did something much worse, my boy. You touched what was rightfully mine. On the night before our vows are to be declared, you touched my wife! And without my consent. After I had just told you that my intentions were to make her mine, unlike the others which you've had your fill of sloppy seconds. Just like the orphan boy I found you as, searching the rubbish looking for the leftovers of others' greatness."

Callum hangs his head, drooling with remorse. "I am sorry- I'm so sorry."

I watch in pitiful horror as this poor creature has bent over backwards to please this monster only to collapse before him. And yet even as he cowers before Serlanos, he still remains loyal. Begging for forgiveness, for another chance. There is never truly pleasing this monster, why are we all dying to do so? Who or what benefits from it? No one. Except Serlanos.

Serlanos picks up one of the tall pikes, like the ones in the chamber next door, Callum trembles with fear. I close my eyes, for I cannot bear a second more of Serlanos' cruelty.

52

llewyn hellsinger

The Only Hope For Me Is You - My Chemical Romance

The Gyanstazi headquarters is an underground fortress of tombs. A labyrinth of darkness that I have found myself locked in countless times. All of the different passages that lead to various points in the city. If Nora even attempts to escape there's no telling where she would end up.

I just hope that we get to the nest before the Blood Rytes begin and Serlanos moves Lenora to the next location.

Where that next location might be, I might have a few guesses.

The dim light from the end of the passage is our only guide through this cryptic maze, which has expanded since my last visit. And we must watch ourselves carefully as any number of these walls or crumbling stone floors could be a trap. The Cosa Nosferati prided themselves on their abilities to trap wandering mortals like rats creeping into the small nooks of the world.

I hear my ragtag crew behind me, just as timid in their steps. They've heard the rumors of what goes on here— being a part of Cynfael's family, they wouldn't have had to witness it. His crew doesn't come here.

And they are counting on me to lead them through here unscathed, while I made no such promise. They know the risk, but I am the reason we

302

are here. I am the idiot that cannot just let Serlanos have this human. And there's no guarantee I will make it out of here, and that's okay. As long as she does.

I am walking into the spider's nest expecting mercy when I have destroyed what Serlanos has worked hard for, he has no reason to keep me now, except to punish me. Which is a good reason but his punishments are lacking their luster, and since my last infraction, I am already on a warning from the Blood Syndicate. Talon and Ordelia wouldn't approve.

What excuses me from responsibility while these laws have governed them for decades?

Nothing. While Serlanos has spread carnage, I have betrayed the oath. And that is way worse.

I also already had a warning against me since Serlanos found out about Emily and Calvin.

I will face execution should we fail.

The tunnels turn and twist and jagged pieces of bone jut out catching our clothes. I hear Leandro curse as his sleeve tears on another sharp edge.

The Gyanstazi nest is empty. The tombs of the recruits are barren, their velvet lined coffins empty.

The elite of our kind have been called for command and have risen for the ceremony.

Which means we got to move fast.

Before Serlanos can sink his teeth into my Nora. I like to think that Lenora is fighting back, but she knows well enough that any attempt to resist will cost her her life.

These vampires could snap her neck at any moment if she chose to disobey. I hated the idea of her being a good girl just for the sake of survival. To submit herself to Serlanos just stay alive. I hope I get there before he takes her for himself.

The tunnels were more narrow and jagged than I remember, the bones of the dead reaching out in their last moments to be saved, only to be memorialized in the foundations of our lair.

We enter the Crimson Hall, the architecture inspired by fifteenth century gothic architecture. The floor was polished onyx stained wood with crimson carpet that extended to the dais where the four clan leaders that made up the Cosa Nosferatis sat on their grim iron thrones, deciding the fate for our kind. Choosing the racketts we've cornered and the ethics of bloodletting and feeding.

Vampires that broke our laws or made too much of a spectacle of their bloodshed were brought before the syndicate, tried and executed. Serlanos has taken the authority on deciding who was worthy of being turned out of the recruits that have been found lurking under the L and sleeping in parks. Those that were desperate for a change. Or craved power that they couldn't dream of. Those that have been wronged transform into vengeful monsters to exert their wrath on their perpetrator, an adulterous spouse or a spiteful colleague that has crossed them. Mortals seek revenge for the pettiest of reasons.

But so does Serlanos.

Cynfael has never taken his seat with the others. It sits there abandoned gathering dust and cobwebs.

Most of the current members of Cynfael's clan, with the exception of those who defected from the Gyanstazi family to join Cynfael, have never made their nest here. Cynfael never agreed with the idea of a governing body for vampires.

"That was the point of vampirism. To escape the pinnacles of humanity. Immortality offers a freedom that should be left untethered," Cynfael would dive headfirst into his typical drunken spiel on his philosophies on freedom and the meaning of afterlife in the private rooms of his clubs.

The Cosa Nosferatis disagreed with this philosophy. Cynfael defected from the Cosa Nosferatis, while he is still recognized as a leader in the underworld syndicate. His reputation buys him what he needs and when he needs it.

Our footsteps echo against the ghastly faint screams of the tormented souls that emanate from the walls. What's below us is far worse than where we are headed. As we approach the meeting chambers I feel a strenuous rasp come from inside.

"Llewyn...." A soft whisper coaxes me inside. It could be her.

Keeping my gun raised, I slid into the room from which I heard the noise. Tapestries have been torn from their hangings and are strewn about the floor in heavy lumps. The light falls dim as the candelabras burn low leaving little to bounce off the obsidian walls. The tall ornate dressing mirror is smashed to pieces. On the floor curled up into a ball, a woman sobbing relentlessly. Her dark hair matted over her eyes.

"Lenora?"

As I inch closer the woman is less corporeal and becomes nothing more than a pile of blood. Darkness takes the room as the blood bubbles and twists into mid air, like a fountain flowing in reverse and darts towards me at bullet speed.

Blood magic.

Zephirah is here.

Before I can flit away into the shadows, a bullet of blood hits me and becomes a monster of its own, expanding and roping around my body, binding me and draining me of any strength I have to fight back.

"How kind of you to join us this evening, Llewyn. I thought I was going to miss the chance of having a dance with you," a cool whimsical voice approaches from behind me.

"I'm surprised you dance outside of all the rituals, it must be tiring finding willing sacrifices these days."

"Not at all, there are hopeless souls ready to give to a good cause. You just have to go looking for them."

I don't need details but she is fucked up. For thousands of years this blood witch has been around, spouting the image of a medicine woman, only to find just a freak of nature wanting to play god. They should have burned her when they had the chance. Normally witches and vampires are amicable and in some ways simpatico. But Zephirah is another breed. Only aligned herself for power. Vampires take bonding seriously. Zephirah does not. When a vampire chooses you, it is written in law your souls are fated together. As Serlanos had with Lenora. As Draxius Khor had with Zephirah. Their partnership was more than just that for the cause.

"So tell me, what will it be? I know you have some punishment for me, stake or coffin?"

"It's going to be so much worse than that, I can assure you of that, Llewyn Hellsinger. You've been a bad boy. It's really a shame, because I love bad boys."

"Lord, don't we all."

The others were right behind me, where are they now? Or were they? Maybe they'd gotten separated from me and all of this has been some grand illusion. Fuck Zephirah and her mind games.

53

lenora holmwood

The Foundations of Decay - My Chemical Romance

Callum's screams of agony fill the chamber as we leave the chamber in an orderly fashion, Serlanos leading the party down the dark, cryptic tunnel. My chest in my heaved and my stomach revolted. No words parted my lips for the horrors that I've witnessed. Serlanos' callousness knew no bounds.

No one was safe.

That was made clear in his display of ruthlessness with Callum.

"You let her escape and after you touched her. You are a writhing pain in my ass. Why should I continue to help you, Callum?" Serlanos screamed in his face.

Callum chokes on the venomous silver consuming him as he attempts to beg for his life. "Pl-Please Serlanos. Don't."

"I've heard that too much from you lately. Here you are just as useless as I found you in that workhouse. Forever failing to rise to the task."

Callum trembles as Serlanos picks up a silver rod from the floor and stands over him, looking him deep in the eyes as he impales him, through and through. Black blood spurts from the top of the wound.

Tears form in my eyes as the horrible scene plays in front of me. The feeling of impending doom was no closer to dissipating. With the help of the two masked expressionless vampires, Callum is lifted into a coffin with spikes protruding from both the bottom and the top of the lid.

As the lid hangs open with threatening intent, Callum and I lock eyes for a hollow moment, tears stinging both of our eyes. Knowing that there is nothing that either of us can do, and in these final moments, I know Callum is saying what he couldn't outloud.

Even monsters can redeem themselves.

He wasn't apologizing to Serlanos, he was apologizing to me. And he didn't have anything to be sorry for.

The lid of the coffin falls shut with with a hard thud that echoes in my heart.

Serlanos advances on me and forces another domineering, rough kiss on my resistant lips.

"Don't worry, my dear. I am sure Llewyn won't miss this for the world. I count on him being here very soon," Serlanos sneers at me. "And then there next to his pitiful brother, he will spend all of eternity. You can visit him any time you want."

I could not hide my fear and hopelessness. And there is no escape.

I tried not to let my feelings display on my face for Serlanos to see, but it was too late. He already sensed it. Gripping my arm again he drags me out of the tomb, followed by our entourage of bloodsuckers and leads us down another narrow hall that darts in every way.

I wanted to tear away and make a run for it, while I still could. But I am surrounded by a throng of fancifully dressed vampires that were ready to kill at will if I were to make a run for it. Each of them glew with an aurora of wicked supremacy and glamor.

I wished to be anywhere but here surrounded by the dead and the undead. The foundation of the walls looks to be held together by the distantly departed, lost souls that got lost in the catacombs or were dragged down there as prey for its inhabitants.

I dare not ask which. I do not say anything at all.

All I can think about is Llewyn. All I want is for him to be anywhere but here.

I am living my worst nightmare and yet, I still think of him. I will always think of him.

After witnessing the gruesome way in which he impaled Callum upon the silver spike for his negligence in watching over my wellbeing, I almost wish Llewyn to stay away from here altogether. Forget about me and start a new life.

Let me endure the fate that was inevitable from the very beginning. Cursed to be Serlanos' wife for all of eternity and feeding him and his army of pureblood vampires.

I don't want him to fall victim to Serlanos' cruelty any longer than he has.

He has a chance of escaping Serlanos' control. Whereas I am doomed for eternity beside this monster.

I cannot imagine losing him just to save me. Vampires may be immortal but they are far from invincible as I have learned, as long as you have something stabby made of silver.

As valiant as a rescue mission would be, he doesn't owe me anything. Not even from the begining. And yet he did. He put his whole life on the line to save me, and even still is going to pay for it.

I cannot be the reason for his demise. I am one human.

"Just think— he will be here just in time to witness us consummate our union. Blood, flesh and soul. Bound together past the afterlife. This union will change both of our lives forever," Serlanos continues on.

I find my spare hand twirling the silver bullet pendant anxiously, remembering what my father said when he clasped it around my neck. *Maybe it will save your neck one day.* Llewyn failed to bite me that first time. He could only feed from me when I took it off. Same for Ordelia, who put it back on me, despite the burns it left on her hands.

Hopefully whatever this fucker tries— he will think twice if he even gets close enough.

54

llewyn hellsinger

Buried Alive - Avenged Sevenfold

Darkness envelops me like an old friend would embrace another here inside the coffin. I feel the wheels of the gurney carting me down the stone floors towards whatever hell hole Serlanos has deemed fitting for me.

A trap set by Serlanos, Zephirah was happy to oblige in participating in that ploy. He believed he finally taught me a lesson on obedience. I was his dog, that was why he turned me. It wasn't too long ago that I found myself in the penalty tombs, sitting in my own shit after the first time Serlanos caught me trying to have a normal life. The things he did to my wife then were unspeakable and I dare not mention it to torture her memory further. I remained in the box for nearly fifteen years.

Mostly missing the decade of Al Capone and where implemented himself further into the Cosa Nosferati. Climbing the ranks of the noblest of vampire families. Before Serlanos, there was no blood shortage. Talon ruled with lenience, and Cynfael was at least amicable. Ordelia was still human. Now everything is strained.

The Blood Syndicate, the lines of vampires across the nation would frown upon what was happening here. No vampire should have the power

311

that Serlanos is trying to obtain. Even vampires have their limits to playing God. Claiming humans was reserved for naming familiars and protected mortals and vassals. Not imprisoning mortals to blood bonds. Those that we turned were willing. Not forced.

And I cannot subject Lenora to the same fate that I have. Not unless she wanted it. Vampirism doesn't offer any freedom. It's a different kind of prison, a lonely one at that. One that I never believed in perpetuating because nothing ever lasts. It was only a matter of time before Lenora would be taken away from me, I was such a fool for believing that we could escape.

I hear a croak of someone choking in the coffin next to me. That fucker's spikes are much sharper than mine. Serlanos isn't done with my torture, he wants mine to be slow and agonizing. The guy next to me has it easy. A quick and painless- okay it's not painless. But you will be dust before the spikes completely impale you.

If I can manage to get out of here then maybe I can help the poor fuck. But I can't do anything for anyone if I stay here. I have nothing to repent for.

I apologize for nothing. No longer will I let Serlanos strip away what shred of happiness that I found. And I certainly won't let him destroy Lenora.

There's no way out of this without a little pain. With all my might, I roll my body against the wall, hoping the weight will knock this tomb off its catafalque.

SMACK! No movement.

Once more. THUMP.

A slight creaking comes from somewhere beneath me.

One more.

THUNK.

The box rolls and tumbles, I fall face flat against the lid of my tomb as it crashes to the ground. The corner of the coffin has busted open, I can probably kick it in and crawl out of here. The spikes jarring at the, now, top of the coffin still threaten to make their mark, one wrong move and I could be in trouble.

I slide down closer to the foot of the coffin and with what little room, raise my leg and kick with all my might, a spike grazing my leg as my foot makes contact with the wood of the coffin, sending pieces flying in every direction. As I draw my leg up once more, a large hand reaches in and grabs the edge of the coffin, ripping it apart. Through the dust and rubble, Riskel stands over me, with Leandro and the twins in tow, looking like they've been through hell just to get down here.

"So much for not getting caught, huh?" Leandro snarks as Riskel offers a hand to help me from the coffin remnants.

"Thank you, Riskel," I say, ignoring Leandro's remarks.

"What happened to you guys? I thought you were right behind me?"

"We thought we were too, and then you disappeared in that room. We looked in and saw nothing."

"A cloaking spell. Should have known."

We are all stilled by a rasping sound coming from the coffin next to where mine was laid to rest.

I slowly walk to the sarcophagus and lift the lid.

My chilled breath catches in my chest and sorrow dresses my face as I look down on my blood brother.

Callum - impaled through the chest with a silver rod that's bent at the end leaving no room for escape, grasping at anything to pull himself up.

My throat tightens and my heart wrenches as I take him in my arms. His chest rippled open at the seams revealing every decayed organ and reanimated tissue kept alive by this venomous curse.

"Llew," he sputters pitch-black blood from his mouth as he speaks. "I-I'm sorry brother."

"Shhh, I know, Cal. I know," I reach for the silver jagged spike pushing through the sucking wound, but he brushes my hand away.

"Please don't. Don't help me," he begs. I couldn't believe he was saying this, he of all people strived to live forever, and an opportunity for revenge was more than enough for Callum to want to stay.

"Callum, I need you."

"You don't. You never did," he struggles as he begins to disintegrate, the silver burning through him like fire burns through paper.

"That's not true," I feel my lower lip quiver as I look over my brother, my eyes redhot with tears.

The reflections of the days of us hunting in London, lurking in the shadows encircling our prey. He taught me everything I knew of this immortal life.

I learned once how to kill as a soldier, but Callum trained me how to kill as a vampire. How to enjoy the art of stalking my prey and feasting on their blood. Those memories were not for naught.

Callum's skin bubbles like hot wax, the wound festers and his bones begin to collapse inward like quicksand around the silver spike.

I've held many brothers in arms as they took their last breath on the battlefield surrounded by others that had fallen to their demise. Surrounded by death only to feel the guilt of surviving on the train ride home.

And still, I am here. Even in immortality, I am left feeling abandoned and guilty by those who somehow find a way to the other side.

"Kill...the...fucker."

You don't have to ask me twice, Callum.

I blink back the tears that I can't stop from bleeding in. Riskel urges me to keep moving with a nudge with his knee. Here, I lay my brother to rest in this dark cavernous, crimson-painted room.

The manic rage poured in. I feel my fangs extend and my claws drawn and the animal instinct to destroy everything in my path. Ripping through furnishings and fine art adorning the altar with the Gynastazi family emblem.

Riskel and the others step back away from the path of my rampage as I tear through the room like a vicious tornado of grief driven rage.

The rage dissipates with the speed of my destruction as I wear myself out and fall to the ground before the altar.

I lay my blood beaten hands on the ground, feeling the stone that was to entomb both me and Callum. Blood brothers torn apart by love and greed. That was what Serlanos wanted. For this to be a reminder that no one was safe from his ruthlessness, not even his supposed sons.

"Come on, man. If we are going to save your girl we need to get going," Leandro said, with a sparkle of a tear in his eye.

I never thought I would see one of Cynfael's men share a shred of remorse over a Gyanstazi. With one hand on the altar, I push myself back up.

CLUNK. What the fuck was that?

I step back as the wall behind the altar roughly glides back revealing the most elaborate embankment of blood I or any other being have ever set eyes on.

The years of ransacking blood banks, shaking down the owners and hijacking shipments from hospitals. This is where it has all gone.

We all look upon it in astonishment. Reaching to the top of the vaulted ceilings, rows upon rows of shelf units housing millions of blood samples.

This could feed an empire for the next millennium, amidst the largest blood shortage this country has seen.

The fucker has been sitting on all of this while we've all been starving.

Hidden behind a wall guarded by the body of his beloved son, Callum. Those would not dare to cross Serlanos to find what lay behind this door. The expansion of the Gyanstazi bloodline.

"What the fuck?" Leandro says, picking up a phial of blood sitting on the table in the middle of the room and examining it with pure envy etched on his face, mirroring the rest of us. Strange etchings carved into the surface of the table tell me this is used for blood magic. Zephirah the Dark Magistrate's area of expertise.

"Don't touch anything," I warn sternly.

But just as the words fall from my lips, the phial slips from Leandros fingers and shatters to the floor, splattering blood in multiple directions.

"Oops."

Oops indeed. I got a spark of madness.

Advancing on the nearest shelf of blood samples, I place both hands and give the biggest shove and step back to watch the carnal domino effect. Catching my drift, Riskel and Leandro run to the other two rows of collected blood and shove them, watching them follow, tipping over and releasing a waterfall of crimson as each shelf topples over.

The cascading sound of shattering glass startled us and we turn and see Fang and Paine throwing phials of blood off the table and anything they could get their claws on against the wall or on the floor.

An absolute blood bath.

Callum would be proud.

55

llewyn hellsinger

Bulletproof Heart - My Chemical Romance

The faint glow in the distance was the only thing that kept me going. I was so close to Lenora, I could feel it in my cold barren chest. She has taken up every space left empty in me. Where once vital organs pumped life into, she is the last thing to keep me going. Without her, I felt as if my chest had been ripped open and everything I had left had been harvested and feasted on. Nothing could help this hollowness until she is safe in my arms. I've never felt an emptiness like this, not even in death. Not even when I passed through the different phases of mortality, only to be left as a revenant trapped in purgatory. Lenora makes me feel alive again.

If I were to lose her— no, I can't let myself think that way.

The glow turns the corner and then comes to a haunting halt. I peek around the corner and watch the ghoulish ensemble disappear through the hidden passage, the wall entrance closing shut behind them.

"Fuck. We're going to have to find another way in."

"I thought you knew where we were going. We're out here risking our necks for this human. And now you don't know if there's another way in," Leandro was about ready to draw his silver knife and slit me ear to ear.

"Up to a point, Leandro. Please lower your voice. We mustn't alert anyone that we are here. Remember I'm supposed to be in coffin repenting," I hissed at him, starting to get impatient with him.

"What's your plan then, Nosferatu? I'm not about to just sit here and wait for someone to find us,' his lips spread thin over his sharp protruding fangs.

"Shut up and start looking for a way out then!"

"There's nothing here!" Leandro roars.

"Um, boss," Faine interrupts, pointing upwards. As a unit we look up.

"A sewer grate. Great."

The break of dawn was just approaching and casting a halo just over the point of the steeple as the last of us crawled out of the sewer opening and resealed it.

"The Holy Name Cathedral?" Leandro scoffs as he climbs out and observes our target entry point. Riskel shook his head at me, in disgust, the others had expressions of spiritual torment on their faces. We were the last of God's creatures that should prevail upon his doorstep, cursed to roam the earth until the end of days with no solace. How long has it been since any one of us have sat for confessional or made so little an utterance of 'hail Mary'?

Despite our group aversion to all things holy, we're going in.

Faine and Paine dash ahead and scale the building, searching for an entrance. Disappearing into the cracks of night. Riskel and Leandro flank left as I go right and brashly rip open the doors to the Cathedral, step into the hallowed shadow of God Almighty, only to be blasted by the roar of the organ playing its macabre tue.

Faine and Paine popped their heads through the dark curtains off to the side and motioned us over to take cover. Creeping up to the upper pew, we had a vantage point. I peek over the ledge and immediately lock eyes on Serlanos who is still discussing details with Zephirah performing the ceremony. Serlanos wears a smug smile.

Some part of me feels he knows I am here.

I've been a ghost for so long, that I forgot that he knew me by my very essence. Serlanos taught me everything I knew about stalking, hiding and getting away. Why shouldn't he anticipate me coming here? I've defied him at every turn he's made. Abandoned his direct orders and lied to his face. Now I've only spat in it since he's found I've been harboring Lenora in my penthouse. Violating her and feeding her.

Because she asked me to. She never said no, nor has she refused me. In fact, we're in love.

Why shouldn't he anticipate my moves? I don't give up. I've never been a quitter, something instilled in me by my father, a strong-willed man of his time. He was proud of me, and that was enough. I didn't need Serlanos's approval in the way that Callum did. I had that family. And I was ripped away from that life.

This rescue mission is predictable. But damned if I don't.

Peeking over the polished banister, I take note of everyone in the room. The masqued revenants have taken their positions, after drawing the ceremonial patterns on the floor in chalk. The black crooked candles are lit and the sacrifice stands before a basin as Zephirah, dressed in a crimson robes and her bald painted head covered in a reaper-like hood reads him his final rytes.

The Ritui De Sangre have begun.

Vampires may be immortal, but we aren't entirely invincible.

And that's what Serlanos wants. Complete invincibility. No stake nor decapitation could keep him down. And with his five bonded blood brides that he's discarded for Ordelia's choosing, all he will need is Lenora's bond, willing or not to seal the deal. The promise of five, Khor had called for, and the one to take it all.

My girl's blood is the last ingredient. Bonding her soul to him will only elongate his existence. She would be an extension of him if he is successful. She would have every power that he would have. It would make her a slave to him.

Dependent on him for existence just as much as I have.

If I kill him, I kill her.

It can't get that far. It's one thing to change her, it's another to damn her for nothing.

Serlanos scans the pews, as if he's searching for me. He will never find me. I will strike - when the moment is right. Right when he thinks he has won. He checks his watch and looks over at Lycidas who shrugs his shoulders.

He looks almost worried, like he was waiting for me to show up. But he needn't to worry. The ceremony was about to begin. In fact, in a few moments, I am going to see my raven, Lenora.

lenora holmwood

Castle - Halsey

The masqued attendees take their places in the pews , filing in one by one, snarling and snapping their protruding fangs and snarling at the converts following in behind, some slightly regretting falling in line with the other monsters of Chicago. The entire Blood Syndicate is here, except for Talon. Ordelia hides in the shadows of the cathedral's atrium watching the show unfold, just like me.

The circle of salt has been drawn on the floor before the altar where Serlanos stands. I am led down to the back atrium, escorted by a horde of succubi, all horrible in their own ways. Each of them dressed in black lace gowns matching their soulless sunken eyes that look lost, sewn over and dangerous all at once.

That was the allure. They sucked men in as their victims and fed them. I read about it in a book on feminine power in vampirism in Llewyn's library. These tenacious wenches will suck a man dry so to speak and use it to impregnate some unsuspecting virgin.

How nice of them.

Serlanos stands at the forefront of the cathedral observing as the dark magistrates prepare for the ceremony. The priest gives the sacrifice his last rytes at gunpoint. Lycidas is quick and agile. He makes eye contact with me, licking his lips. I hesitate to react. I can't give any number of these beasts the satisfaction that I am theirs to feast on. Even now I am forced down the aisle and marry the worst of them.

The sacrifice, the priest and I share in our fear, while everyone around us feeds on it. Serlanos stands before us, unmoved by emotion, holding our hearts in his claws ready to crush them at once.

The Dark Magistrate then nods to Serlanos who then nods to the organist. The ceremony is about to start. The two succubi behind me smile maliciously.

"It will be a pleasure watching Serlanos tear you apart later tonight. The night we consummated our bond, I could barely walk for a month," the red hair striga beside me whispered as we walked down the aisle.

I didn't respond. I won't give them the satisfaction.

"Don't make her too nervous, Lilith. She's probably a virgin still, after being locked up. Serlanos will ruin her for eternity," the blonde maiden giggled and averted her eyes as I turned to meet her envious gaze.

These sucky-bitches don't frighten me, nor am I envious of them. I feel sorry for them even as I feel sorry for the fate that I am faced with.

With each step, I mourn each of our lives. Here I was, fated to be like them, but hold no joy in that. Will I become like them? Bitter about mortality and feed from the essence of men and victimize unsuspecting women? Could I bestow a fate like that upon someone that was once me? A victim of circumstance and poor deals for riches. Is my blood really that special or is that what Serlanos has told these other women to lure them into this soul bonding trap? How many souls does he need in order to become invincible? That part was left out in the legend.

Part of me feels they're just saying these things to feed into my fear. They were hungry for suffering, as if their own was not enough.

My heart sinks deeper into the pit of my stomach, the closer we step towards the altar.

Serlanos stands proudly at the altar to receive me, his eyes glinting with victory. Lycidas and Norryx at his side, acting as best men in this cozen wedding. I stand before them, like a prized sow ready for slaughter.

With one fell swoop, Serlanos casts my veil over my head and looks me in the eye as he kisses my cheek and takes my reluctant shaking hands and leads me to the center of the salt circle. There's a silver basin set before the altar and a knife and chalice carved from bone sitting beside it on a table. I choke down my fear.

Llewyn will come for me.

The lights were dimmed and the only sound that could be heard was the faint whimpering of the priest who was still being held at gunpoint.

The dark eyed hooded magistrate lights the last ceremonial candle, the largest as she hums and sings an incantation under her breath, too low to hear. She steps up to the platform and surveys the morbid congregation before her, the gleam of the flames reflecting in her protruding wicken black eyes.

"Revenants and worthy Converts, please rise to recite our immortal vow," she bellows.

The congregation stands in unison behind us. In unison, voices from the shadows began to recite:

"Blood for blood,

Ash to ash,

From blood mist

And bone dust

We rise Again,

When the moon rises,

Our cravings cease

When the sun rises
the feeding halts,
Our blood brothers and sisters
I will keep close until the end,
For when time is spent,
And we are nothing left but corpses
blood in and blood out
Walking this barren plane forevermore
Till then my undead soul belongs to
God of Crimson and War, Draxius Khor"

"My dear undead revenants," the Dark Magistrate addresses the room, breaking the chilling, eerie silence following the cryptic chant. "I call those pure in blood and malice to come forth and make your offering."

Those suited in black in red robes and elegant suites snaked through the pews and approached the altar lined up. The first vampire takes the knife that the Dark Magistrate offers him and he takes the silver blade and cuts deep into his arm and lets the black blood spill into the basin. He makes direct eye contact with me as licks his wound and the cut heals. He smiles as he steers away and I fail to hide my disgust. One by one, each of the pure blood vampires come forth and pour a bit of their blood into the basin.

The Dark Magistrate smiles as the basin fills with the obsidian offerings. The sacrifice and priest stand beside, one in chains and the other at gunpoint, shaking with fear. We share in our fear, as the others around us feed from it.

God I hope Llewyn gets here, before innocent blood is spilt. I fear for the bald naked man in chains, trembling and avoiding my eyes. Serlanos leans in and whispers, "This is my favorite part."

Once the last offering has been made and the congregation has settled, the Dark Magistrate takes the same knife and leads the trembling man before the basin and forces him down on his knees and pulls his head back by his hair. He winces, closing his eyes and whispering a few prayers before she opens up his neck from ear to ear and lets his blood pour like a waterfall into the basin as she hauntingly chants:

"The Blood of the sacrifice,
Offerings of the loyal servants,
Here on this Hallowed Ground
We come to bond these souls,
As one"

Letting his limp body fall to the ground, the callous woman offers the knife to Serlanos who takes the knife in hand and turns and looks me in the eye as he slices the knife through his hand and lets his dark blood drip into the basin.

"Do you Serlanos Gyanstazi take Lenora Holmwood as your blood bond, until eternity fails?"

"I do."

Attempting to fight against him, Serlanos grabs my hand and slices through my palm and squeezes my stinging wound over the basin. I wince in pain, letting the tears flow down my face.

"Lenora Holmwood, you have been chosen by Serlanos Gyanstazi to be his blood bond, relinquishing your life, submitting yourself to him, and pledging your allegiance to Draxius Khor. Do you accept these terms?"

"She accepts," Serlanos speaks for me as I choke on my tears. Every drop that falls objects but my words cannot form to be heard.

"You may commence the turning."

The what? Before I could form any sound though, Serlanos grips me violently at the neck and dips me over his knee, exposing my neck and with his white protruding threatening fangs he bites into my flesh.

Searing and stinging pain and then a strange euphoria takes over as he drinks from me, draining me of life. It was nothing like how Llewyn fed from me, or Ordelia. I can feel my very essence leave me as he siphons from me like a drunkard would for his last drop from the bottle. Blood squelches against my strain veins. His hold on me grows tighter, painful even, yet I don't have the strength to fight against him. He draws away from me as I can feel myself barely hanging on to life.

The Dark Magistrate hands Serlanos a goblet filled to the brim of the offerings of the entire vampire clan.

He takes a deep sip before turning to me.

I mustn't drink it.

It can't be Serlanos that turns me. I'd rather die from blood loss.

It should be Llewyn to turn me. I'd rather it be Llewyn. He should be the one.

He was the one from the beginning.

Serlanos forces the goblet to my lips and with little strength left in my body, I resist, pressing my lips tight.

"Drink it!" the dark freak shrieks at me attempting to pry my lips open as Serlanos forces the goblet to my lips, but I turn my head away hitting Serlanos' hand.

Almost spilling it, Serlanos maneuvers to a choke hold around my neck bringing me close to his menacing pale face.

"Do not make a fool of me now. You're mine! " Serlanos stops and his eyes grow large with fear as he looks down at his chest.

The sound of ripping flesh and the sudden impalement from behind.

Llewyn pierced Serlanos with the same silver stake he had used on Callum.

The congregation of vampires roars with snarls and shrieks of terror.

"This is for my blood brother. Now get your claws off my girl."

But Serlanos doesn't budge. Fueled by the fresh quenched thirst of my blood, he grips Llewyn's arm and throws him across the cathedral - crashing into the stained glass window.

llewyn hellsinger

To the End - My Chemical Romance

Blood stained glass shatters and falls around me as I crash to the floor. Shrieks and snarls erupt in the pews and the sounds of bullets ricocheting off the ceiling fill the room. Serlanos, with one arm still holding tight on to my struggling raven, wrenches the silverstake from his chest pulling it the rest of the way through, gritting through the searing pain and tossing the silver stake to the floor with a clang.

Lush with fresh blood, Lenora's blood, the gouging in his chest heals before my eyes. Ribbons of flesh and tissue sew together on their own. Serlanos' malicious smile crawls up his face as he makes eye contact with me. Beads of blood drip from his hand, his hold on Lenora is so tight he's killing her.

"It's funny you mention Callum at such a time like this. I understand you didn't make it in time to save him from turning to bone dust. Yet you had all the time in the world to bring in backup to save Ms. Holmwood. Oh, sorry, Mrs. Gyanstazi. So much for loyalty, eh boy?"

I stand on my feet, pulling my drop gun from its sheath as I rise.. "You're the last person that should talk about loyalty. How does it feel knowing I fucked your wife and she liked it?"

I raise my gun, pointing it at Serlanos' head.

"Do you think that's a wise choice, Llewyn? I have the girl in a death grip and I could just let her bleed out right here. Besides, if a silver stake doesn't take me down, what good will your bullets do?" Serlanos taunts Llewyn.

"I should've aimed higher, I admit. With a head that big, it makes for an amazing target." I open fire on Serlanos who drops his hold on Lenora, who drops to the floor and crawls away, taking cover from the cascade of bullets that Serlanos absorbs, holes tearing through his body only for them to mend. He advances towards me. I open fire on him again.The bullets ricochet off of him, hitting some of the brawling congregates against my raucous team of bloodsuckers.

My clip empties as he closes the gap between us. Gripping my collar with one hand he catapults me once more into the air. I crash into the pews, destroying them upon impact.

Through the dust, snarls and hail of gunfire I crawl from the debris and watch as Serlanos returns to terrorizing Lenora. He grabs a handful of her long dark hair and drags her toward the basin of blood. She thrashes and screams.

For a moment I see her fumble with something at her neck.

She mustn't drink the blood in the goblet. Please have strength left to fight back. I push through the corpses of vampires that lay choking on silver venom, gurgling noises sputter from their fanged mouths, some reach out for me to help them. Lycidas lost his hold on the priest dodging one of the bullets and became lost in a crowd of vampires, the wailing priest who was now making his escape, crawling in the shadows towards the emergency exit door.

I hear Lenora scream and struggle against Serlanos' death grip on her. He's got her pinned to the floor as he forces the goblet of blood to her lips. I can hear her heartbeat fading from here as she refuses his attempts to turn her with the blood of the whole syndicate. A warm welcome to the whole family.

I reach the altar only to be cut off by Zephirah who jumps on my back. The bloodthirsty witch sinks her tiny sharp teeth deep in my neck. Her loyalty and derangement drives her attack, determined in seeing through with the ritual no matter the cost.

Lenora is dying. If she doesn't get help or consume blood soon— she will perish.

I manage to pull the witch from me and yeet her across the room like a ragdoll, crashing into the ceremonial candles.

I turn back and watch in horror as Serlanos rips the silver pendant from Lenora's neck, the silver chain steaming in his hand but he does not flinch an inch as he twists the casing from the bullet, letting it fall to the floor.

"Since you've refused the blood of our family, I've no choice but to just let you die. Such a shame. And now my dear, it's time for me to take what is rightfully mine," Serlanos declares before he peers into the bullet casing. Ice-hot rage consumes his face as he realizes it's empty. He looks to Lenora, who has gone limp in his grip.

Her lips wet with crimson, playing a triumphant smile on her porcelain face.

"NO! You little bitch!" Serlanos roars, moving his death grip to a choke hold. Her eyes grow wide with fear. "Do you realize what you've done? You've ruined everything. Your weak mortal body won't be able to handle the blood you just drank. I should just kill you now and save you the pain and agony."

Before I could reach her— Riskel appears from the mist and smoke billowing among the bodies of massacred vampires and jabs his revolver against Serlanos' head. "Kill her and I will put seven rounds of silver into your fucking skull."

Holy fuck he can talk!

Serlanos releases his hold from Lenora's neck and steps away with his hands in the air. Faine and Payne have Lycidas and Norryx at gunpoint, both spitting black blood on the floor.

The wail of sirens echo in the distance for the whole city to hear.

They're coming. We must scatter.

I scoop Lenora up from the floor, her small arms wrap around my neck. Her fading warmth carries us out of the cathedral, past the bodies and through the front doors. Her clutch on me becomes weakened and limp as we flit down the steps to an SUV waiting for us with the engine running. Slamming the door shut on the last vampire to stuff himself inside, we take off into the night.

58

llewyn hellsinger

Don't Fear the Reaper - The Spiritual Machines

We keep driving until we are well out of town limits. Headed north. We know that there are going to be road blocks up the minute the chaos inside the cathedral is discovered by Chief Warren. A warrant for each of us will be issued. Not one of the new recruits made it out of there alive. Mortal lives were spent. The basin spilled, not leaving a single drop for the other depraved minds that sought out Serlanos' favor in return for the immortal life. How tragic that is, indeed.

No fresh-blooded minds to be fuddled with by Serlanos's warped views of immortal life. He will have to rebuild. Leaving only a remaining few will give us some time before the Crimson Wars begin.

Lenora's breathing is ragged and gaspy. She is going down the dark tunnel as I hold her head in my lap, keeping her mind present by listing off the things that I see out the window. Her tiny hand clutches mine for dear life.

"My love, it will be okay," I whisper to her as she is near death itself. Her body grows cold as she slips in and out of consciousness, fighting against the venomous blood that is coursing through her body. Mutating and mangling each cell. The veins on her chest and arms turn black and her body grows stiff as it is tormented by the rigor mortis.

The blood, whomever it came from, was acting fast. I feared that for once Serlanos may have been right about something. She may not be able to handle this fast transformation. I hold her close, begging that this not be the end.

"Cynfael, we need to stop soon."

"How bad is it?" He asks as he turns back from the driver's seat to catch a glance himself and sees her failing condition. Her skin is chalk white and lips blue .

"Oh fuck. Heard. We are well into Wisconsin by now. I think somewhere past Milwaukee?"

"You think? Why aren't you using Google Maps like I showed you?" Gabriel, a new recruit of Cynfael's, cries from the front seat. He's been offering to drive since we started, claiming Cynfael needed to rest. I don't disagree with him. But Cynfael is stubborn like that and he will have to get used to it for all of eternity.

"I don't want to give away our location if we are being tracked. I turned it off. I don't think Serlanos is that tech savvy, but I cannot say the same for his minions."

"Good thinking, boss," Riskel said from the back. I know it pained him to not be in the front seat letting the little rugrat take the copilot seat. I could see it in his eyes saying *that's my seat twerp*. It's funny how possessive vampires can get at times.

Cynfael exits somewhere off the interstate and pulls into a cheap travel lodge. I took the lead, looking the least threatening and injured and got us four rooms for eight of us. This will give us a chance to recoup and stay out of sight.

"Be as human as possible. We don't need to draw attention to ourselves. We will figure out a blood supply once we get settled," I warned them all. The last thing we needed was to be surrounded by mortal officers. giving Warren the cheese he's been dying for on a silver platter.

I carry Lenora's limp body up the stairs and into the small dank and smelly motel room. The walls were stained yellow from years of inhabitants chain smoking and drugging. From the looks of the parking lot this is a popular trucking stop. Many of the meaty truckers climbing in and out of their truck are too appetizing for the others to deny. I cannot deny, I am feeling a little hangry myself. But Lenora comes first.

"We will go out hunting and bring you back something. I know you won't leave her side,"Faine says to me, winking. "If you want her to survive this, you have to take care of yourself too, Llew."

"Thanks Faine."

"You're one of us now, brother."

My Melancholy Baby – Ella Fitzgerald

I sit in the armchair by the queen bed she lays listlessly on. The glow of death emanated from her. It's almost as if I can feel her soul being ripped away from her body. I never wanted this for her. I know she chose it. She drank whatever was in that bullet casing. Whatever her dad stored there, it was what Serlanos wanted. Was this what he was after all along?

After seeing Serlanos's large library of blood samples in the hidden wall chamber, I couldn't help but wonder if he had picked up where Draxius Khor, vampire Lord, left off. The purification of the bloodlines of vampires. The strengthening of our powers. To never die and to be the dominant species in the world. No more hiding. No more finding willing victims. Pure anarchy. The mortals could pledge their allegiance or die. Serlanos would not know anymore about Draxius Khor had he not linked up with the Blood Witch, Zephirah. That's when he focused on cornering the blood market. Taking over blood and plasma donation centers, buying up hospitals and medical centers. Trying to find the direct lineage to Draxius Khor. To rebuild his empire.

I let the tv run as I held Lenora's hand, watching the news for any sign of Serlanos or his movements. What did the Chicago PD find when they arrived? I doubt Serlanos is in custody. And if he was, it wasn't for very long. Not with the strings he can pull in the Police Department. I am sure it won't be long until he has his fangs in every officer on the street. At his beck and call to find us.

He won't let her go so easily. The ritual was incomplete.

Whatever blood she consumed, he coveted so.

He will do whatever it takes to get her blood.

59

lenora...gyanstazi?

Become the Beast - Karliene

Death was peaceful, while it lasted. I awoke into this after life gasping for air, my throat raw with thirst. All of my senses burn with intensity. The darkness of the curtains wasn't enough to shield my fresh vampire eyes from the raw sunlight. My surroundings were unfamiliar.

Llewyn was nowhere in sight.

My body lays exhausted and unwilling to move from this fanciful bed. Hooked up to an IV bag, my newborn thirst is being kept at bay. I sit up and still find myself reaching for the bottle of water on the bed table. There's going to be a huge adjustment period I feel. Even in my constant questioning about vampirism in my evenings in the library with Llewyn, I still felt clueless what to expect.

Not all vampires had the same abilities. Like for Llewyn, he doesn't transform into a bat but rather an omnipotent mist that can drain the life force from anyone that crosses his path.

From what I gathered from observation, Norryx could transform into a snake and Lycidas had super speed.

Serlanos had amplified strength, not that he needed it to subdue me.

I was such a small, fragile weak human.

336

I let my reality sit in with me. I am no longer human. I am a vampire now.

I resign to keep myself further secluded. My mind races with questions that need answers and if I am going to get them I have to go find Llewyn.

As I dress in the robe and slippers left out for me on the armchair by the ornate armoire, I notice something written on the blood bag hanging on the IV hook.

Written in Sharpie are the words : NOT WINE.

I giggle to myself and shake my head.

He thinks he's so funny.

An eternity of Llewyn's jokes, what have I gotten myself into? I ask myself this only for a split second before knowing the answer. Probably the best thing ever.

My heart races at the thought of seeing him.

My love, my Llewyn.

The silk black robe hugs my body in all my curves. Things feel tighter, like I got a tummy tuck overnight. I feel light on my feet as I slip my feet into the soft house shoes.

I take a deep breath and exit the bedroom and follow the wide white painted hallway to the main living area that was open and bright.

Llewyn and Cynfael are sitting at the large glass dining table with the patio door open letting the sun cast in, paying no mind that their ghoulish natures were showing.

Llewyn looks up as I walk into the bright light of the room, shielding my sensitive eyes.

He rises from his chair and says nothing as he rushes to me.

We crash together like a violent car wreck. Llewyn's soft lustrous lips claim mine like it was the first and last time. Rubicund with immortal bliss.

Caressing my face in his soft hands, he breaks the kiss and whispers, "Good morning, my love."

I never thought I'd hear those words pass through those languid lips again. I crave them against mine like my life depends on it and pull him back in.

"Would you like something to eat?" he asks, offering the table full of food. My stomach growls with hunger that I didn't expect. I also felt at the same time relieved at the sensation. I don't think I could fully give up food like . Especially bacon.

Llewyn pulls a chair out for me and then promptly begins piling my plate with food.

"So, Ms. Holmwood, how are you enjoying the immortal life? Is it everything you've ever dreamed?" Callum asks, glancing up from his paper.

I don't know how to answer that question. "I think it's too soon to tell, it's only just begun."

"And you have so much to learn, baby girl."

"But first breakfast. You need your strength back before we even think about training."

"Training?"

"Learning how to hunt. It's in our nature, dear."

Deep down, I knew that. But imagining myself hunting down something and feeding from it, well that's another.

"Don't worry, we will start small. With animals, and then we go for the real thing."

"Cynfael, don't make her lose appetite before breakfast. She's still waking up."

"Fine, fine. I guess I am more excited than I am."

"You just love having a new vampire to corrupt."

"Reminds me of when I first met you, sick as a dog coming over on that boat. I got you right as rain."

I barely hear their continued banter over the bacon, activating every carnivorous need in my body. I felt my fangs extend for the first time as I savored every bit of blood run-off from the raw meat pooling in the middle of my plate.

Llewyn watches me, with an amused look on his face. I feel my face glow red with embarrassment, wiping away the red dribble from my face.

"Chief Warren has issued warrants for all of us. Looks like the cats are almost out of the bag. I don't think Serlanos could cover up all of that carnage in the cathedral," Cynfael laughs as he reads aloud from the paper.

"Where is he now?"

"There's no telling now. And that's when he's most dangerous."

"And you're still not out of the shit yet. That blood you drank from that little necklace of yours put an even bigger target on your head."

"How so?"

"That was supposedly the blood of Draxius Khor."

I nearly choke on my bacon.

"I'm sorry, what? How the fuck did my dad come across the blood of some vampire god?"

"That's what I would like to know," Cynfael adds.

My heart froze for a moment. "Llewyn, did you happen to grab anything from the penthouse before you left?"

"I'm sorry, my dear, there was no time."

Fair. But now we need to go back. We need that notebook before it falls into the wrong hands. It is my duty to remember my father's request and honor it. And while I have been turned in to a vampire, I must protect the rest of humanity. Which feels overwhelming when I say it like that.

"What is it, Lenora?" Llewyn asks, recognizing the look of deep thought on my face.

"We are going to have to go back to the penthouse. There's something there that is important that I left."

"I don't know if that's possible right now," Cynfael interjects. "The city is searching for us all, which is why we are nowhere near Chicago."

"Where are we?" I didn't ask to begin with and it felt silly sitting here.

"Canada, love. And we may have to stay here for a while so hope that whatever it is you need stays put."

Looking beyond the breakfast windows, I see miles and miles of snow covered plains only being covered with a new midafternoon dusting.

I sulk. How long might that be? Months? Years?

Serlanos did a number on my family's house and my grandfather's house. I don't doubt that he took his time tearing apart Llewyn's penthouse the moment we skipped town. All I can do is hope that Serlanos hasn't found it. That he doesn't even know what to look for. And he's back to square one, looking for me. And I am now looking for him.

"When do we get to kill Serlanos?" I ask, feeling a heat rise within me.

"When we figure out what other than silver can kill the fucker."

"Good. The sooner we do that, the sooner I can breathe again."

"My, don't we have a spicy little vampire."

"While I find your thirst for revenge ever so alluring, do we have time to fit a wedding in? I'd like to claim you for the rest of eternity," Llewyn declares.

Did he just—

Pulling an elaborately set garnet engagement ring from his pocket, he reaches for my hand and takes it in his. He holds the ring, ready upon my answer.

Tears form in my eyes, as I reply "I have all the time in the world for you."

Llewyn's tears prick my cheek as he consumes my lips, slipping the ring on and intertwining his fingers with mine.

Cynfael drops his paper on the table. "You two did NOT just get engaged in front of me."

"I think they did," Gabriel and Austin call from the couch, still immersed in their video game.

"So on top of revenge, we have a wedding. Great. How are we to do this in the middle of rural Canada?"

"It doesn't have to be anything big. My last wedding was a disaster," I tease.

"I wouldn't even count that as a wedding, my love. That was coercement, dismemberment and sacrifice, and some other shit."

"Sounds like a wedding to me!" Faine interjects as he walks in rubbing his eyes from a deep death.

"Looks like we've got a wedding to plan then," Cynfael announces with a twinkle in his eye. He winks at me.

"And then revenge," I add between Llewyn's tender kisses.

"Yes, and then revenge. I like this one, Llew," Cynfael says returning to his paper.

"Just what I need - you two are plotting together."

"All for a good cause, my love."

"I alway knew there was a little monster in you," he smiles as he presses lips against mine, whisking me away once more, burying me in an eternity of happiness.

I was on the prowl now, on the run, nevermore.

To Be Continued in BLOOD LINES & BAD VEINS